Nine-Iron John

Nine-Iron John

❀

A Tale About Men Who Play Golf

Alan Shapiro

Writers Club Press
San Jose   New York   Lincoln   Shanghai

Nine-Iron John
A Tale About Men Who Play Golf

Writers Club Press
an imprint of iUniverse, Inc.

For information address:
iUniverse, Inc.
5220 S. 16th St., Suite 200
Lincoln, NE 68512
www.iuniverse.com

Any resemblance to actual people and events is purely coincidental. This is a work of fiction.

ISBN: 0-595-21337-5

Printed in the United States of America

Grateful acknowledgment is made for use of the following:

"Passing the Strait" by Wendell Berry

"The Name I Call You" by Marge Piercy

The symbolism borrowed from the Grimm Brothers' fairy tale, Iron Hans, as depicted in Robert Bly's, Iron John (Vintage, 1990)

Cover design by Jeffrey Radden/Animated Arts

For Sandy...
the love of my life

"The greatest breakthrough is taking your own sweet time to reach your goal, be it par or enlightenment."

–Shivas Irons

CHAPTER 1

Somewhere over Virginia, Jim pulled out his Holiday Golf brochure and read to Arnie for the umpteenth time. "With deep–green forest and golden water, playing over 7,000 yards, the island course is one of a kind. Still inhabited by a variety of wildlife..."

"I know, I know," cut in Arnie. "No need to remind me. I'm not thrilled by the prospect of running into a wild animal while I'm looking for my ball. I don't know why I ever let you talk me into this trip. At my age, I don't even know why I took up the game, let alone play with you. I was perfectly content on the executive courses."

Jim continued reading. "Featuring meticulously manicured Bermuda greens, well protected by contoured bunkers, the masterpiece known as Wild Links was rated by *Golf Digest* as one of the fifty most challenging courses in the United States. Experience a gut–check of the noblest variety as you tee off on the world famous 16th hole. Known as *The Savage*, it is rumored that this 458–yard, par four beauty has *never* been parred."

"Well I'm certainly not going to be the first to par the hole," protested Arnie. "I'm lucky to make par at the miniature golf course. All this must be great for you and your six–handicap."

"Come on, Arnie, nobody twisted your arm. You know how much I've always wanted to play this course."

Arnie, red in the face, stopped talking and blew a sigh in the direction of Jim. He turned away, pushed the button on his armrest that reclined the position of his seat. Why *did* I allow Jim to convince me to come on this goddamn trip? He's twenty–five and single, no kids, no responsibilities. I'm forty–four, with a wife, two kids, and my own business. I must have been crazy to let him talk me into this. Playing with a hacker like me must be great for his ego. But what about me? I wish I had taken up the game as a kid. But my father never played. Didn't even like sports. Arnie reminded himself to not get worked up. He agreed to the trip and would make the most out of it. He slipped his *Discman* earphones in place. Anxiety was momentarily blocked by the sounds of Joni Mitchell singing "They paved paradise, put up a parking lot, wa wa wa wa…."

Ten minutes later, the jolt of the wheels hitting the runway knocked Arnie out of an unsettled sleep. He had dreamed of being in a grocery store, filling his cart with candy. His parents were arguing. There was no use trying to remember the sketchy details. He could never remember his dreams.

"Getting psyched?" his younger companion looked down at Arnie with a hopeful expression.

"I'm going to rest some more," responded Arnie, momentarily locking gazes with Jim before turning away. Jim's pale blue eyes were wide open, their whites glistening with the clarity of youthful enthusiasm. Arnie recalled the sight of a ten–year–old Jim in his Little League uniform. He was sitting on the edge of one of the orange vinyl chairs in the waiting area of Arnie's carpet–cleaning business. He was waiting for his mom to finish her work for the day. Jim's mother, Carol, had been Arnie's bookkeeper for seventeen years now. Ever since the time when Jim's dad left the family to try and make it as a pro golfer. Arnie had come to care deeply for Carol and had taken her son under his wing. And nothing was more important to Jim than a shot at the Savage. He had talked endlessly about it to Arnie for years, had driven his mother crazy with his obsession. And Carol wanted nothing more than to see her son happy. Arnie remembered why he agreed to go with Jim on this trip.

Interrupted by the flight attendant's voice, Arnie was startled into an upright position. He removed his headphones, stretched, and yawned. "After deplaning, please head to our courtesy booth for information about connections and delays. Thank you for flying…"

Jim had already pushed his way to the front of the cabin. "Let's go Arnie," he shouted back. "We can't miss this connection. They're very tight with starting times."

Arnie chased Jim through the airport at Charlotte. With forty minutes to spare, they arrived at Gate 12A and boarded the small twelve–seat plane. The tight cabin was crowded with oversized men who were too busy talking about their golf games to worry about seating comfort. Jim and Arnie were fortunate enough to be opposite each other in the only two emergency exit seats on board.

Arnie shouted above the engine's roar to Jim. "Did you see that pilot? He looks eighteen. I don't think he shaves yet."

"Will you lighten up. They make hundreds of commuter flights everyday and you never hear of crashes. Only the big planes go down. Hey, do you think we'll have any problems getting a taxi to the Hydroshuttle? You know that's the only way you can get to Caramus Island. I hope they transferred the luggage. If I have to rent clubs, I'm screwed."

Arnie did not respond. The small plane bounced and vibrated as both men, tired of yelling, leaned back in their seats. The engine's loud, syncopated roar drowned out the voices of the others.

Forty–two minutes after takeoff, the miniature aircraft settled on the Jetport's runway, located just six miles from the Atlantic coastline.

The Jetport's terminal was crazy on this April day. Small, servicing only two airlines, it made LaGuardia look like the reading room of the New York Public Library. Hundreds of people dashed in all directions. No lines, no sense of order.

"Where do we get our luggage?" Jim yelled.

Suddenly, Arnie broke stride and darted to his right, through the crowd. Like a halfback breaking tackles, he edged into fifth place in line at an information counter.

The line moved quickly, and when Jim found him, Arnie was next in turn.

"I didn't know where the hell you went! Jesus Christ, all we have to do is lose each other. It's already 1:20. If we don't find our clubs and get out of here, we're dead!"

"Can I help you?" The clerk was a tall, erect black man with a wide, white, toothy smile and a calm and deliberate manner of speaking. Just another workday.

"Where do we get out luggage?" asked Jim. "Where can we store it? We only need our golf clubs now. And what's the quickest way to get to the Hydroshuttle?"

"All luggage arrives in the back–center portion of the terminal. Do you see that large red sign with the two white arrows…?"

Jim cut him off. "I'll get the luggage, you get the cab."

After two full strides, he stopped, whirled around and shouted, "Where can we store our luggage?"

Once again, a slow deliberate speech from the clerk. "Ask one of the redcaps to give you a storage form. Make sure you keep the claim ticket. The cabs are lined up right outside these automatic doors to my right. Please have a pleasant vacation."

Jim was gone. Arnie, feeling like this day had already lasted three, went out front and was greeted by a chorus of cabbies.

CHAPTER 2

Bill Ayman, a retired Navy man and deep–sea diver, owned and operated the Hydroshuttle. Every twenty minutes from dusk till dawn, the old Captain took out his thirty–four foot, fourteen passenger boat named *The Serpent*, dropping off and picking up tourists from one of three stops. First come, first served. When Jim and Arnie arrived, the boat was already loading.

"How many going to Wabaugh?"

A man, woman, and their three children put up their hands.

"Who's going to the Bay?"

"We are," an elderly couple responded in unison.

"Then I guess you four other fellows are going to Caramus. That'll be six bucks a head."

Before manning the wheel at the front of the boat, the Captain played entrepreneur as he collected, counted, and organized bills in order of denomination, all right side up.

"First stop, Wabaugh."

The passengers rocked back as the Serpent made a sudden burst straight toward the center of the horizon. The engine's roar and the blinding sea spray ruled out any possibility for socializing.

Arnie eased back into his seat. For the first time all day—in weeks—he felt himself relax. Away from the routine, he reflected that his life wasn't half bad. He laughed when he thought of Jim

getting stuck with two bags of golf clubs in a wrong way automatic door. But already, Arnie missed his wife and kids. He
worked long hours during the week and rarely got to see them.
And here he was, on the weekend, vacationing without them.
Arnie's chest tightened and stomach growled. So much for relax-
ation. Arnie worked as hard at relaxing as he did at everything
else in his life.

"Next, the Bay," bellowed Ayman from his cabin.

Jim watched white foam sliding up the side of the boat. Like
Arnie, but for different reasons, he couldn't relax either. He
looked up at the surrounding sky—a heavy blanket of thick gray
and white clouds. Not a trace of blue. No sun. A very good chance
of rain. 2:05. They'd make their 2:52 tee–time, but there would be
no time to practice putting or to hit balls at the range. Jim wondered what the first hole was like.

As the Captain cut the engine and began to dock at Caramus,
the foursome aboard introduced themselves.

"Ralph Peterson's my name, and this is my partner, Bud
Stillwell." The younger and healthier looking of the two older
men offered his hand, "You fellow's just get in today?"

"About an hour ago. We had to leave our luggage at the airport." replied Arnie reaching to meet the handshake. "I'm Arnold
Weiss, and this is my friend, Jim Carlson."

"You boys must be serious golfers to be in such a rush to play
Wild Links," said Ralph, smiling.

"He's a serious golfer," said Arnie pointing with his thumb at
Jim. "I'm just out on a weekend pass from the psychiatric hospital."

The men laughed as the boat banged against the dock.

The four got out, then made the steep climb up a narrow dirt
path cut through thick woods about 100 feet from the shore.
Racing ahead, Jim was the first to clear the woods, the first to get
a look at the Wild Links clubhouse. A massive structure of tan

bricks with red tiled roof, the Clubhouse rose like a turreted medieval castle from the broad meticulously manicured lawn under a pewter sky. Looking back, Jim waved the others on, then waited.

Flushed and breathing heavily, Bud was the last to reach the clearing.

"What do you think, Buddy? Did I lie to you?" Ralph looked at Bud, waiting for a response.

"It's a goddamn palace!" gasped Bud.

"When the hell was this thing built?" questioned Arnie. "It looks like freakin' Camelot."

"Yeah, the architecture is definitely awesome. But we better find the pro shop and sign in now." Jim's words faded, and once again he led the charge toward the fortress.

Inside the extraordinary structure, the pro shop was like any other. Sets of irons and woods lined the walls. A practice green, putters, bags, clothes, and shoes filled the center of the modest-sized room. Up front, on the wall behind the counter, was a small, blue sign with white letters that read, Hans Keeler, Head Professional.

The man behind the counter was all business. "You boys will be playing together. Your green fees are already paid, but you owe eighteen bucks each for the carts." He turned, reached for two keys, and rang up two $36.00 charges on the register. As he bent over and pointed out a wire-mesh covered window, the man said, "Take the first two carts out front, the first hole is over there. The starter will give you scorecards. Better get moving. You tee-off in twenty minutes. You can use the locker room to change your shoes and store anything you want to keep behind."

As Jim pulled on the door, it was being pushed from the other side by a young woman. He stepped back, frozen. Jim stared and said nothing.

"Hi guys. Hi dad." The young woman breezed around a motionless Jim, her long, lush, blond curls bouncing as she walked through the shop, exiting through a door behind the Ping measurement chart and demo display.

"That's your daughter?" asked Jim.

"That's right, young fella. Now you better get your ass out to that first tee, or there won't be no golf played today."

Understanding all levels of the point being made, Jim opened the door and left with the other men.

"Did you see the body on her? Unbelieeevable!" Jim exclaimed, barely out the door.

"Come on, son," countered Bud. "She was beautiful all right. But the feeling will pass. And you got to concentrate on hitting a little white ball for the next four hours."

Arnie added, "Her old man would rip off your balls and shove 'em down your throat if you went anywhere near her. Already, he doesn't trust you. Smart man."

But Arnie wasn't too old to notice. She did have a great body. That loose fitting, white blouse revealed her small, well–shaped breasts. And those tight, faded Levis. Arnie was a child of the sixties, still a sucker for a great ass in tight–fitting jeans. Her long, slightly bowed legs didn't quite meet at the top, leaving space for daylight and imagination. Arnie had seen the small frayed hole just beneath her back left pocket, where her panty–line would be—if she had been wearing panties. No, Arnie wasn't too old to look and to long.

At the first tee, Jim was back to the business at hand. Everyone figured that he would be the first to hit. He placed his Titleist DT 100 and tee in the ground two–thirds over toward the right tee–marker.

"I don't really mind starting off with a par five. How long is it again?" Taking easy practice swings with his Hogan Edge driver, which he referred to as Big Boy, Jim rotated his upper body ninety degrees right, then left. He paused and looked back at the other three still sitting in their carts.

"Five–hundred and forty–five yards, dogleg–left," shouted out Ralph, looking down at his scorecard.

"Jesus Christ," exclaimed Bud. "This should be a par eight for me and my old 4–wood."

"Don't worry," reassured Arnie. "You're not alone. I'll be happy just to get it out into the fairway. I'm hitting my 5–iron off the tee."

Bud shushed and gestured with his hands palm down as Jim began his waggle. With a graceful, powerful swing—the kind that requires a six–foot, 185–pound lean frame—he got all of it. The ball sailed for 200 yards in the air before rocketing into a second level that carried for an additional sixty yards, finally coming to rest in the center of the dark green, striped fairway.

"Whooooeee!" screamed Ralph.

"You're off to a great start, young fellow," added Bud.

Arnie gave him five as they passed each other while exchanging positions.

Trying to downplay the drama of the moment, but noticeably beaming, Jim called out encouragement to his partner and friend. "Come on, Arnie. A nice, easy swing. Just get it out there."

Arnie couldn't get himself comfortable over the ball. He buckled his knees several times, improved his posture by straightening his spine, and rechecked his grip. He told himself that this was the par three, 153–yard hole at Oakwood Executive. The stark white, perfectly round sphere became fuzzy against its green backdrop; as if someone had changed the focus knob on a television set. Arnie's last thought before he began his takeaway was that he couldn't do it. And his instincts proved correct. To get the shot off, he made an awkward, chopdown lunge at the ball. The tee, buried in a divot like a spear in a small animal, traveled almost as far as the ball.

Arnie didn't attempt to retrieve his tee. "All right. No big deal. Plenty of golf to be played today."

Jim sat behind the wheel of the cart and stared ahead, saying nothing.

"I'm going to hit uglier shots than that before the day is through," said Bud.

"Hey, we're out here to have a good time," added Ralph. "Who gives a shit how we play?"

Both men hit perfect drives off the tee on that first hole.

After nine holes, Jim was smoking to the tune of one over par. Ralph and Bud played steady, good short–game, bogey golf. Arnie showed a 63 on the scorecard. What the scorecard didn't show were the balls kicked from behind trees, the forgotten strokes, and Arnie's shame and humiliation.

"I'm ready to eat," suggested Arnie, as the men walked up the hill from nine, in the direction of the clubhouse. "I know I can eat as well as you guys."

Jim, who didn't want to risk a cooldown, wanted to play through. He was, however, outvoted by Bud's tiebreaking request for some rest and ice tea. It had been a quick hour and three–quarter frontside, and despite a few gusts of chilly air, the weather had cooperated. There was plenty of daylight and time left for the guys to grab a bite at the turn.

CHAPTER 3

❀

Located in the backside of the clubhouse, the snack bar was
about half–full. Like the pro shop, it was very ordinary, with
Formica tables, wooden chairs, and a self–serve counter with the
menu on display behind the servers. Hamburgers, hot dogs, fries,
and pizza were the basic choices.

"Arnie, grab a table and I'll get us food. What do you want?"
Jim hurried up front, afraid of wasting time and losing the magic.

Lagging behind, Arnie answered, "I'll go up and see what they
have for myself."

Jim stopped in his tracks and turned to face Arnie. "No use in
us both getting on line. Get me a burger, medium, and a coke."
Walking in the direction of Bud and Ralph, he added, "Might as
well let the man with the dying hunger spring for lunch."

Bud nodded approvingly at Jim. "Let's let Arnie and Ralph
serve us, you and I'll find ourselves a table and rest up our legs.
Still a lot more golf to be played today. Hey, Ralph," he shouted
ahead. "Get me an ice tea. Not too much ice."

Jim and Bud found a relatively isolated table with three chairs
near the back of the snack bar. Bud grabbed a fourth chair from
an unoccupied table and the two men sat down across from one
another.

"You've got a real nice swing, Jim. Where'd you learn to play?"

"I've played since I was about three or four. My dad owned a driving range, and he used to give me a penny for each ball I'd retrieve. I had this old cutdown 7–iron, and I was always taking whacks at the balls. For as long as I can remember."

"I had a feeling that your game went way back. Could see it in the way you stand over the ball. Real comfortable. Like the game's a part of who you are. I sure do envy that. I myself still feel a little nervous most of the time out there. Started the game way too late in life."

Arnie dropped Jim's burger and his own two chili dogs—both on doubled–up paper plates—onto the table, pulled out a chair, sat and rubbed together the palms of his hands in gluttonous anticipation. A moment later, Ralph joined them with two iced teas and a slice of pizza.

Ralph bit into his pizza and pulled it away from his mouth, severing a string of cheese with his fingers. "That was some display you put on out there, Jim. You must play lots of golf."

Jim had a quarter of his burger in his mouth, leaning forward to keep the ketchup from dripping onto his sky–blue Jantzen golf shirt. He held up his hand while he began to chew the swollen contents in his mouth.

Bud answered for him. "He's been hitting balls since he could talk. His old man owned a driving range."

"Is that so." Ralph put down his pizza, wiped his mouth with a napkin, and looked straight at Jim. "Doesn't that figure. You've got the swing of a professional. Could spot it first time I saw you hit the ball. Was your dad a pro?"

"I'm getting another Coke. Anyone want anything?" Jim was already out of his chair and walking as he spoke.

"Yeah, could you please get some more napkins?" asked Ralph.

"I'm all set," replied Bud.

"Get me another hot dog with chili. I didn't realize how starved I was. This *has* been a long day," added Arnie, still chewing his first hot dog, mustard on his lower lip.

Ready to protest, Jim threw Arnie a disgusted look, but grudgingly complied with the request as he looked at Bud and Ralph.

"Well, don't you want to know how I developed *my* swing?" Still embarrassed by his play, Arnie sought some sort of resolution, real or imagined.

"How long you been at the game?" asked Bud. Physically, Bud was beat, but he still had the energy to soothe another man's hurting ego.

"Last year was my first full season. Made a lot of progress, too. I'd say I was shooting pretty consistently in the one–oh's—broke fifty for nine about a half–dozen times. I could never hold it together for eighteen, but I came close. One–oh–one, one–oh–three. And I'm talking about full–size courses, without cheating." Arnie spoke with enthusiasm until the reality of the moment hit. He might never hit another solid golf shot in his life.

"How old are you? Thirty–eight, forty?" asked Ralph.

"Forty–four," replied Arnie.

"Tough game to learn at mid–life. You've got to get out there when you're a kid and get the swing programmed. Look at Jim. You can't hit a golf ball like that unless you've spent years at it. I took up the game in my thirties and always regretted it—wished I'd done it when I was a kid. Never been a big hitter. The short game is where you got to do it. That's where you score and frustrate the hell out of those big hitters."

"That's right. The short game's the ticket," added Bud.

Arnie was really depressed now. It was too late to change not having played as a kid. Forget golf. He had never even been encouraged to play baseball or football either. His dad wasn't into *any* sports. Although he grew up on Eastern Parkway in Brooklyn, his father didn't even root for the Dodgers. Arnie's mother and sister did. But not his father.

As Jim dropped the chili dog in front of Arnie, there was a deep, distant sound that caused the floor to vibrate. The conversation and activity in the room ceased. No one was sure what had happened.

"Must be an aircraft," Jim offered. This theory proved false as hard rain began to hit against the roof and two side windows.

"Looks like we can take the spikes off. We're done for today," said Bud, already reaching down to untie his shoes.

Jim ran to the window. "Not so fast, guys. It's just one of those ocean storms that'll pass real quickly. Look how bright it is out that way."

Ralph laughed and said, "Talk about wishful thinking. But I can't blame you, son. If I was playing like you, they'd have to shoot me to get me off the links. But I'm not. And I'm not particularly partial to playing in damp, chilly weather either. I can feel my arthritis starting to act up right now." Ralph looked down at his fingers, alternately stretched them apart, and clenched them into tight fists two or three times.

Jim continued to stare out the window, reality setting in. "Shit, I was heading for a 75. Maybe even par."

"You can pick up where you left off tomorrow, Jim. Have a great front–nine, and you can still have your dream round," suggested Arnie.

Jim glared at his traveling companion.

"Our problem isn't whether we're going to get anymore golf in, but how the hell we're going to get back to the mainland," offered Bud. His concern was verified when the power and lights shut down for several seconds. A sudden flash of lightening was followed by more rumbling sounds in the distance.

"It's five–after–five," said Ralph glancing down at his Wilson sports watch. "Cocktail hour. I don't know about you boys, but I'm going to find me a brew."

Arnie pointed to a Michelob Light sign on the wall behind the service counter. "Let's go, Ralph. Bud, Jim, you want one?"

"Well, the doctor wouldn't approve. But what the heck." answered Bud.

Still staring out the window like a little boy hoping to see his lost dog return, Jim waved his right arm and said, "Yeah, get me one."

"Staring out that window ain't gonna help," consoled Bud. "Come here and pull up a chair. Might as well make the best out of a difficult situation."

Jim closed his eyes, threw his head back and sighed before turning from the window and taking a seat with the old man.

"You know, you should be damned proud of the way you hit that golf ball today. I've played with some mighty fine players in my day—scratch golfers, even pros—and I can't say that I've seen a better looking swing than yours. And you play gutsy. Real tough. Like when you saved par on that water hole with the long lateral trap. Now that was some scrambling golf."

"I really was zoned–in today. I mean I usually play pretty well, but to come through after traveling all day. And at Wild Links. I've dreamed about playing this course since I was a kid and my dad talked about it. Why the hell did it have to rain?"

Ralph banged down four bottles of Moosehead on the center of the table and shouted back, "Get a couple of bags of those pretzels, too." Turning around, he added, "First round's on me, boys."

Following tradition, the four men clanged the bases of the green bottles as Ralph proposed a toast. "To the great game of golf...and to friends, old and new."

Another burst of thunder, this one closer, resonated in the floor and chairs. Holding up his half–empty bottle, Arnie said, "To our surviving the night. Or getting too drunk to care."

Looking toward the window, Jim started to feel concerned. "You know that rain's not letting up, and we've got no way back except for the shuttle boat. And shit, all our luggage is at the airport."

"They must have rooms here," said Arnie. "There's got to be something in this castle besides the pro shop and this hole."

"I've been here twice before," stated Ralph. "Once in 1967 and again in 1983. Back in '67, there was a different owner. We stayed here for three days. Most beautiful accommodations you ever saw. The castle was a magnificent hotel. Cheap too. Probably the best three day golf vacation I ever had."

"What happened in '83?" asked Jim.

"When I called for reservations, they said the management had changed. Some European golf pro had bought the place and was running it just as a golf course. No hotel accommodations. So we stayed at a condo on the mainland. It was terrible. No maid service. A real rip–off. This time we decided to stay at the Breakers. Got to have that maid service. Where you boys staying?"

Arnie jumped in first. "At the Holiday Inn. The one downtown. At least that's where we were planning to stay."

Battered by a strong gust of wind and water, the door to the snack bar flew open. Rushing in quickly, shutting the door with her back as water dripped off her yellow, hooded slicker, was the beautiful woman from the pro shop. Once inside she took a moment to catch her breath, rested against the door, and threw back her hood. Freed from the protection of the slicker's hood, golden curls framed her gorgeous face then narrowed into darker, wet clumps which covered her shoulders. She walked around the outside of the tables and stood in front of the service counter, ready to address the men. Bright blue eyes, a soft full mouth, she had everyone's undivided attention.

"Needless to say, the weather is pretty awful and Captain Ayman just called to say that he definitely won't be out again today. The forecast calls for the rain to slack off soon, but the waters will remain treacherous."

"I'll show you something treacherous, babe," Jim bent over and whispered to Arnie.

"Will you shut up. I want to hear what she has to say," retorted Arnie.

"Those of you who will be missing flights or need to contact family, may use the pay phone outside the snack bar or one of the two phones at the pro shop. We have a limited number of rooms available in the south wing of the old building for your accommodations tonight, as we've booked reservations for wedding guests this weekend. So please, just bear with us. The snack bar will remain open till midnight, then will open again at 6:00 A.M.. We've got plenty of food on hand. Any questions?"

"Yeah, how much beer do you have?" A voice shouted from the back of the room. This was greeted with loud, tension–breaking laughs.

"Unless you guys need more than a case a man, we should be okay."

"That should just about do it," shouted out the same voice.

"Other questions?" asked the woman as she scanned the room-ful of men.

"Yeah, how much is this going to cost us?" shouted another, higher–pitched voice, obviously not the beer man's.

"Twenty bucks a man. We're not looking to get rich off you guys."

Jim watched the blond—still wet but no longer dripping—speak gently, yet firmly. Composed and confident, she knew how to handle a roomful of men and a situation. She smiled as a few men gathered to ask about some follow–up details and to joke with her. Perfect, white smile. She raked her fingers through her hair to join the dry and wet strands. Jim fully appreciated the grace of her movements and that body. He could still envision her body very clearly even though it was covered by the rain jacket.

"Oh, one more thing. Guys? Could I have your attention for another moment?"

The men stopped talking and once again turned to listen.

"I know some of you are going to want to get into your room and freshen up. It would make matters a lot easier if you could all come down to the pro shop within the next hour to get your room assignments and keys." Pausing to look out the window, she added, "It looks like the rain has just about stopped, so we'll see you down there shortly."

As the young woman walked toward the door at the front of the snack bar, and the men picked up the chatter and laughter to full volume, Jim darted between two tables, bumped into three men, and stubbed his toe. Barely beating the blond to the door, he held it open, walked out with her, and asked, "Do you need any help? Tell you the truth, I get thoroughly bored hanging around and drinking. I'd much rather keep busy, doing something productive."

"Thank you very much, but we've got it covered."

"My name is Jim. Jim Carlson." As he offered his hand, he noticed the open clasp and the white fabric beneath the shiny, yellow slicker. The wet blouse molded around her small breast, revealing clearly her erect nipple.

Tina pulled the edge of her slicker together at the neck and shook his outstretched hand.

"Hi Jim, nice to meet you, but I've really got to get back to the pro shop. My dad and Mr. Keeler are going to want to talk to me before the men start coming down." Walking away, she turned and said, "Good–bye."

Jim did not reply. Standing motionless outside the front door to the snack bar, he thought about her. Reliving the image of her in the pro shop, addressing the men, talking to him just moments ago. Jim knew that he had met the perfect woman. She was beautiful, bright, warm. He was determined to know her, and the unexpected overnight stay would make it possible.

Jim managed for a moment to put her into a corner of his mind, but he could not shake off the rush that had soaked his senses and demonized his spirit. Absently, he went into the snack bar to join the others who already had a new round of Mooseheads.

"There he is." Ralph was the first to notice Jim. "Where the hell were you? Sit down, we got you a fresh beer."

Jim pulled out the empty wooden chair, threw his leg over the back of it, and sat down.

"Was she receptive?" Bud leaned forward and looked Jim straight in the eye.

"You son of a bitch," added Arnie. "You're trying to make it with the pro's daughter. I'm telling you, that guy's got your number. Don't even try it."

"Will you relax." Jim cut Arnie off. "No one said I'm trying to make it with her. Besides, that guy in the pro shop was not Hans Keeler."

"I was wondering about that," said Ralph. "From what I can remember, the last time I was here, Keeler, the new owner, was a much smaller and older man."

"What difference does it make," added Arnie, into his fourth beer—two more than he had consumed at any one time in the past ten years. Looking at Ralph, he said, "Forget about the head pro. Let's talk about Wild Links. We know Jim's had this longing to play here since he was a kid. What brought you to the place, Ralph?"

Ralph pointed the base of the green bottle straight at the ceiling. Liquid and foam bounced and emptied into his throat. "To answer your question, Arnie, when I came in 1967, it wasn't my own choice. My sales manager arranged the whole thing. A solid, straight–ahead golf vacation. Great time, too. The next trip was different, though. I told you that the hotel was closed because of this new European owner."

Jim broke in. "My father came down here a few times and told me that some men died on the course."

"That's true," answered Ralph. "They drowned. On the sixteenth hole. The Savage. In the pond right in front of the green."

"Give me a break," said Arnie. "I can find my way into any water hazard in North America. But I can't imagine anyone drowning in one."

Bud who had been listening quietly, offered his opinion. "I was skeptical myself when Ralph first told me about the drownings. And whether the story was true or not, I had no interest in playing the damned course. But then Ralph showed me the newspaper clippings and the article in *Sports Illustrated*. It's true. There were two confirmed drownings on the sixteenth hole."

"What's the big deal?" asked Jim, arms crossed, legs fully extended. "There are freak accidents all over the world, every fucking day."

"I know, I know," countered Bud. "For fifteen years, old Ralph here hasn't stopped bugging me to come and experience the feel of this place. Says something special always happens here."

Ralph interrupted his friend. "It's no lie. The place has a magical grace to it. Think about the first time you saw that magnificent clubhouse. For me, it's like my grandson seeing that castle at

Disneyworld for the first time. And I saw the looks on your faces when you guys first saw it."

"Yeah, but that's just a building," argued Jim. "What about the golfing? I'll admit—that even today, with the miserable weather and all—that it's an interesting, challenging, well–kept course. But hell, you find great courses all over the world."

Ralph didn't let him finish. "It's more than the great golf and the beautiful landscape, Jim. Both times I was here, I left feeling like I was different in some way. I don't know. It's hard to explain. Let me just say that I had somehow changed from the experience. Ah, forget it. I'm not that good with words. You guys will have to see for yourselves. Wait until you play the backside. And just wait until you play the Savage."

"That's another question," said Jim. "My dad always talked about being the first to par the Savage and this brochure I've been reading says that the hole has *never* been parred. That's got to be bullshit. It's four–hundred and fifty–something yards, and unless there ain't no cup, I'm goin' to get it home in four. At least every now and then I am."

"I'm telling you, you're not getting over that pond in two." Ralph argued. "There's this great old big oak tree off to the side of the pond that just bends over and whacks those on–target balls straight on down. I swear to you, sometimes it seems to stretch. To reach out and knock those balls right into the pond."

Bud broke in again. "Okay, so the hole's never been parred. Who the hell cares? For God's sake, I'm happy just to be here. We're four men, hopefully looking at eighteen sunny holes of golf tomorrow, with ample opportunity to relax and shoot the breeze tonight. Doesn't sound all that bad to me."

"You're absolutely right, good buddy." said Ralph.

"I'm having a great time," added Arnie. "I'm finally starting to forget my nine holes of horror."

"You really did have a time of it out there," said Jim, laughing. "I can't believe some of the shots you pulled off today."

"Can't say I appreciate your humor, Jimbo," replied Arnie.

Ralph swallowed a gulp of sudsy air from his nearly empty bottle. "Well, I'm real happy I finally convinced Bud to get away with me to some place other than Florida. Took fifteen years but I finally did it. I know the news from the doctor played a big part, but I still think I deserve some of the credit."

Arnie, slightly drunk, reacted immediately. "What *is* the matter with you, Bud? You gonna be okay?"

"Ah, Ralph, I wish you hadn't said anything." Bud sat up, pulled his chair in, and got right to the point. "I've got cancer. But then, half the men in the country who are lucky enough to have made it to my age have freakin' cancer."

"What kind of cancer?" Arnie pressed for details. He was no stranger to the disease that had tortured his father for six years. That finally killed him.

"Started out in the colon. Almost ten years ago. They cut out half my large intestine and I was fine for years. Up until about six months ago. Now they say it's in my stomach and liver. I have surgery scheduled in about three weeks. It doesn't look real good."

"Jesus, Bud," said Arnie. "I'm sorry to hear that. But maybe the surgery will be successful. Or chemo. There's so many treatments these days."

"Don't give it a second thought. I've already told you, I'm damned lucky to have made it this far. I've had a good life. What the hell's a man supposed to expect anyway? Now enough of the doom and gloom, next round's on me!"

"Let's hold off on the next round," suggested Jim. "Most of the men have already been down to check–in, and you heard what she said about getting that settled."

"Well, aren't you the considerate one," retorted Arnie. "You wouldn't happen to be interested in checking out the blond's dinner plans? Now, would you?"

"Fuck you." Jim got up and left the snack bar on his own.

"Man, I'll tell ya'. You boys really know how to irritate each other, now don't ya'?" said Ralph.

"Where did you boys meet anyway?" asked Bud. "He seems more like your son than your friend. I don't mean the age difference part. Just the way you two carry on."

"I know exactly what you mean."

CHAPTER 4

Looking through the wire–mesh window into the pro shop, Jim looked for her. There were a dozen or so men milling around, taking down irons from their wall mounts, looking at shoes, trying on hats. He did manage to see her father, the man who greeted them, behind two very large men near the clothing racks. He was smiling, seizing an opportunity to give his sales pitch and pick up some unexpected dollars.

Jim walked in and went through his usual golf browsing routine. The putting green was open. A good time to practice his stroke. He picked up an Odyssey mallet, felt the weight of its head, and went through his preshot pendulum routine. Felt pretty good. Lining up four of the practice balls in the direction of the furthest cup, he smoothly sunk three out of four. Smiling to himself, he realized that he still had it, and for a moment longed for tomorrow's play.

The clothing was outrageously expensive. LaMode and Mark Scott designer labels were not his usual fare. Suddenly, a woman's voice permeated the chorus of male tones. With a hunter's infallible instincts, Jim did a half–turn and immediately focused on that face. She was down on one knee, checking the size of a pair of DryJoys on one of the two large men he spotted earlier. In an attempt to overhear the conversation, Jim edged closer and picked up a pair of wing–tipped Etonics. As he checked the pliability of the leather, he managed to catch what was being said.

"I'm still surprised a little out–of–the–way shop like this would carry 13EEEs. My own club man won't stock them. He always kids me. Says he doesn't carry freak stock!" The large man laughed loudly.

"Well, my dad's got a big foot himself, and he knows that if you have an odd size, and find what you need, you're going to buy it."

"I'll tell you, Tina. You're some smart gal. Smart and pretty. And you and your dad really know how to run a golf operation."

"Thanks. We do our best. How do they feel?"

"Great, just great."

"Will you be paying cash or using your credit card?"

To keep from being noticed, Jim scurried around the corner of the shoe display area and pulled down the 5–iron from a set of Titleist DCIs. Folding his fingers around the Tour Wrap grip, getting into his stance, he processed the new information. Her name was Tina and she could sell. That guy hadn't known what hit him. He'd probably pay a fortune for those shoes.

Tina handed the shoe box over to her father who was working the register. Jim watched her turn to line up the next available sucker. He was ready.

"Excuse me, Tina," he shouted across the room. "I have some questions about these irons."

Tina's cheerful expression faded when she discovered who had called. Pausing, looking around for an out, and finding she had none, she approached Jim.

"Looking for a set of irons?" she asked.

"Well, maybe. I play with these forged clubs that I've had for years. I understand that the new cavity–back designs are much more forgiving. What do you think?"

"What's your handicap?"

Jim hesitated. "Single–digit. Somewhere between five and seven. Shot a 37 on the frontside here today. Until the rains came and ruined…."

"It seems to me that you'd be foolish to give up the irons you've been playing with. What type are they?"

"Hogan Apex."

"That's a great iron. A classic iron that's still popular. Sounds like you're using the right irons for your game."

"Maybe you're right." Jim placed the iron back on the display rack. "So, how's business tonight? Looks like you and dad found a small gold mine with that storm."

Tina glanced around the room, then down at her watch. "As you can see, we're pretty busy. Why don't you keep looking and I'll be back if you have any other questions. Please excuse me."

Jim would not. "So your name's Tina. I wouldn't have guessed Tina. You look more like a Kimberly or Heather. How do you survive on this island? What do you do for fun?"

"Look…I don't mean to be rude, but I'm really kind of rushed right now."

"Hey, I'm just trying to be friendly. I thought disaster situations helped people lighten up. Everyone reaches out a little more. That's all. Any harm in that?" Jim watched Tina's expressions carefully. He thought she was beginning to soften.

"Well I don't mean to be rude. It's just that this is a very trying situation that demands all of my time and attention. Now, if there's anything I can help you with."

"Actually, I was interested in some clothing. I'm not the kind of person who can wear the same thing two days in a row."

"Why don't you take a look over here and when you…."

"Hey Jim, did you get us checked in yet?" Jim recognized Arnie's voice. Mr. perfect timing.

"Excuse me, Tina."

"No, I didn't," Jim shouted back. "Why don't you take care of it."

Jim tried to buy more time. But it was too late. Arnie, Ralph, and Bud were all heading in his direction.

"Hey Jim," Ralph led the charge smiling broadly. "What are you doing? Looking for some new clubs to shave a couple strokes off your game?"

"Actually not, Ralph. I was thinking about picking up some new playing clothes for tomorrow." Pulling on Ralph's ketchup–stained shirt pocket, he added, "Something that you might want to consider."

"Excuse me, guys." Tina broke in. "I've really got to go and help out. You should get your room assignments, keys, and linens. If you want to get anything from the pro shop, we're going to stay open until midnight, along with the snack bar."

"Where do we check–in?" asked Bud. "I can really stand a hot shower."

"Right behind the front desk there's a table with registration sheets," she turned and pointed as she began walking away. "My dad will take care of you."

"So how'd you do? Get to first base?" Bud whispered to Jim as soon as Tina was out of earshot. "Man, she *is* a beautiful woman. The kind I could go for myself if I was about forty years younger." He glanced back at her and added, "Make that fifty years younger."

The men shared a laugh that relieved some of the earlier tension. Jim was feeling up and very hopeful. He figured that Tina didn't have to make a point of letting him know she'd be around all night. Maybe she was starting to come around.

CHAPTER 5

The door to Jim and Arnie's assigned room was heavy solid oak with an ornate brass knob and knocker that opened into a spacious room with a twelve–foot ceiling. Above the ivory stucco walls, four parallel beams ran across the ceiling creating five equal rectangles. At the far end of the room, heavy green and gold tapestry curtains covered all but a center slit that gradually broadened from ceiling to floor. Particles of dust danced in the spear of incandescent light that pierced the opening. Two large cherry armoires stood about twelve feet apart on one of the side walls opposite the queen–sized beds. Joining the armoires was a waist–high dresser. An authentic 18th century desk with Queen Anne legs and several antique chairs and tables completed the furnishings. The royally expansive room was airless, with the stale, musky odor of a basement with water problems.

Arnie began to pull down the emerald green and deep red flowered bedspreads, preparing to get the clean linens in place. Jim's first order of business was to find the air conditioner.

Looking out the window into the dark night, Jim recognized some landmarks. "There's the light at the corner where we turn to get to the snack bar from the pro shop. That means that the first hole is over there, and the woods that lead to the ocean are in the other direction, down that way." Jim held the heavy curtain with his left arm, while he pointed out the directions with his right.

"You know, this has been some day," said Arnie. "Can you believe we were in LaGuardia this morning at six? That seems like days ago. Thinking about what Ralph said, I think there *is* something special about this place. Just think about the events that went down today. I mean, I already feel like I've known Bud and Ralph for years."

"It *has* been a long day," Jim responded. "Some good. Some bad. The weather sucked, the golf was great—little we had of it—and I could do without all the hanging out. I feel sorry for Bud, I really do. But this is my once a year golf vacation and I don't need to hear about cancer."

Arnie understood how Jim felt. A kid of twenty–five. Thinks he's immortal. Then Arnie remembered Bud's comments about how Jim and Arnie carried on like father and son. Arnie thought of his own son. Ryan turned fourteen a month ago. Last year, when Arnie's father was dying, Ryan had refused to go see his grandfather in the hospital. When the old man died, a reluctant Ryan went to the memorial services, but not to the burial. This infuriated Arnie.

"Arnie...hey Arnie, you there?" Smoothing out the clean linen, Arnie heard the voice and looked up to see Jim standing in front of the bed, clad in his underwear.

"Listen, I'm going to go check out the shower. What time are we supposed to meet those guys?"

Arnie glanced down at his watch. "Nine–o–clock. It's about ten–of–eight right now, so we still have some time. Tell me how the shower is. I think I'll stretch out for a few minutes now."

Walking toward the bathroom in the direction of the front door, Jim said, "We may have accommodations, but I sure wouldn't mind some clean underwear."

Arnie shouted after him, "Only the finest for your delicate genitals, right Jimbo? Why don't you turn those inside–out?"

The door to the bathroom squeaked as Jim closed it, pushing it several times to get it shut securely. Arnie propped two pillows behind his head and stretched out to relax after a very long day. The bed was comfortable, Arnie's body was at rest. It was his mind that came to life during these quiet moments, that made relaxing impossible.

He thought about Bud...his cancer. How life could be so cruel, so sad. And how ugly it can be to die. The normal process of aging—dried up leathery skin, achy, swollen joints, broadening girth, sleeplessness, dulled senses—is hard enough without piling on the rapid and destructive invasion of malignant cells. Why must a good man like Bud have to face such a horrible fate? Arnie knew the answer to that question, which brought about the next disturbing thought. That everyone faces the same potential circumstances. Arnie and even his children. His stomach began to tumble and talk, his pulse thumped the back of his neck.

Closing his eyes and breathing deeply, Arnie pictured his daughter, Lisa. Only five–years–old, so beautiful, so pure. Those great big brown eyes, the hugs. "I love you, Daddy," streamed out of Lisa as naturally as breathing. And Arnie had no trouble saying it right back to her. "I love you, Lisa. Do you know how much Daddy loves you? Come here and give me a great big kiss." Arnie and Lisa had an easy, loving relationship. Why was it so much more difficult with Ryan? Why did Arnie have so much trouble telling Ryan how he felt about him? That he loved him.

Arnie gave up trying to relax and got up to retrieve the *Discman* from his travel bag. Lying back down, he browsed through the CDs he'd brought along. Carole King, Cream, James Taylor, Joni Mitchell, Beach Boys, and the Dave Matthews Band. Music always helped Arnie to unwind. Michelle and the kids had given him the *Discman* for his 44th birthday, and while he did his best to fake a pleasant surprise, he hadn't wanted to trade in his old LPs for compact discs. Arnie loved the music from an earlier time. A time of hopes and dreams. Of youthful delusion. He laughed as he looked at the CDs he'd bought. Changing without changing. He remembered Ryan's reaction to his listening tastes. "Come on, dad. You're into the world of CDs now. It's a new millennium. Lighten up. There's some great music out there." That was the day Ryan gave him the Dave Mathews Band CD. Arnie still hadn't listened to it.

He got off the bed, wrapped the headphones around the *Discman* and dropped it into the travel bag. He pulled off his shirt and stopped to look in the mirror above the wide dresser. He leaned forward and stared into his eyes. He pulled down the bags beneath his eyes with his thumb and forefinger. Two small clear brown perfect circles. When he released his flesh, the base of his eyes sunk like setting suns. Arnie kept staring until body and image separated from each other in a moment of marijuana–reminiscent magic.

Arnie backed away, stood sideways and sucked in his gut before releasing it again. Not terrible for forty–four. Five–ten, still under 200. Arnie tightened and then released the muscles in his arms. Not much there. Never was. Still, he didn't look nearly as bad as some of his previously rock–solid college buddies. Forty–four. An age when the hardbodies begin to resemble forever flabby types like himself. Some justice in the aging process. Arnie didn't mind that part of getting older.

The bathroom door opened and Arnie looked to see Jim stumbling in, his hair soaked, his underwear inside–out.

"Man, that shower felt great. Plenty of hot water and great pressure."

"Well, I'd better get myself moving," said Arnie, opening his belt buckle.

"You got a comb or a brush I can borrow?" Jim asked as he towel–dried his hair while looking in the mirror. "I wish I had a blow dryer."

"You got plans I don't know about?" asked Arnie sitting on the bed, pulling off his trousers.

"What's your problem? Are you supposed to be watching out for me or something?"

Arnie paused before responding. "Jim, I don't care what you do. But is there anything wrong with my being a little curious? Can't a dirty old man get a vicarious thrill?"

"Why not," answered Jim, raking his wet brown hair around a left–centered part. "Actually, I was planning on stopping back down at the pro shop later to check things out. I'll still be eating with you guys, though. I have to. I'm starved. But I don't need to hang around all night talking about the good old days."

"That's fine with me," answered Arnie. "And I can't blame you for giving that girl your best shot. She *is* something."

"What a babe. And I think she's coming around. You know her type. Puts on that cold, standoffish front when she feels attracted to a guy. And with her father looking over her shoulder, what can you expect?" Jim slipped his shirt carefully over his hair and pulled it over his smooth and lean, muscled torso. He leaned his face closer toward its image in the mirror, licked his hand, and pressed down a few hairs that stood up on the top of his scalp.

"So, what do you think'll happen? Screw her tonight and take her phone number?"

"I'd like to." Jim backed away from his reflection and straightened his collar. "But this isn't about getting in her pants for just one night. She's something special. This might go the distance."

"I wish you all the luck in the world, buddy. I'm taking a shower."

CHAPTER 6

When Jim and Arnie reached the snack bar, Ralph and Bud were already seated in the center of the noisy, crowded room. A bluish cloud of cigarette and cigar smoke hung in the french fried greasy air.

"Hey guys," Ralph called from across the room. Waving his arm, he yelled, "Get yourselves a beer. They're out of Moosehead, but there's plenty of Michelob and Bud long neck."

"Sit down, Arnie," offered Jim. "I'll get the brew."

"So, how was your room?" Ralph asked Arnie.

"Actually, quite good. I see what you mean about this place. It must have really been something in its day."

"I took a nice, hot shower, laid down and fell right to sleep," added Bud. "Feel great now. Ready to go."

Jim returned and banged two bottles down on the table.

"Hey, Jim. How's par man doing this fine April night?" Ralph scraped his chair sideways to make room for Jim to sit down.

"You really impressed me and Ralph here," added Bud. "You smacked the living tar out of that ball today."

Jim sat down and edged his chair toward the table. "I only hope that I can pick it back up tomorrow. The weather's looking good. I saw the moon out there before. Still cloudy and breezy, but it looks good for tomorrow. Anyone hear a forecast?"

"I'd take a handful of well–struck balls in a blizzard," broke in Arnie.

"Oh, stop putting yourself down so much," consoled Bud. "From what you say, you've had some decent rounds in your day. And you hit some decent shots today."

"I've got to tell you," added Ralph. "Your swing's not half bad. Good rhythm. You don't swing too hard. And you've only been at it a couple of years. Give it some time. Golf's the hardest and most frustrating damn game in the world."

"To the hardest and most frustrating damn game in the world." Arnie lifted his bottle and the four men banged their Bud long necks in the second toast of the day.

"Actually, Arnie, they're right," said Jim. "You're not nearly as bad as you looked today. You're just not used to playing on really tough courses. You were too nervous out there today. Tight as a drum."

"So you've played some golf with Arnie before," said Bud. "I've been kind of curious about that. How do you two come to be traveling together?"

Arnie jumped in with a reply. "Jim's mother works for me. She's been my bookkeeper for years. Way back from the time he was a little kid, Jim always stopped at the business after school. Sometimes, on vacation days, he'd spend the day." Arnie flashed a smile at Jim. "You were such a cute kid back then. What the hell happened?" Turning to Ralph he pointed his thumb at Jim and added, "This good–looking young man used to come by in his Little League uniform. We used to talk all the time about baseball. We'd argue because he was a Met's fan and I rooted for the Yankees. His big hero was Keith Hernandez. Remember those days, Jim?"

Jim, shoving a piece of pizza crust in his mouth, nodded without speaking.

"So, Arnie, Jim's mom is your bookkeeper," said Ralph. "What kind of business are you in?"

"Carpet cleaning and repair. Used to do installations but got out of it a few years back. Couldn't compete with the big companies."

"So is the recession kicking your ass like everyone else?" Ralph asked.

Before Arnie had a chance to reply, Jim cut in. "Are you kidding? Don't worry about old Arnie here. He always knows how to rake in the bucks."

"Yeah, we do okay." Arnie sat up straight, and rubbed his hand against his swollen chest. "I've been around a long time. Eighteen years. I have some solid contacts and they come through for me. But you know how it is in business. You never want to count your next dollar too quickly."

"You're right about that," said Ralph. "Before I retired, I was in the pet products' business for thirty–seven years. Never took anything for granted. Had some tough times, too. Some real scares."

"That's why civil service did me just fine," added Bud. "Forty–two years with the Feds and never lost any sleep. Good pension, benefits. Yup, the Feds did me just fine."

"I agree," said Jim. "I've been a programmer with Nassau County for three years now and I think it's the way to go. I'm not going to bust my ass working eighty hours a week. For what?"

"Sounds sensible to me," said Bud. "Besides, when would you play golf? You got to keep that beauty of a swing grooved in. Right?" Bud reached beneath his chair and added, "I don't know about you boys, but I'm getting a little stuffed from all this junk food and beer. Anyone up for a different kind of adult beverage? Something with a little more gitty–up?"

Bud came up with an unopened bottle of Cuervo 1800 premium gold tequila. He placed the bottle on the center of the table.

"What the hell!" exclaimed Ralph.

"Where did you get that?" asked Arnie.

"All right, Bud! Coming through in the clutch!" Jim straightened his posture, pulled his chair toward the table, and reached out for the bottle.

Bud was laughing, scanning the expressions on the faces of the three men. "I always carry a little something in my suitcase when I travel. You never know what might come up. Hardly ever use it, though. This here cactus whiskey and me have been together for a good six, seven years now. Seemed like a good time to part company with it."

"I'll get some cups and see if they have any lemon." Jim was off in a flash.

"You sure your gut can handle straight liquor?" asked Ralph.

"You know he's right, Bud," added Arnie. "Don't do anything you'll regret. Hey, I have trouble handling booze myself. I might have one, but that's it."

"Hey guys, lighten up," replied Bud. "I'm a big boy and know what I'm doing. Had a half dozen beers and feel just fine. And besides, I'm better off with the damn tequila than I am with the beer. It's more efficient and to the point!"

The men laughed in agreement as Jim came back with four plastic cups and a sliced lemon on a paper plate. He grabbed the salt shaker from the middle of the table and proclaimed, "Let's do up the first round!"

Bud poured four "short" ones and the men went through the ritual. Passing the shaker around, they sprinkled some salt between their thumbs and forefingers, on top of closed fists. Then, each one licked the salt, gulped the shot, and sucked on a lemon slice.

"Ahhh, that was nice." Bud was the first to register a reaction.

Grimacing, Ralph said, "Man, I don't remember the last time I did that."

Arnie, head turned off to the side, eyes pressed closed, his mouth curled against the bottom of his nose, was the only one to leave some liquid in his cup.

Jim stared straight ahead. Ready for another.

Ralph proposed the first post–ceremonial topic for discussion. "So you boys ready for the Savage tomorrow?"

"Please don't remind me." Arnie barely got out the words, his eyes were tearing, his chest on fire from the straight whiskey.

"I've had enough talk about this goddamn hole," said Jim. "I'm just goin' to go out and par the fucker tomorrow."

As Jim spoke, he reached over and poured himself a second helping of Cuervo. "Anyone want to join me?"

"Not right now," replied Ralph.

"I need some pretzels to go with this," said Arnie, getting up slowly from his chair. "Anyone want anything?"

"No thanks," Bud answered. Turning in the direction of Jim and pointing at the bottle, he said, "I *will* have one of those."

Jim poured the shots. "What do you think about all this Savage bullshit, Bud? You believe it's never been parred? And that there were two drownings in that pond? What do you think?"

"I don't just think—I know for a fact that nobody's ever parred it. Those drownings were real too. Sad but true. Lots of superstition connected with the Savage. It *does* have a reputation. Of course, people usually blow these things out of proportion. It's just like the trash they sell at the check–out counters at the supermarket. Nine–year–old girl gives birth to alien monkey with two heads."

Jim and Ralph laughed.

"No, you got the story wrong." Ralph held the index finger of his right hand pointed straight up and shook his head. "It wasn't a nine–year–old girl. It was a nine–year–old boy! And the monkey wasn't an alien. It was South American!"

"What's so funny?" Arnie returned and tossed four bags of Lay's rippled potato chips onto the table. "What'd I miss?"

Still laughing, Ralph explained, "Bud was just telling us about the gynecological habits of South American monkeys...or something like that. I don't know." Pointing his thumb at Bud, he added, "Just ask him. Bud'll explain it to you."

Arnie sat frozen, expressionless. A deep sigh jump–started him into tearing open two of the bags of chips with his teeth. He threw a bag of ranch flavored chips across the table, picked up some barbecue chips, scooped out half of the bag's contents, and shoved them into his mouth. Chewing loudly, he looked at Bud to find out what he had missed.

"These boys are just getting a bit carried away." Bud flashed a good–natured grin. "You know, some people just can't handle their liquor all that well."

All the men joined in laughter now.

Arnie, thirsty from the salty snacks, queried the group, "So, we ready for another round?"

"Set one up, buddy," said Jim.

"Yeah, I'm ready for one," said Ralph.

"I'm goin' to take me a leak first," Bud began to stand up. "Go ahead and get mine ready. I'll have it when I get back. Don't wait on me though. Pissin' ain't what it used to be."

Walking away, Bud stopped and turned back toward the table before adding, "Don't you boys take a good, strong piss for granted. Someday, when you and your prostate's seen a little more experience, you'll be dribbling the night away."

The men laughed and shook their heads as Bud went off.

"How does he do it?" Arnie asked Ralph. "He's got such a great attitude. And to be out playing golf at this stage. He's unbelievable. I hope I can have that kind of strength some day."

"What do you want him to do? Roll over and die?" said Jim.
"And what better way to go than on a golf course."

"Easy for you to say," countered Arnie. "I've seen you lose it
over a blister on your finger. I can imagine how you'd be if you
had cancer."

Jim maintained an eye sparkling smile aimed right at Arnie.
"Cancer would be okay. As long as I could still play golf. A blis-
ter's a problem. Can't grip the club. Come on guys. Bottom's up.
We'll pour another and join Bud when he gets back."

The men drank up and were sucking their lemons when Bud
returned.

"That was fast," said Ralph. "We would have waited for you if
we knew you were going to be back so soon."

"False alarm," answered Bud as he got back on his seat. "The
place is pretty crowded and I didn't want to keep anyone waiting.
Can't piss with someone staring right at my damn back. I'll go
back a little later. So…where's my shot?"

"Right in front of you," pointed Jim, now officially in charge of
the bartending responsibilities. "Hold on. We're going to join
you."

Ralph placed his palm over his cup. "Not for me right now. I've
got to slow down a bit. We've also got an early tee–time tomorrow. You forget about that?"

"That's tomorrow; tonight's tonight," responded Jim.

"Well, that thinking's okay for someone your age. I've got to
pace myself."

Arnie was well past the point of rational self–monitoring.
Pleasantly numb, he slumped back in his chair and listened to the
sounds that filled the room, that floated past his conscious
awareness. From the next table, a deep voice echoed, "…well, it's
still good to be away from the wife and kids." The wife and kids.
Arnie, jarred from his fog, abruptly sat up and looked first at Jim,

then Bud, and finally Ralph. He didn't recognize any of them, not even Jim. He was 1000 miles from home—from *his* wife and kids. Arnie rubbed his eyes, then rotated his head around, loosening his stiffened neck and shoulders.

"Hey, Arnie. Grab some salt and pass it down this way." Jim's voice helped complete Arnie's return to reality.

"Uh, I think I've had enough." Arnie reached across the table and handed Jim the salt shaker. "Where did they say the phones were?"

"There's one just outside the front doors," pointed Ralph. "I used it earlier to check in with the Mrs."

"Who you got to call?" Jim asked as he took a slice of lemon out of his mouth and threw it into a cup.

"I want to give Michelle and the kids a call," slurred Arnie. "They don't even know where the hell we are. They weren't expecting a call until tomorrow, but just in case they have to get in touch with me, gotta let 'em know where I am."

"That's a good idea," said Bud. "You never want to worry folks unnecessarily if you can help it."

When Arnie returned to the table after calling home, the Cuervo was nearly gone, along with everyone's energy level. Arnie hadn't been able to wait to talk to Michelle, to hear her voice. And when she answered, she said all the right things. "Just make sure you have a good time." "You need a break from all that stress, honey." "We miss you." "I love you." Arnie knew that she was a great lady. Very giving, a great mother. But for reasons he could not comprehend, as soon as he heard her voice, his excitement about talking to her transformed into agitated annoyance.

"Everything okay on the homefront?" Ralph asked.

"Everything's just fine." Arnie yawned and slumped back down on his chair. His buzz was already beginning to wear off and his head ached like hell. "Lisa, my five–year–old was sleeping, but I got to talk to my wife and to Ryan."

"So, you've got a son, do you?" asked Bud. "Son's are great. Not that there's anything wrong with daughters. Got three of them myself and love the hell out of all of them. But I always wished I could have had at least one boy."

"Well, I've got two of them," chimed in Ralph. "And I always wished I could have me a little girl. Seems like you've got the best of both worlds, Arnie. What we call a rich man's family. How old's your boy?"

"Fourteen. Ryan's a good kid. Gets good grades and doesn't give us any trouble."

"You got him playing golf yet?" asked Ralph.

"No, not yet. He's wanted to go out with me. But...I don't know, I've only been at it for two years myself, and I don't have that much time as it is. I'll get him into it eventually."

"Now's the time," persisted Ralph. "Remember what we were talking about before? If you want that good swing, you've got to get it grooved down when you're young. Get him out there!"

"That's right," added Bud. "Now's the time. Just look at Jim here. Hitting those balls on his dad's driving range when he was a kid. That's where he got it. That's why he hits that ball a mile." Bud turned his chair in the direction of Jim and continued. "I'll bet since your dad owned a driving range, he knew a little about the game himself. Must have taught you a few things."

"My dad taught me shit."

Bud, Arnie, and Ralph stared silently at Jim.

"Yeah, he was a good player, maybe a great player. Gave lessons at the range. Loved to teach pretty young women. He was so full of shit. I remember listening to the lines he would hand some of those ditzs." Jim stopped to grab a handful of chips. The others remained quiet.

"He used to try and teach me how to play, but mostly he just worked on his own game. I'd just sit there and watch him hit balls, sometimes until his hands bled. He was a crazy mother-fucker. And totally into himself. The few times he did give me a pointer, he'd wind up yelling at me. He had no patience. I could never do anything right. Never could please him; neither could my mom. That's why he did us all a favor when he decided to take off."

"Where'd he go?" asked Bud.

"Big man at the local club—everybody's hero—thought he could make it on the Tour. So he ran away with one of his bimbos and went down to Florida. Got into the mini–tour down there and even managed to win a couple of events. But it didn't go anywhere from there."

"Did you ever see him again?" Bud followed up.

"Nah, and it was better that way. My mom and I did just fine. She got the job with Arnie and we moved out of that old piece of shit house by the range. Found a real nice apartment. We did just fine on our own." Abruptly, Jim pulled his chair back from the table and stood up. "Hey, what time is it? We do have some seri-ous golf ahead of us tomorrow."

"Ten–thirty–five," answered Ralph.

"I'm getting myself one more brewski and then I'm out of here. Anybody want one?"

The others deferred as Jim left the table.

"Whew, that boy's had a rough time of it," whispered Bud. "Got a lot of anger vented up."

"He's doing okay," said Arnie. "His life's not half bad. He's got a decent paying job, no one to take care of but himself, and as you can see, has no problems meeting women."

"Would you want his life?" asked Ralph. "It seems to me that you have a good, loving family and a good business. Would you want to have no one to take care of but yourself?"

"Shhh." Arnie put his finger to his mouth as he saw Jim heading back with his beer.

"So what time do we tee off tomorrow?" asked Jim. "I think I saw us down for 7:22."

Ralph had made the arrangements. "We were originally scheduled for 8:18, but I was able to move it around, so we'll all be going off at 7:22. The whole damn schedule is screwed up, with the storm and all. The fellow at the pro shop tried to be as accommodating as possible."

As Bud, Ralph, and Jim discussed the next day's round, Arnie withdrew into his thoughts. He knew that Ralph was right, that his life *was* great. But he just couldn't appreciate what he had. He understood it intellectually—a great life on paper—but he just didn't know how to feel the joy that should rightfully be his. What was his problem? He didn't have the problems growing up that Jim had. His father wasn't the easiest man to be around, but at least he was always there.

Arnie's dad was a factory worker who commuted every working day of his life, forty-one years, to and from Patterson to the city. Two hours each way. It was no wonder that when he got home at night, he did nothing but eat, drink, yell, and fall asleep on the sofa. Arnie swallowed hard and dry, noticed a tingling presence in his gut that glided up and came to rest behind his moistened eyes.

Six months into retirement, his dad was hit with cancer. Terminal. Arnie felt ashamed for having spent so much of his life blaming his father for his own inadequacies. Blaming him for not being a baseball fan; for not teaching him how to play golf or for not taking him fishing. Blaming him for being so critical—relentlessly critical at times. Arnie was past the point of believing in his ill–placed blame. It was absurd and it was selfish. Unlike Jim's father, he had been there. "Brat!" Arnie screamed silently to himself. "Spoiled, fucking brat!"

Jim swallowed the last of his beer, slammed the base of the bottle on the table. "Guys, I'm outta here. I've got some business to take care of at the pro shop and I need to get some rest. Tomorrow morning the Savage awaits. Right?"

Arnie sat up and smiled at Jim. "Oh that's right. And you probably need a new golf shirt to play in tomorrow. You know, now that I think about it, I can use some clothes myself. How about you guys?" Arnie winked at Ralph and Bud. "Wouldn't either of you guys like some new golf pants? Or a new pair of shoes? How about a hat. You can always use a new hat. Let's go boys, let's keep Jim company."

Ralph and Bud grinned but did not speak.

Jim surveyed the men's facial expressions. His shoulders dropped as he sighed, the redness in his neck and cheeks softened. "Come on guys. It's no secret I'm interested. I'm not trying to hide it. Arnie here's just a little jealous. You guys understand, don't you?" Jim gave Ralph and Bud his own wink.

"Go ahead, young fellow," encouraged Bud. "She's a beautiful girl. Arnie's not the only one at this table who's jealous."

Ralph nodded in agreement. "Just don't wear yourself out tonight. You've got some unfinished business to attend to tomorrow."

"Don't worry about that." Jim was already backing toward the snack bar's exit. "Beautiful woman are nice. But pars are where it's at. I've got my priories straight. You guys have a good night. It's been a pleasure."

Ralph waved to Jim and then turned to Arnie. "Well, I guess it's time we all called it a night. We got a flight out tomorrow night. How about you? How long are you guys staying?"

"We're supposed to stay three nights. Until Sunday. We're scheduled to play again tomorrow. Then on the weekend we've got tee–times on a couple of Mainland courses. Seems like a lot of golf to me. We haven't even gotten our luggage out of the airport or checked into our hotel and I'm already burned out. After only nine holes, too. I don't know if I'm up to playing fifty–four holes in the next three days. Jim wanted to go for thirty–six a day. Can you believe that?"

"Yeah, I can believe it," answered Ralph. "He's young and strong and he can hit the cover off a golf ball. I can't say my game was ever at that level. But I used to hit thirty, forty yards further than I could now. Didn't mind playing thirty–six every once in a while myself. Remember them days, Bud?"

Bud sat still, staring ahead, his face white as chalk.

"You all right, Bud?"

No answer.

Arnie slid his chair closer to Bud and placed a hand on his soggy shoulder. "You don't look well. You want to get back to your room? Do you need a doctor?" Arnie lurched forward, his eyes widened as it hit him. "Shit. Suppose you need a fucking doctor on this island!"

"Just relax, will ya?" Bud spoke weakly, gripping the sides of his chair with both hands. "I just miscalculated the booze a little, that's all. Give me a few minutes in the can and I'll be fine. Some cold water on my face. Sleep it off and kick both your asses on the links tomorrow." Pushing himself up from the table with both arms, trying to steady himself, Bud grasped the back of his chair.

"Go with him," Arnie urged Ralph.

Ralph's eyes carefully monitored his friend's progress. "Don't worry about Bud, Arnie. He'll be just fine. Right, good buddy?"

Bud, who had managed to steady himself on his feet, didn't hear his friend's comment as he walked toward the restroom.

"You can't let him go by himself. He could fall and kill himself." Arnie was half out of his chair, ready to offer assistance.

"Oh, let's give him a few minutes to get settled, and then I'll go in after him." Ralph spoke calmly, but his unwavering stare over Arnie's shoulder belied his concern.

"Will he be all right?" Arnie asked. "Is it just the booze or could something else be wrong? Has he been like this before? Does his doctor know about the trip?"

"I'll go and see if he's okay." Ralph got up and went to the restroom to check on his friend.

Ten minutes passed and Arnie couldn't wait any longer.

As he slowly opened the door to the men's room, he saw Ralph, leaning with one hand resting on the sink, talking quietly. "Just take it easy, good buddy. Don't rush. Take your time."

Arnie heard the sounds of a sick man coming from inside the stall, the toilet flushing.

Then Arnie heard Bud's voice.

"Jesus Christ, I'm making a fucking mess in here. I can't believe how stupid I was to drink so much. What a fucking mess."

Arnie listened carefully to the sound of Bud's voice as it echoed in the tiled confines of the bathroom. He recalled visiting his dying father in the hospital, helping him to the tiled bathroom with the chrome support bars.

"Don't worry about a thing, good buddy," soothed Ralph. "I'll clean up after you. Just take your time and make sure you're okay."

Arnie, unnoticed, heard Bud crying as he quietly closed the door and went back to the table.

CHAPTER 7

Jim peered into the window of the pro shop and saw Tina piling up scattered boxes of golf shoes. There were only a few customers milling around, and there was no trace of her father.

"Hi there." Jim closed the door behind him. "Been busy tonight?"

"Oh hi. Sure have. I'll be glad when this day is over."

"It doesn't look like you'll have to put up with any of us after tomorrow. The weather has really cleared up. Turned into a beautiful night."

"That's what I heard. I can't really complain. This is such an infrequent occurrence." Tina glanced at her watch and turned to look over her left shoulder. "Excuse me, please. I have to get some boxes from the back room."

"No problem. But I can use some help when you get a chance. I wanted to pick up a shirt or two. Possibly a pair of slacks."

"I'll be back in just a couple of minutes." Tina glared at Jim, through him, without smiling. After a moment's hesitation, she sighed through a pouting lower lip, turned, and walked toward the door that led to the stockroom in the back of the shop.

Jim picked up a red, white, and blue La Mode golf shirt, removed it from its cellophane bag, unfolded it, and placed it against the front of his torso. He kept the shirt pinned against his shoulders with the three middle fingers of each hand and walked

up and down the aisles until he found a mirror on the wall dis-
playing golf bags. He looked at himself without noticing the
sweater, instead staring at his face. He turned his head to the right
and studied his strong, stubbled jaw, watched his Adam's apple
enlarge and fall as he swallowed. Facing the mirror again, he took
note of his round, usually alert, sometimes blue, sometimes green
eyes. He noticed the puffy, grayish half–circles beneath them and
suddenly realized just how tired and drunk he was. Still, the blue
in the shirt he held before him brought those eyes to life; sun
sparkled oceans. Tired or not, his eyes were still, no doubt, his
best feature. He studied his long lashes, pink cheeks that rounded
like pale apples atop high cheek bones when he smiled, his soft
skin. His mother always told him that he was the kind of hand-
some that would also be beautiful on a woman. He thought that
the hard edge of being unshaven made him appear more mascu-
line. He liked that.

He turned around and spotted her at the front counter. She was
handing two towels—white with one solid green stripe—to a
frightfully short man with slicked back, greasy black hair. Jim
noticed that she had changed her clothes since earlier in the day.
The wispy, outer edge of her soft and golden hair captured the
glow of the yellowish fluorescent that lighted the pro shop and
transformed it into brilliant rays of midday sunshine. She must
have just showered. When they talked just moments before, he
recognized how great she smelled. Obsession, he thought. One of
his old girlfriends had worn it.

Tina finished her business with the small man, bent over to pick
up a stack of four shoe boxes, and headed in Jim's direction. He
moved quickly from the mirror, back toward the sweater rack,
stopped and looked over the top of a pile of Goretex rain gear. She
had stopped to talk to another man. A man seated in a chair. Jim
threw down the unfolded sweater and stepped out from behind

the rack into the open center portion of the pro shop. He decided to take a few more practice putts while he waited. Grabbing a Tommy Armour Zapp, he began his pendulum preshot practice routine. He could see her clearly now. She was talking to an old man in a wheelchair.

Jim continued stroking putts. He did not sink one, nor was he keeping track. He wondered what a man in a wheelchair would be doing on this island. The only people on Caramus were golfers, Tina, her father and…. It suddenly hit Jim that the old man had to be Hans Keeler, the owner of the place. Head Professional, as the sign behind the counter said. Jim looked more carefully. The old man was small and frail, the width of his bottom only covering the middle portion of his seat. Several thick ropes of flesh ran down diagonally from a point in the center of his balding scalp, forming parentheses around his eyes, ending at the outer edges of his mouth. When he talked, his forehead appeared to jump, swell, and during pauses in his speech, to deflate. The sickly looking, leathery old man still had an animated youthfulness about him. He spoke excitedly, conducting his speech with both hands flailing. And even from this distance, Jim could feel the radiance of his icy blue eyes. The eyes of a beautiful young child encased in a decrepit, weather–beaten corpse of a man. It was obvious that Tina was very much at ease with him. She bent toward him, laughing, her long blond hair brushing his shoulder.

Jim stood transfixed, ankles crossed, leaning on the top of the putter with his left hand and watched Tina, her back now facing him. She had on tight, black cotton chinos and a navy blue, satin blouse. Jim stared hard. The shiny fabric of her blouse that kissed her shoulders and back, the imprinted lines of her low–cut panties. Jim imagined her naked, taking her from the rear, penetrating those perfect buttocks. Parting her blond curls, gently kissing the back of her neck; reaching around that fragrant body with both hands and stroking her breasts.

As Tina stood upright and turned to face him, Jim quickly placed the putter back on the rack, and turned his back to her. He needed time to recover. To conceal his thoughts.

As Tina approached, he grabbed an ugly lime, pink, and purple sweater from the rack and held it in front of himself.

"Do you like that sweater? It comes in three color combinations, and there's twenty–five percent off. It's one of our most popular."

Surrendering his woolen figleaf, Jim answered, "No, I don't think so. I was just looking around. What I really need is a shirt."

"Let me show you what we have. I just got the word that we should start closing up." Tina walked ahead of Jim to a different section of the shop.

As he studied that butt again, close up, in motion, Jim asked, "Was that man in the wheelchair Mr. Keeler?"

"Yes it was. A great man. He's a pleasure to work for." Tina pulled down several shirts from a shelf. "You're a large, right?"

"Yeah, I guess so. Sometimes a medium fits. The sign says that he's a golf pro. Is that true?"

"Sure is." Tina pulled four different styles of shirts, two medium and two large, from oak storage cubicles. "He was the European champ in 1972."

Jim's face lit up. "Really? Did he ever play in this country?"

"Very little. Actually, he never visited this country until 1981, when he purchased Wild Links."

Jim reached for one of the shirts Tina was holding, held it at arm's length, and examined it. "There's something I've been meaning to say to you. I mean about before. I didn't mean to offend you. I was just trying to be friendly."

"That's okay," answered Tina. "I may have been abrupt, but we were very busy. Now, do you have any particular colors in mind?"

Jim picked out two of the shirts Tina was holding. One was a solid navy with a small, red logo on the breast pocket. The other a teal, black and white, divided into three wide horizontal stripes. "These look good. How much?"

"Let's see." Tina looked for the price tag inside the collar of the navy shirt first. "This one's seventy–five." Looking for the price of the other shirt, "And this one's sixty, with 20% off. So that's...forty–eight dollars. Looks like the bargain choice."

Without any hesitation, Jim stated, "I'll take them both. You do take Visa, right?"

Tina paused before answering. "Right. Mastercard, Visa, and American Express. You want to try them on? The fitting room's..."

"That's okay, I'm sure they'll fit just fine."

"Okay, then let's take them up to the register."

He followed her, once again studying his subject matter with intensity and purpose.

"I really like this navy blue one," she said as she folded it up and put it into a bag.

"I really like *your* navy blue blouse. That's why the price didn't matter. You had me thinking navy blue."

Tina turned away and ran his credit card through the imprinter. "That comes to $131.61. Please sign by the X."

Jim took the pen from her and signed his name. He looked around to make sure that no one could hear, stared directly into her eyes, and whispered, "Look Tina, I can't keep playing games with you. You're a beautiful girl and I'd like to get to know you. I don't need these stupid shirts. Why do you think I'm here at this time of the night? I happen to think you're incredible."

Tina took back her pen, ripped the top layer off the credit slip and handed it to Jim. She placed her hands flat on the counter–top, looked Jim straight in the eye, and calmly stated, "I'm engaged to be married."

"You're what?"

"Engaged," she repeated. "And the wedding we're getting ready for—that I mentioned in the snack bar—it's mine. I'm getting married on Saturday."

"Why didn't you tell me before?"

"I had no reason to."

"You knew I was interested."

"Maybe so. But you should have realized I wasn't."

"That's not true. I thought you might be. Why did you make such a point of letting me know you'd be here tonight?"

Tina locked the register, her neck reddening and taut, she turned to close the blinds on the wire–mesh window behind the pro shop's counter. "I made a point of letting everyone who walked in here today know that we'd be open late tonight. As you said earlier, we *are* in business to make money."

Jim stood perfectly still, shoulders slumped, mouth open, his eyes glazed, focused on nothing.

Shutting one set of lights, Tina said, "It's late. I have to close up now. You'll have to go." She handed him the bag that contained his shirts and led him to the door.

Jim walked out into the black night.

CHAPTER 8

Arnie was in his grandmother's house, and she was giving him chocolate–covered halvah. Then his fourth–grade teacher appeared and scolded him for keeping candy hidden in his desk. A steady beeping sound created a backdrop for Arnie's dream. The garbage truck? Was today garbage day? Where the hell was he? Where was that sound coming from? The Fossil chronograph on the nightstand. Arnie reached out, knocked the watch around, and grabbed it. Squinting, he put it in front of his face and pushed the alarm button. Quiet restored, Arnie buried his face in the pillow. Disoriented, not quite fully awake, it took him a moment to realize where he was. Finally, he got it together. Golf, Caramus Island, Wild Links.

Managing to sit up, he looked again at the watch. 6:07. Sunlight streamed through the vertical opening which separated the room's heavy curtains, striping the wall and floor opposite Arnie's bed. He looked around and saw Jim sprawled across the bed, face down, quietly snoring, wearing only white jockey shorts—inside–out. The blanket and spread lay beside the bed. Arnie wondered about Jim's night. About how it went with that girl.

Getting out of bed, Arnie didn't feel too bad. A small miracle. After a shower, a couple of aspirin, some breakfast, and six or eight cups of coffee, he should be just fine. Then he remembered Bud. Arnie worried about the old man. He walked over to the window, and drew back the curtain. The bright sunlight filled the room—too much for waking up eyes. Retreating for the moment, Arnie walked over and attempted to wake Jim up. Jim mumbled, "I'm up, I'm up," but made no effort to move. Arnie decided to be more forceful after his shower.

Twenty minutes later, Jim lifted his head, and asked, "What time is it?"

"Six–twenty–seven," answered Arnie, revived, dressed, combing his hair in the mirror.

"Shit, I'd better get going. I hope there are some clean and dry towels," he added as he sat up. Running his fingers through his hair, breathing deeply, he finally pushed himself off the bed and toward the bathroom.

Arnie yelled to Jim as he passed by, "So, how did it go last night? I can't wait to hear about it."

No reply. The sounds of the toilet flushing, water running in the shower.

Arnie had his answer.

Five minutes before 7:00, the snack bar was nearly empty when Jim and Arnie got there. Ralph and Bud hadn't arrived yet.

"Let's get some breakfast," suggested Arnie.

"Coffee will be just fine for me."

By the time they got seated, Ralph walked in alone.

"Where's Bud?" asked Arnie.

"No need for concern now, but as you know, Bud had a rough time last night." Laughing, Ralph added, "Man, I don't remember the last time I saw him overdo like that. Like a teenager. Just like a damn teenager."

"Are you sure he's all right?" Arnie pressed for more details.

"Absolutely!" exclaimed Ralph. "He's suffering from nothing worse than a good old fashioned hangover. Plain and simple. Problem is, he's no kid anymore. He figures he'll be best off just taking it easy today. He's goin' to take the shuttle back and relax at the Breakers. Can't say it sounded all that bad myself. Excuse me, I'm goin' to get me some breakfast."

"So Bud wound up getting sick," said Jim. "I'm not surprised. He was really belting those shots down. Well, I guess he might as well push it here and there. I mean, what's he got to lose?"

Arnie sat back and sipped his coffee. Arnie knew what Bud was losing. His life. His goddamned life. Arnie felt a deep pain sear his chest. His stomach knotted as he realized that he would never see Bud again. And, that he had never said goodbye.

"Nothing like some easy–overs cooked in bacon grease to start off the day." Ralph dropped his plate on the table and went off to look for some ketchup.

"How can you eat this shit?" Jim asked Arnie, who had finished everything his empty, grease soaked paper plate had to offer.

"I like it, that's why."

"You'd think you'd take better care of your body than that," Jim retorted, as Ralph pulled in his chair and spread a napkin across his lap.

"Well, we have one helluva day in store for us," said Ralph, banging his fist on the bottom of the unopened bottle of Heinz.

"The guy at the grill said it's supposed to get into the 80's," said Jim. "With plenty of sunshine."

"Did you see that sky out there this morning?" asked Ralph , cutting up his easy overs into several small pieces, before taking his first bite. "Not a cloud in the sky, fog sitting on the ground, ready to burn away. I wonder how the fairways and greens will be after all the rain we had yesterday."

"Should be okay," Jim had already considered the problem. "These ocean courses usually have pretty good drainage. They have to. They get a lot of big storms. Hurricanes. Yesterday's was probably not that bad."

Ralph, scraping up egg yolk with his toast, nodded in agreement.

Arnie had trouble thinking about golf. He wondered how Ralph could be so relaxed, why he wasn't back at the hotel with Bud. Then Arnie remembered the scene in the bathroom the night before. Ralph knew what he was doing.

"So, I guess we'll go off as a threesome," said Arnie.

"Not necessarily," said Jim. "They might want to slot in a single."

"Either way, we can't lose," Ralph said as he hastily swallowed the last of his coffee. "Let's go boys. Time to see what the fates have in store for us today."

CHAPTER 9

Jim practiced on the putting green while Arnie and Ralph paid for the carts. Still wet from yesterday's rain and the morning dew, the green was slow, and Jim's putts consistently short.

"Let's go, Jim," said Arnie, driving the cart as close to the practice green as he could. "They're backed up, and we have to get in line."

"Great." Jim picked up his two putting balls, placed them in his pocket, and headed toward the cart.

Two foursomes were lined up in front of them. The delay didn't look too bad. The men took the time to do some stretching and to take some practice swings.

"Man, I feel stiff as a board," said Ralph as he swung his elbows from side to side. "Still think some of that dampness is settled in my bones."

"If there's ever a day that will loosen you up, this is it," reassured Arnie.

While Jim and Ralph continued their calisthenics, Arnie went back to the cart and got organized. A handful of tees and a Wilson Prostaff ball in his pocket, two more balls in the pop–in rack on the cart's dashboard. He put on his tan Footjoy cabretta golf glove, opened and closed his fist several times. Getting behind the wheel, Arnie entered the names on the scorecard with a stubby red pencil. Jim first, Ralph second, his own name last. Arnie studied the scorecard's green and blue diagrams for each hole. Par 5, 545; par 4, 427; par 4, 432; par 3, 207. Arnie became aware of his heartbeat, noticed his mouth starting to become dry. This course was ridiculous for a player with his skills. He didn't belong here. No wonder he had shot a sixty–three the day before. Today he might reach 150! That's why there were drownings on the sixteenth hole. Those people weren't killed. The poor bastards committed suicide.

Laughing to himself, Arnie looked at the morning sun making its way up the eastern sky, and remembered that this was only a game. He took a deep breath and smelled pine as the sun began to soothe the crisp, morning chill. Arnie felt glad to be alive, determined to just enjoy this round. Like Bud said, any damn game is meant to be fun.

Arnie turned around as he heard two carts pull up behind him on the path. Four athletic looking young men. The audience for his tee shot. Arnie noticed a hot, prickly sensation in the back of his neck, his hands started to shake. He got out of the cart to take a few practice swings.

The foursome in front of them had hit their tee shots. Two in the woods to the left, two in the heart of the fairway.

Jim pulled out Big Boy as he approached the tee area. "I'll be happy with the shot I hit yesterday."

"No shit!" exclaimed Ralph. "Nothin' wrong with two–fifty down the middle."

"I'll be happy just to lay it out there," added Arnie. "I'm going with my 5–iron again. Just want to hit it…"

"Excuse me. Excuse me, please."

Arnie stopped talking, and turned to respond to a bearded man wearing a solid gold cap with no lettering on it, bag on shoulder, who was trying to get his attention.

"Hi there, what's up?" asked Arnie.

"I'm a single, and the starter suggested I hurry up to find out if I could play with you guys. Would you mind?"

"Not at all," said Arnie. "You guys mind if...what's your name?"

"John."

"If John plays along with us?" Arnie looked at Jim, then at Ralph.

"It'll be a pleasure, John. My name is Ralph, welcome." Ralph reached out his hand.

"Thank you, sir," replied the young man.

"My name's Arnie." Arnie also shook hands with the new player.

Jim walked back to meet John halfway from his position at the tee, and offered his greetings with a handshake.

"You can ride with me," offered Ralph. "My playing partner was not feeling real good, so I'm riding solo today."

"Thanks very much," replied John. "But I prefer to walk."

"That's great," said Ralph. "I'll tell you, walking on the golf course is a dying art. Best thing in the world for you. These damned carts are bad for your back, and don't give you that nice rhythm you get from walking. Especially on a day like today. But, you're welcome to strap your clubs on my cart if you like."

"That's okay, I'd just as soon carry my bag. But thanks again. You're very generous."

Jim glanced back with a strained, annoyed expression before setting up behind his teed up ball, and glancing out at the fairway on one. In front of him, the final player was hitting to the green. Jim backed out again and took a moment to check out the new member of his foursome. Big dude. Must be about six-two. And a wide body. Not fat. Just big and solid. Probably around 220. Jim figured he was a player; coming along as a single, carrying his bag, appearing very relaxed. Jim knew that today wouldn't be like yesterday. Today, he was going to have some competition.

"I think you can go hit now," said Ralph, getting ready on–deck.

Jim looked out at a clear fairway and nodded in agreement. Standing behind his ball, Jim picked the spot he wanted to hit to, visualized the shot, and got into his stance. Waggling the driver, Jim paused and looked back at John. He stepped out and regrouped.

Back to his waggle, he focused on the white ball, the black print, Titleist 1. See the ball...see the ball. Low and slow. Jim swung, but never saw the ball's flight. On the screws, perfect impact felt like no impact. He knew he got it all.

"Whoooeee!" screamed Ralph.

"Great hit. Perfect position," added Arnie. "Looks like you haven't lost it."

Jim bent down to recover his tee, which flipped end–over–end, just like a long field goal that bisected the goal posts. Walking back toward his cart, he smiled at the others.

"Nice hit," said the stranger, as he moved up and waited for his own turn.

Ralph was next to hit. Swinging a Power–bilt, graphite shafted, 3–wood designed for seniors, he lifted the ball 175 yards out, on the left side of the fairway, close to the trees. Not a great spot on the left bending dogleg, but a decent start on the long par five.

"I'll take it," said Ralph walking toward the others.

"So would I," said Arnie on his way to center stage. "Nice hit, Ralph."

Arnie placed the ball in the ground and noticed that there were now two foursomes behind them, taking in the action. So far, they had witnessed one great shot and one decent shot.

Soling his 5–iron behind the ball, Arnie was not going to stand over it too long. Thinking only about keeping his head still, he whacked away. It felt good, and the cheers from Ralph and Jim confirmed a good shot.

"Way to go, Arnie," said Ralph.

"Looks like you're on today," offered Jim, holding out his palm for five.

"Good play," added John. "You're in great shape."

Turning to face the others, Arnie stated, "Not so fast, let's not overdo it. I just covered 150 yards. I still have 6900 left."

John was already at the tee area, smiling in response to Arnie's comment. Carefully, he spotted his Titleist X–out, bent down again, and pushed it a little further into the ground. He looked out at the fairway, and took a gentle practice swing with his weathered, MacGregor persimmon 3–wood. Once over the ball, he swung almost immediately. A gentle, graceful swing that gave the impression that, for such a big man, he might be holding back. The clear, hard knocking sound announced a clean hit. The ball, climbing higher than Jim's, seemed to pick up speed in the air. Hanging, loping, it disappeared into the pure blue sky, until suddenly it landed, right in line with Jim's ball, about fifteen yards further out.

"Did you see that?" Ralph was ecstatic. "Look's like we're going to have us a longest drive contest today!"

"Great shot, John," said Arnie. Was that a 3–wood? Holy shit!"

"Good drive," said Jim.

Arnie was away and decided to go with his 5–iron again. It was going to take three more shots to reach the green anyway. Why push his luck? Walking up to his ball, the others waited for him to hit. Arnie was reminded of the penalty for being short off the tee. Feeling some confidence after his first hit, he was determined not to hurry and screw up. He took his time. There was plenty of wide open fairway to aim for. Arnie's mind was clear as he took a nice easy swing. He hit another perfect 5–iron.

Ralph's second shot hooked into the woods, and his third shot was an effective chip out to the fairway. He was still away. With a clear path to the green, he topped a 5–wood, but hit it straight and got plenty of roll. He dropped his club in his bag, got in the cart, and took a deep breath, happy to be out of trouble for the moment.

Jim had about 280 to the front of the green. He placed his palm on his driver, paused, and then went for his 2–iron, before switching to the 3. Although slightly fading, his solidly struck lay–up stayed in the right side of the fairway, about 90 yards from the green.

John went to the 3–wood again. The ball started off to the right, only to draw back and land on the right, front fringe of the green. No reaction, he calmly picked up his bag and headed up the fairway.

"Ride ahead without me," Jim told Arnie. "I want to walk with John."

Jim hurried and settled into a brisk stride alongside John. "Nice shot. You always hit the ball that well?"

John smiled. "Are you kidding? No one can. It's impossible. Besides the game wouldn't be any fun if you hit great shots all the time."

"I guess that's true," replied Jim. "How do you usually score?"

"I don't really keep score. Just play one hole, and one shot at a time."

"I understand that logic, but you must have some idea of how you score."

"Well, let's just say that I aim for par."

Practically running to keep up with John's pace, Jim said, "So then, you're a scratch golfer, right?"

"I don't know about that. Sometimes I make par, sometimes I don't. I get my share of bogies, too."

Jim stopped asking questions.

When the hole was completed, John got his birdie, Jim his par. Arnie was elated with his bogey six, and Ralph was down, but not out, with his triple for a snowman.

When the men reached the tee of the par four, 427 yard second hole, the foursome in front of them was just getting ready to hit.

They pulled the carts up the path near the tee area, under a huge oak tree. The gusty breeze was a chilling reminder of the early hour.

"I should have brought a jacket *and* a sweater," said Ralph as he shuddered and wrapped his arms across his body.

"Don't worry," replied Arnie from the cart behind. "Soon you'll have your sweater off. Just look at how sunny the tee area is. You'll be warm as soon as you get there."

Under the oak tree, sun spots dappled the dense leaves, highlighting the ground brush. Motion and light , but no warmth. The oak tree had won out. It was cold in this place.

Blowing on his fists, Ralph turned around and commented, "Well, it looks like everyone's off to a good start. Everybody but me that is."

"Guaranteed, you'll be ten strokes ahead of me before we're through," replied Arnie.

"I don't know about that. You really have that 5–iron cooking."

"Well, get ready for something different and totally unpredictable," said Arnie. "I'm hitting my 3–wood this hole. What is it…427 yards? It's still like a par five for me, but I feel like such a wimp hitting off with that 5–iron all the time. Paid a fortune for these Big Berthas and never use them."

"Use whatever you're comfortable with." Ralph turned back around, rocked back and forth, blew again into his right, ungloved hand.

"I'm gonna go take a leak," said Jim. "All that coffee's finally caught up to me."

"Don't get lost now," cautioned Arnie. "We're up in a couple of minutes."

Jim found a path that led down a short and steep hill. He reached a small clearing covered with fallen leaves. Standing behind a large tree, he relieved himself. He looked around and then straight up. The tree tops in the distance were bending and scraping against the high, blue sky. Jim looked at the stream that bordered the clearing, running effortlessly across its rocky bed. Everything was perfect, yet Jim felt empty. It was a beautiful day, a great course, and he even parred the first hole. Still, Jim felt no excitement. He felt nothing.

By the tee area of the second hole, Ralph said, "You've got the honors, Johnny boy."

John walked up to hit, and Ralph and Arnie walked up with him to get an idea of how the hole laid out.

"I don't see the green," said Arnie squinting, his hand across the top of his eyes.

"You have to drive the ball over that crest," said John pointing. "Right beyond it is a valley. Get over the ridge, and the ball will roll forever. Try to stay on the right, because that's the only way you'll have an angle toward the green. It's still a tough second shot, because the green is elevated with large bunkers on either side."

"Five–iron," shouted out Arnie as he headed back to his cart to switch clubs.

"I'm just goin' to hit the damn thing out there," said Ralph. "Bogeyed the sucker yesterday. Don't know how I did it, but I did."

From the edge of the woods, Jim looked long and hard at the stranger. Figured he was probably in his mid to late twenties. It was hard to tell with that untrimmed beard. And his clothes. Black denim trousers sporting at least a half–dozen zippers and a bright yellow, collarless shirt with two rows of buttons running down the front. Jim looked at John's feet. Black high top sneakers.

"Woooosh!!" The sound of rapidly moving, battered air got Jim's attention. Running up to see where the ball went, all four men watched. Silently.

"Where'd it go? I lost it," said Ralph. "Sure did sound good."

"I never saw it," added Arnie.

"I got over the crest, but hooked it a little. I'm going to have to lay up on my second shot."

John smiled at the others as he picked up his tee and walked back to the cart area.

"You use a driver?" asked Jim.

"Yes I did."

Jim grabbed Big Boy and proceeded to crush a perfect drive. Just the way John had outlined it before.

Arnie and Ralph hit their tee shots straight out, short of the rising crest. Again, Arnie was away.

CHAPTER 10

The only one off the green, Ralph blasted out of the right side bunker. The ball rolled to a stop, ten inches in front of the pin, right on line.

"That's good." Jim was first to concede the putt after the great out.

Arnie met Ralph at the flag, put his left arm around the older man's neck, and with his right hand, pinched his cheek. "Tell me. Who do you think you are? Huh? Who do you think you are? You have no right doing that. You have no right making that shot."

"Get away from me," said a laughing Ralph, pushing Arnie away. "I do it all the time. All the time. Nothin' but a bogey anyway. You'd think I'd at least get a par on a shot like that."

"Beautiful play." said John. "I thought it was going in the cup."

Arnie was next to putt. He made it to the green in four. His second shot was a straight, low 3–iron. He topped the ball a little, but hit it square enough for it to travel the customary 170 yards. With about 100 yards left, he was feeling as confident as he ever felt on a golf course. All that practice on the executive courses gave him a pretty solid short iron game. He got all of his 9–iron, but miscalculated the distance, and hit too far, onto a mound in back of the green. Hitting the only chip in his repertoire—a little choked down 7–iron with a putting stroke—he pushed the ball much too hard. It rolled eighteen feet past the hole.

Still away, Arnie didn't panic. Putting didn't scare him the way long range, power golf did. Much less opportunity for humiliation here. It was just like miniature golf. Arnie remembered being a kid and his family going to the Catskills for the only vacation they ever had. They all played miniature golf—even his grandmother. Arnie smiled as he thought of the holes–in–one that his sister and Grandma had made. He remembered how much his father had laughed that day.

Behind his ball, Arnie bent on one knee to study his putt. He was unsure of how to approach the shot, but he'd make it look good. Arnie was just happy to be on the green. And in four. Not bad. Get it close, and get your double bogey.

Arnie stroked the ball.

"Pack a lunch!" kidded Jim after Arnie's putt rolled ten feet past the cup.

"Shit, can you believe it?" cried Arnie. "I hate this fucking game."

Arnie knew it couldn't last. Early on, he'd hit the ball crisply, and had already fantasized about the prospects of a good round. That last putt signaled the return of reality. Arnie remembered how long eighteen holes of golf could be. It was such a frustrating game. So many ways to screw up.

Jim was next. His drive couldn't have been any better if he'd walked out into the fairway and placed the ball. He got the roll down the right side, and had a wide open 6–iron to the flag. He executed the easy shot and looked now at a twelve foot, relatively straight downhill putt for birdie.

Jim studied his putt, distracted by the long morning shadows and John's perfect, sixty–five yard sand wedge that missed hitting the stick by less than a foot. John's ball settled about eight feet away. Jim knew that if he made his birdie, he could be even with John.

Jim walked around his putt again. Aware that the rains and morning dew had slowed the usually fast greens, he knew he had to hit it. Couldn't come up short. But it was downhill, and the ball could potentially roll well past its target if he wasn't careful. Concentrate. Get the line. It looked like a two inch, late break to the left. Jim visualized the ball rolling along the projected path, right into the cup.

As Jim struck the ball, he thought he headed it out too far to the right, that he didn't give it enough. Rolling smoothly, the ball kept rolling as if motorized. Rotating, spinning inward, the old Titleist bit the turf and veered into the right edge of the cup.

"Yes!" Jim pumped his right fist in the air.

"Way to go, Jim!" exclaimed Arnie.

"Chirp, chirp. Chirp, chirp." Ralph cheered the birdie.

John offered his hand in congratulations. "Excellent read. Excellent putt."

Arnie was next. He had to get it close. Triple bogey would be bad enough. This time he didn't study the putt. He lined up straight at the cup, thought about keeping his head still, and was absolutely shocked when the ball fell into the heart of the cup.

"Arnie, Arnie, Arnie!" shouted Ralph as he ran over and patted his friend on the back. "You're goin' to keep me honest today, aren't you? Goin' to give me a run for my money."

Jim, his hand high in the air, slapped Arnie's hand. "Nice putt. Way to bear down."

John smiled broadly. "Good recovery. You've got a nice putting stroke."

Arnie reveled in his success until he remembered that the next hole was a 432 yard, par 4. Arnie felt like calling it a day.

John's eight–footer for par seemed pretty basic. Straight putt, slightly uphill. With the haste that matched the rest of his game, John hit a smooth rolling, on–line putt that slid just past the left edge of the cup. He tapped it in for a bogey, picked up the flag-stick, reset it in the cup, and headed to join the others.

"You were robbed," said Ralph. "That was in the cup."

"Tough break," said Arnie. "It looked good."

"It was a good roll," added Jim, walking alongside John. "Don't those frustrate the hell out of you?"

"Not really," answered John. "They're going to happen. Nothing I can do about it."

Jim didn't respond, but kept his eyes fixed on John while they headed off the green toward the next tee. He's so full of shit, thought Jim. Pretends that nothing bothers him, but inside it's really tearing his guts up. Jim hated guys like that.

John turned to meet Jim's glare and said, "You have a very nice game."

"Thanks. I've been playing the damn game long enough."

"I could tell."

The men walked single–file along a narrow path which wound through a thick pine grove. John led. Jim followed and watched him closely. John was a powerfully built man, with a touch for golf. He knew the game. Jim felt good as he remembered having played the first two holes one under. One stroke better than John.

As they broke into the clearing by the third tee, the sight was breathtaking. Twenty yards in front of the tee area, a pond mir-rored the tall pines that ran down the right side of the hole. The sun's dazzling light topped the scene with a rippling, golden cover-ing. Off to the left, the green, aged mountains rested under a sap-phire sky.

"Lord, you can take me now," said Ralph. "That's about as pretty as it gets."

"I think Mark Twain was right," said Arnie.

All three men looked at Arnie.

"Well, are you going to tell us what you're talking about?" asked Jim.

Pausing another moment, Arnie went on to explain. "Mark Twain referred to golf as a perfectly good walk, spoiled. Looking at this wonderful spot, I can't help but think what a shame it is to have to try and hit a little white ball over that beautiful water."

Ralph and John laughed.

"Come on Arnie," said Jim. "You're playing real well. You can enjoy the sights *and* play the damn game."

"I know, I know," said Arnie. "I am having a great time. And I love this fucking game. Don't you know how much I love this fucking game?"

Arnie grabbed Jim behind the neck and had him laughing too, now. It was a magnificent day, smack in the center of paradise, and the men were all laughing.

Chapter 11

Within the next hour, the men completed four holes, and the temperature went up eight degrees. The golfers, jammed at the start, had opened up, and spread out deeper, into the sun–baked, green island. It had taken Jim twenty–five strokes to complete the first six holes. Even par. John remained one stroke behind this pace, while Arnie and Ralph were both ten over. As they approached the tee at the par four, 361 yard seventh, play had again backed up.

"What the hell!" cried Jim as he noticed the pot–bellied gentleman from the foursome in front getting ready to hit his drive. "How did this happen?"

"Play backs up at this point a lot," said John. "The eighth hole is a very difficult par three. The fifth handicap hole. There are a lot of balls lost off the tee."

"Goddamn," said Jim. "I hate this shit. I was into a nice rhythm, and now I have to sit here and wait while these guys go looking for lost balls."

"Well, I personally don't mind the break." Ralph had his hands behind his neck and his feet up on the cart. "The way you boys are burning it up, and the way I'm stinking up the place, I'd just as soon take me a breather."

"I hope you're including me, when you talk about hot rounds," said Arnie.

"I sure am," answered Ralph. "I can't believe you're the same fella I played with yesterday."

"Thank you very much. I accept your assessment with grace and humility." Arnie bowed his head.

"You said you started to play just a couple of years ago?" asked John. "You get yourself a little pitch shot, work in a wood off the tee, and you'll have a very nice game. It takes a long time. You've got to hit thousands and thousands of balls."

"Why thank you very much, my good friend," said Arnie continuing his noble manner of expression. "Kind of you to offer your astute and generous observations."

"Have you had enough?" asked Jim.

Arnie ignored Jim and asked of John, "What do you mean, I have to learn how to hit my woods? Might I remind you of the par 3 fourth hole?"

"You're right," replied John. "That was a great 3–wood. I stand corrected."

Both men shared a laugh while Arnie slouched down in the cart, cap over his eyes, and relived that spectacular moment. A par 3, 207 yard hole, water 100 yards out, elevated green, surrounded by some major bunkers. There was no point in laying up, and he needed all of his 3–wood to get there. Ironic that the first time he took out a wood all day, was on a par 3. Although expecting nothing short of disaster, he hit the ball solidly—low, and well left of the target. His old banana shot finally rewarded him as the ball sliced and landed right on the green, about eight feet from the cup. He and John scored the only pars on that hole. Arnie would see that tee shot a thousand times over in the weeks to follow.

"Hey John," said Jim, looking up from his scorecard. "Any tricks on this hole? Looks pretty straight ahead to me."

"It's one of the easiest holes on the course," replied John. "Straight out, no trouble to speak of."

"How often have you played this course?" Jim asked.

John, hands on hips, stretched from side to side, and replied, "Many times. I help out with the groundskeeping a couple of days a week. When I have a little extra time, like today, I try to slot in somewhere."

"Oh yeah? What kind of grounds work do you do?"

"Routine. You know, mowing, whipping the greens, moving the hole placements. That kind of stuff. Except for the flowers. That's my own little project."

"What flowers?" asked Jim.

"I don't know if you noticed the flower garden off to the side of the clubhouse," explained John. "I put a lot of time into that. Did you notice the small, boxed–off section of flowers at each tee area?"

No response from Jim.

"Yeah, I noticed those," said Ralph. "I was thinkin' how beautiful they were. Those yours?"

"Yes they are. I put whatever free time I can find into the flowers. I really enjoy it."

"That's great," said Arnie. "They really are beautiful."

Jim couldn't believe what he was hearing. This guy who's built like a linebacker is into flowers? He needed to know more. "Do you have a regular job? I mean, where do you live? What do you do?"

John smiled, stopped stretching, and walked toward the cart where Jim and Arnie were sitting. "Yes Jim, I do have a regular job. I work in the kitchen at the Beach Cove Resort. They also give me lodging and meals. The hours are tough, but it gives me plenty of time for golf."

"Sounds like a great life for a young man," said Ralph. "To be free like that, all that time for golf."

"I can't complain," answered John.

Listening to these conversations, Jim decided he had John pegged. No wonder the guy was such a good golfer. He was basically a bum. Has a shitty job in a kitchen, screws around with flowers, and plays golf all day. Probably knocks up all the pretty young tourists, too. Jim definitely had his number.

"Looks like we can hit now," said Ralph. "Jim, you have honors, right?"

The relatively easy, straight ahead, seventh hole gave everyone but Arnie problems. The wide fairway was not broad enough to contain Jim and John's duck hooks, both of which landed behind a big weeping willow. Ralph hit a "worm burner" that made it only 100 yards out, while Arnie hit a perfect 3–wood smack down the middle. Jim, John and Arnie all scored bogey, while Ralph's game continued to suffer with his second triple on the front side.

The men reached the tee at the par 3, 199 yard, eighth hole. It was obvious why the hole was so tough to score on.

"Jesus Christ!" exclaimed Ralph as he looked out from the tee area. "They're trying to kill me! I tell you, this hole just might mark the end of my time on earth. Bury me right down there in that ravine. Hey John, you can put the flowers on my grave."

"It's not that tough," said Jim over the other men's laughter. "You just got to hit the green, that's all."

"That's all? That's all?" Arnie put his face three inches from Jim's and shouted. "Are you out of your fucking mind? If you don't hit the green, you'll need to take a mule train down that ravine to find it."

"It's a very tough hole," verified John. "I've had my share of problems on it more than once."

The eighth hole at Wild Links had no grass except for the tee area and the green. Between these two points, the yardage looked like a miniature version of the Grand Canyon.

"Suppose you hit your ball down there?" asked Arnie, pointing to the reddish brown rocks out in front of the tee.

"Well, then you have two options," answered John. "You can either tee up another. Or…you can take a mule train down and try to retrieve the one you hit."

Arnie and Ralph laughed.

Jim said, "Hey Arnie, you bogeyed the last hole, why don't you show us the way?"

"Sure," replied Arnie. "Why the hell not. It'll be my pleasure. I'm so zoned–in right now, I can't miss. How far is it, about two–hundred?"

"That's close enough," answered John.

"Well, then, I guess it's my old trusty 3–wood again." Arnie took the Calloway 3–wood from his bag, kissed the head, and said, "Please Momma, don't fail me now."

"Hey, Arnie," Jim yelled from the cart. "You've got a forty with only two holes left. Don't tell me you're goin' to break fifty. What a difference a day makes, huh?"

"I don't need to think about that now," replied Arnie, teeing up his ball. "It's just another shot, that's all."

Arnie whispered to himself. Just another shot, that's all. Just another shot. Just another shot. Forget it. The devil in his subconscious awakened. Hi Arnie, I'm back. Just wanted to remind you that…you *cannot* hit a golf ball!

I know I can't, I know I can't, were Arnie's last thoughts before his ball spun thirty yards to his left, straight down the ravine.

"Fuck!" screamed Arnie, ready to slam his club into the ground, before catching hold of his temper and composing himself.

"It's just a game, right? It's just a game." Arnie talked to himself as he walked to the cart. "It's just a game, just a game…"

"What club you hitting?" Jim asked John as he approached the tee area, 3–iron in hand.

"With the slight breeze at our backs, I'm going 5–iron."

Figuring he was about a club shorter than John, Jim thought about switching to a 4, but reconsidered when he took a look at the trouble in front of the green. After hitting, he didn't regret his decision.

"Unbelievable shot," said Ralph. "Man what I wouldn't give to hit a golf ball like that."

"Beautiful," added John. "You must be fifteen feet from the cup. That was really pretty."

Behind the action, feet up in the cart, Arnie declined comment.

"Okay, Big John," said Ralph. "Put it right up there."

In an instant replay of Jim's shot, John hit the ball. A mammoth trajectory, right at the flag. His ball settled into place, opposite side of the stick, equidistant from Jim's ball.

"Are you really going to make me hit this?" Ralph implored, ready at the tee. "Oh well, I'll do it for Arnie. He can use some help gettin' that mule train together."

Ralph used his driver and hit a fast ball down the middle. Low, hard, and straight, the ball just cleared the ravine and stuck in the front edge of the green.

"Way to muscle it out there." Jim patted Ralph on the back.

"You hit it well enough," said John. "You deserve to be on."

"Nice shot," said Arnie.

Ralph nodded apologetically at Arnie.

After his descent into the ashes, Arnie three putted for a seven. The others made par. The results on the ninth were more balanced. Jim and John, both fighting the tendency to duck hook off the tee, bogeyed the par 4, 408 yard hole. Ralph and Arnie scored doubles. Arnie, relieved to be at the turn, was grateful that his missed shots still found their way toward the target. He was not looking forward to the backside.

Only Jim wanted to play through without a break. However, the majority ruled, and the men left their carts in a parking area near the ninth hole. Climbing up the hill behind the ninth green, in the direction of the clubhouse, they noticed that the day was getting hot. Even Ralph had removed his sweater.

"I'm starved, we gonna have some lunch?" Arnie asked.

"Give me a break," retorted Jim. "How much can you eat? My god, you had two pounds of grease and fat three hours ago, you couldn't possibly be hungry again. And besides, the course is pretty crowded. If we break too long, we'll be lucky to finish before sundown."

"I'm with Arnie," interrupted Ralph. "If I don't eat at the turn, I get awfully cranky come the fourteenth or fifteenth hole."

"Don't you have a plane to catch?" said Jim.

"Plenty of time for that. Plenty of time. Our plane doesn't leave until 7:30 tonight. So don't you worry about me."

"Actually, it would work out pretty well for me if you guys broke for lunch." John joined in. "I've got to check and see if I'm needed around here. I'm not sure I can even play the back nine."

"Well that would be real disappointing," said Ralph. "You and Jim have put on quite a show for Arnie and me, and I must say I've enjoyed it. What do you think, Arnie? Hasn't it been fun watching these guys play the game the way it's supposed to be played?"

"I don't know about that," answered Arnie. "If I want to see great golf, I can watch the pros on the tube. Now if you want to know if I want John to keep playing with us, the answer is yes. Very definitely."

Turning to John, "It's been a pleasure playing with you. But feel free to hit a few crummy shots on the back nine. I assure you, I'll still enjoy playing with you."

It wasn't the first time Jim excluded himself from the group's camaraderie. In fact, he hoped John had to go trim a couple of trees or fertilize a flower bed. Let him fertilize every fucking flower on the island if he loved working with "his flowers" so much. Jim would just as soon lose him on the backside.

As the men came to the top of the hill, the clubhouse came into full sight.

"Jesus Christ, will you take a look at that," exclaimed Ralph.

"Every time I see that structure in full view, I get a little chill. And today, with all that blue sky around it—well words just can't describe it. Don't do it justice."

"It's magnificent," added John.

"And look over there," noted Arnie. "There are John's flowers. Look at those colors, they're absolutely beautiful."

"Thank you."

"Hey look," shouted out Arnie. "There's…, you know, the young blond. I forgot her name. She's in the flower garden, pushing someone in a wheel chair."

"Where?" Jim stretched his neck in a frantic effort to spot Tina.

"Never did ask you how that went," Ralph inquired. "You ever get to first base with that pretty young woman?"

Jim finally located Tina and Keeler. "Are you kidding? She's good looking all right, but that's where it ends. What a tease. She practically invited me to meet her last night, ripped me off for two shirts, then tells me she's getting married. I mean, I couldn't believe it. What a con artist."

"Well you might be wrong about that," said Ralph. "Look, she's waving at you right now."

"She is?" Jim stopped in his tracks and looked. "What the hell, I don't get this at all."

Tina had stopped waving and was heading toward the men. She was wearing yesterday's jeans with a pink cotton turtleneck. The wind tousled her straw–colored curls, and her full mouth curved into a smile as she neared the group.

Jim stood frozen.

John dropped his golf bag, and Tina fell into his arms. He picked her up, and spun her around.

Tina stroked John's cheeks with her hands and kissed him on the mouth.

"Great to see you, hon. I got here early, and had to get right out if I wanted to play. I hope you're not mad."

"Oh no. Just glad to see you. Didn't think I'd have a chance today."

The young lovers celebrated with more hugs and spins.

CHAPTER 12

"You really put your foot in your mouth that time," said Arnie as he shoved a hot dog, mustard, and relish into his mouth.

"I don't care," responded Jim, quickly turning around when he heard the door to the snack bar open.

"You seem a little edgy. Maybe you'll get lucky and John won't play anymore."

"Listen. I have nothing to be uptight about. It's not like I lied or anything. I can't help it if John's about to marry a woman who likes to flirt."

"Now wait a minute." Arnie took a minute to swallow his food and take a sip of Diet Coke. "You're making some pretty bold assumptions here. Don't forget. Just yesterday, you were madly in love with this so–called slut."

"Bullshit. I never said that. I'll admit, she's a good looking woman, and it was a boring night. That's all."

"Don't I remember you saying that it was more than that. Remember when we were in the room…"

"Why am I sitting here arguing about this with you? Shit, I might as well get something to eat before you clean the place out, Arnie."

Arnie put down his fork, leaned back, and smiled to himself.

Just as Jim returned to the table, Ralph and John entered the snack bar.

"Hey Ralph. Hey John. Pull up a couple of chairs," suggested Arnie. "Did you get through to Bud?"

"Sure did," replied Ralph as he and John sat down. "Son of a bitch is having a great day. Took a sauna and whirlpool. Read the paper by the pool. Now's he's goin' to take a little snooze before lunch. Signed up for a massage this afternoon. A full one hour deal. Can you believe that guy? I told him, the way I'm playing, I'd just as soon be with him."

"How's he feeling?" asked Arnie.

"Are you kidding me? We should feel so good. I'm telling you, he just had a little too much to drink, that's all." Studying his outspread fingers at arm's length, Ralph went on, "A nice whirlpool would do these old arthritic fingers just fine right about now."

"Why don't you call it a day?" John spoke for the first time since he reached the table. "Go back to the hotel and join your friend."

"Are you kidding me?" Ralph sat up straight, pulled his head back, his eyelids pulled back to reveal the rounded, white portions of his eyeballs. "On a beautiful day like this? I got nine holes to play yet. And I got some catching up to do. Need to hit a couple greens, drop a couple putts. I'll be back. Don't go counting me out yet."

"Sorry," laughed John. "I didn't mean to offend you."

Sitting sideways, legs crossed, hunched over, Jim stayed as far outside the circle, as far away from John, as circumstance would permit.

"So John," asked Arnie. "You joining us for the backside?"

"He sure is," Ralph answered for him. "Right John?"

"I'd love to, if you guys don't mind," confirmed John. "I checked with my father and he didn't have any pressing work for me to do. Nothing that can't wait for later in the day, or in the morning."

"That's great," exclaimed Arnie. "We'd love to have you."

Jim said nothing.

"Did you say *your father* had nothing for you to do?" Arnie questioned.

"Yeah. I guess I didn't tell you guys, but my dad owns Wild Links. The man in the wheelchair."

"Your father is Hans Keeler?" Jim asked quickly, facing John.

"Yes, he is. I hope I didn't offend anyone by not mentioning this before." John turned to Jim. "And Jim, I'm sorry that I never said anything about Tina. I just didn't see the point. Tina told me what happened. She said that as soon as she told you she was engaged, you backed off. I think I understand why you made the comments you did, and I'd just as soon forget the whole thing. What do you say?"

"I don't have any problems with it," mumbled Jim. "It was no big deal."

"Well now that we have all our business squared away," cut in Ralph, "I'm goin' to get me something to eat. Hey John, you want anything?"

"No thanks, I already ate."

"What, those apples? Is that it? You call that lunch?"

"I'll be fine. Thanks just the same."

"I'll tell you," Ralph pulled his chair back and slowly stood. "You should have seen those two in that garden over there. I'm on the phone watching them sitting on a blanket, in the middle of all those flowers, eating those golden apples. You had to see it. I'm telling you, it looked like a freakin' fairy tale. I'm not kidding. Hey John, you sure that apple's goin' to be enough for you? You're a big boy now."

"I'm quite sure. Thanks again."

Jim wiped his mouth with his napkin, threw it into his plate, and sat back, his legs stretched straight out, crossed at the ankles. He was beginning to understand John. His father owned the damn place. Was probably worth millions. Tina loved a buck and would obviously do anything for money. It all made sense now. That's why she was so nice to Mr. Keeler. She was probably counting the days till he died. Then she and "Mr. Golden Apples in the Garden" would have it all.

Ralph dropped two slices of pizza on the table and announced, "I think it's time to start getting ready for the backside. I figure we might as well pick John's brains here and get caught up on all the local knowledge. What can you tell us, John?"

"Well, for the most part, it's pretty basic golf. A little longer than average, but nothing out of the ordinary. Except, of course, for the sixteenth."

"Yeah, you're the person to ask about that," jumped in Arnie. "What is it about this legendary Savage? Is it true it's never been parred or have *you* parred it?"

"No, I never have. I've come close, but never parred it," replied John. "As far as I know, no one else has either. At least not since my dad's been here. And that's been seventeen years."

Jim broke in. "You mean to say, that your old man owns this place, that you play here all the time, and you have never parred the sixteenth hole? Why? I saw you play. You can reach any *par five* in two. Why can't you make par on this hole?"

"It's the pond and the oak tree," answered John matter–of–factly. "The front of the hole plays uphill, so even if you hit a good drive, you're looking at 200 to clear the water and hit the green. Now that's not normally a problem, but that big old, hanging oak tree makes it one. The tree's on the right side of the pond, but bends way over to the left. I've hit many perfect second shots, only to have them hit a branch and fall right into the water."

"But couldn't you hit a knockdown? Maybe punch a 2–iron under the branch?" asked Jim.

"Have to hit it awfully low. The branches almost scrape the top of the water."

"Whew," added Ralph. "I can tell you right now that I'm not going to be the first to par this hole. But couldn't a good player start the ball left, have it fade around the old tree, and find its way to the green?"

"That's what most people try," answered John. "And that's what I tried for a long time. But that tree hangs so far over the water, that the ball always seems to find a branch. Sometimes, it seems like a branch reaches out and finds the ball. As if that tree is determined not to let anything get through."

"That's right," said Ralph excitedly. "Seen it myself. I told you boys. That big old oak tree just stretches out and whacks them balls down. Like a big old hairy arm. Just whacks them down."

"Come on guys, get real," said Jim. "Apparently, it's a very large tree that's hard to get around, that's all. What about going over the top?"

"That's my current strategy," answered John. "Only problem is, the tree's so tall, it's hard to get enough height on a shot from 200 out. Also, the pin placements are one of three spots, all on the right side of the green. Right behind the tallest part of the tree."

"So, what are you hitting to get on in two?" asked Jim.

"I've stopped trying. My new strategy is to get on in three and one putt. I've only tried it a few times, but I'm convinced that it's the only way."

"That's crazy," argued Jim. "To count on a one–putt for par."

"You're right," said John. "It is crazy. And I don't think I mentioned the fact that the green has two tiers. If you don't hit the green on the level of the pin, you're looking at going up or down a swale with a two foot bend in it."

"It'll never work," said Jim. "I'm going to find a way to get over in two. If you're laying up, what club do you hit?"

"Nine–iron all the way," answered John. "Three 9–irons and one putt for par."

"That sounds like my kind of strategy," cut in Arnie. "Except at 450 something yards, I'd need five 9–irons and a putt." Arnie closed his eyes, inhaled through his nose, smiled before adding, "Hey you know, that wouldn't be bad. I'd have my double bogey."

"You know, Arnie," said Ralph. "You do a lot of talking about how bad your game is. Here's a news flash for you—you had a hell of a frontside. You beat the tar out of me."

"You did play well," added John. "You hit a nice, straight ball, and you have a good putting stroke."

Finding the scorecard from his back pocket, Arnie examined it. "Twenty–eight plus twelve, plus thirteen...I had a 53. Hey, that's pretty good for me...on any course, let alone this mother of a course."

"Damn good, said Ralph. "Don't go figuring my score. You'll need an adding machine."

Arnie had already begun. "Twenty–three, plus twelve, plus sixteen. You had a 51, Ralph."

"No shit?"

"That's right. After you opened with that eight, you only had one triple. And don't forget that par on the eighth. That's where I got my seven."

"Well that's where it's misleading," said Ralph. "Get rid of that one hole, and you played much more steady golf than I did."

"Well, I'm not complaining," replied Arnie. "Especially after yesterday's round from hell. You know, now that I think of it, I only lost one ball today. The one I hit in the water on the third hole. And I still managed a double."

"That's right," recalled Ralph. "That was on the Mark Twain hole. Sure, I remember."

Arnie laughed, and softly added, "I just wish I hadn't finished on such a bad note."

"Hey, let's forget *our* scores for a minute," said Ralph. "What about these guys? Both you boys must be flirting with par."

"I'm two over," responded Jim immediately. "I can't believe I was one over yesterday."

John addressed Jim. "You have a very nice game. Looks like with some time and effort, you have the potential to be a professional."

"Now wait a minute," answered Jim. "You're only one stroke behind me, and you play all the time. And your father was the European champ. You're the one who should be thinking pro."

"Is that so?" cut in Ralph. "Your father was a champion?"

"Yes, he was," answered John.

"Well, I guess you and Jim here have something in common," Ralph went on. "His dad was a pro. Owned a driving range and played on the mini–tour." Turning to Arnie. "See that? You got to get that boy of yours out there. Look at the way these fellows hit the ball. You gotta start 'em young."

"So your dad was a pro?" asked John. "I don't know about you, but I learned very little golf from my father. Learned mostly from my grandfather. My dad left for the States when I was about eight. I didn't see him for years."

"My dad gave me some pointers here and there," replied Jim. "But he never had any patience with me. I learned mostly on my own."

"Well, I was very fortunate to have my grandfather around after my dad left. He was an excellent teacher."

"Sounds like your grandfather's passed on," cut in Ralph.

"Yeah, he died when I was fifteen. That's when I left home."

"And came here to be with your father?" asked Jim.

"Not quite." John pulled his chair in and added, "Look, I don't want to bore you guys with my biography. Getting time to head out for the backside."

"One more question." Jim stared directly at John. "You said you left home at fifteen. If you weren't with your mother or dad, who took care of you?"

"No one. I took care of myself. I looked older than my age and always managed to find some work. Actually, that's where I got my experience—for Beach Cove and Wild Links—working in kitchens and gardens. Those jobs were always available."

"How long did you do this for?" asked Arnie.

"Oh, I bounced around Europe for about five years. I thought then about going back to live with my mother, but decided instead to come to the States and see if I could locate my father."

"And you wind up finding your father *and* that beautiful bride as well," added Ralph.

"One big, happy ending," said Jim. "Now, who's ready to play some golf?"

CHAPTER 13

The day remained perfect. Temperature just under the eighty–degree mark. Gentle, warm breezes, and still, not a cloud in the sky. The sun was almost directly overhead as the noon hour approached. To get to the tenth tee, the men had to ride along a path that ran parallel to the western shoreline. The waters were calmer than they had been the day before.

Arnie looked out at the ocean and marveled at its beauty. These were the times that momentarily convinced him there was a God. There had to be. Inspiration came easily and often to Arnie, but it never locked in. It filtered through his consciousness like sand through a strainer. For an instant, an hour, a day, Arnie believed, understood, felt at peace. But it never lasted.

Arnie turned to Jim, who was driving the cart. "Twenty–four hours ago, we were on the plane. Can you believe that?"

"Sure," answered Jim. "Why shouldn't I believe it?"

"Come on Jim. Cut the shit. You know exactly what I mean. Sometimes you play dumb, but I know you think beyond what's right in front of your face."

"Yeah, maybe I do. I know a lot's happened, that it seems like years, not days since we got here; that it feels like we've known Ralph forever. But shit man, what more do you want me to say about it? This is life."

Arnie leaned back, closed his eyes, and felt the warm breeze on his face. Maybe he did make too big a deal out of everything. But Arnie couldn't help it. Life *was* a big deal to him; and during the past twenty–four hours, his past, present, and future played out across Wild Links. He had hurt for Bud, felt the loss of his father, and recognized the fragility of his own life. Time was racing by, and there was so much to do. Suddenly, Arnie thought about his son. How much Ryan needed a father. There was a good place to start.

Jim spotted the "To 10th Tee" sign on a tree alongside a path which led through the pines, bearing left, away from the ocean. Arnie looked back and recognized a familiar sight.

"Look Jim, there's the Serpent, heading to the dock."

Steering the cart onto the wooded path, the ocean no longer in sight, Jim did not hear Arnie's comment. He was already playing the tenth hole in his mind.

"Come on guys. Looks like we're in pretty good shape." Ralph was in his cart, up by the tee area waving his arm. "The foursome in front of us has already hit off."

"Where's John?" Jim was hoping his old man snagged him for some unexpected work.

"Oh, he should be along any minute. He wouldn't take a ride. Wanted to walk a path through the woods. Can you believe that guy?"

"So this hole is a pretty severe dogleg left," noted Jim. "Only 361 yards, I wonder if you can cut it?"

"Don't ask me," said Ralph. "I'll be happy to hit it straight. Look at that fairway. Must be twenty yards wide. Two of the fellows up front already found the woods."

Jim walked up to the tee box to get a closer look. "Shit, the dogleg breaks left more quickly than I thought. Let me see a scorecard."

Jim walked back to where the carts were parked and took the scorecard from Ralph. Studying the diagram of the tenth hole, he said, "I'm right. Most of the hole plays out after the corner. Shit, if I don't cut it, I'll have to hit a 6 or 7–iron off the tee. And then I'll be looking at a long second shot."

"Those trees look pretty tall to me," said Arnie. "Why don't you ask John what he thinks when he gets here. Easy choice for me." Looking at Ralph, Arnie smiled as they said in unison, "5–iron."

"Where the hell is John?" Jim asked. "Figures that the first time I want to ask him something, he disappears."

Two carts pulled up to get in line. Turning around and greeting the other golfers, Ralph said, "I think somebody better hit. I don't know what happened to John, but we don't want to back these people up. Unless, you want to let them play through..."

"No. I'm hitting." Jim grabbed his 7–iron and headed out to the tee.

Taking a couple of light swings to feel the club's length, Jim thought about his decision. Couldn't risk losing a ball in those woods. Could ruin his whole round. Just get it out into that clearing, and he'd have an open shot to the green.

Jim executed the shot perfectly.

Arnie and his 5–iron were next. As he spotted his ball, Arnie noticed John appear from the woods behind the tee area. "Hey, John, we thought we lost you."

"Had some work to take care of. Hope I didn't hold you guys up."

"Perfect timing." shouted Ralph. "We couldn't have hit any sooner."

Arnie's swing was a little late, causing a mild slice. The ball appeared to stay in the open area, off to the right of where Jim's ball had landed.

"That'll play fine," said Ralph on his way up to hit.

John added, "Don't worry about it. There's plenty of room up there."

Jim turned to John, who was holding a 5–wood. "You're not going to cut it, are you? Those trees are awfully tall."

"If I tee it up high enough, I could get it over with my 5–wood. If I lay it out, I seem to always find one of the frontside bunkers. Those traps are real deep, and if you get a bad lie, it's nearly impossible to get up and down. Besides, I'm not a very good sand player, so I usually take my chances getting up close. At the very worst, I'll lose a ball."

Jim couldn't believe what he was hearing. Very worst, I'll lose a ball? The guy was so full of shit. And why did he show up right after Jim hit off with a 7–iron? He knew what he was doing all right. Any way to get an advantage. It wasn't going to work. Jim was going to bear down and find a way to outscore the sucker.

Ralph hit a beautiful 5–iron that landed alongside Jim's ball, just to the left.

"Way to go, Ralph," shouted Arnie. "Can't stop us and our 5–irons."

"Perfect hit," said John.

Jim gave a nod of approval as he watched John walk up to the tee.

Setting his ball up a good two inches off the ground, John took an easy, sweeping swing. He hit the ball straight into the sky, aimed at the woods off to the left. The ball disappeared from sight once it reached the top of its arc.

"Looks good," said Ralph. "Think you made it?"

"It should be okay," answered John, bending down, picking up his tee, heading up the fairway.

When they got to the clearing, the green was in clear view. They could also see John's ball, sitting in the middle of the fairway, about 85 yards out. Arnie's slice just barely avoided the woods and was off the fairway in some mulch, about 210 yards from the green.

"What the hell," proclaimed Arnie as he grabbed the 3–wood from his bag. "What the hell do I have to lose? It's only a god-damn game, right? Right?"

"Right, right," said Jim. "Just hit the ball."

"Come on Arnie," added Ralph. "That 3–wood's been working all day for you. Just another tee shot. That's all it is. Come on pal, right on the green."

As Arnie stood over the ball, he felt relaxed. He didn't expect much. In his short golf career, he had experienced it all. He had whiffed on countless occasions. Once, he even caught his own tee shot. Arnie laughed at this memory. Normanside Country Club. While playing with some VIP businessmen, Arnie used his driver and hit the ball straight up in the air. Then, he hustled three steps to his left, and caught the damn thing. No one had ever seen any-thing like that before. Back then, Arnie felt disgraced. At this moment, it was funny—he thought it was great.

"Whoooeee!" Ralph's shriek echoed through the clearing as Arnie hit his best shot of the day. Probably the best shot of his life.

"Where'd it go? I don't see it," asked Arnie, his hand flattened across his brow.

"Are you kidding?" said John pointing at the target. "You're right on the green, pin–high. Look."

"Great shot, Arnie." Jim spoke softly, his squinting eyes contin-ued to stare at the ball sitting on the green.

"I'm proud of you, Arnie," said Ralph, patting him on the back. "You really showed me something there."

Jim was next and decided to play a 4–iron. His ball was sitting up nicely, and there was plenty of green to aim for. He had to make sure he cleared those bunkers. It's just one swing, that's all, thought Jim. Another day at the driving range, that's all.

As soon as Jim made contact, he knew he'd blown it. He quit on his swing, caught it thin, and hit it short into the right, frontside bunker.

"Fuck!" Jim shouted as he smashed the head of his club into the turf.

Only Ralph spoke. "Okay, Jimmy. You'll be okay. You can get up and down from there."

No response. Red–faced, Jim stifled his anger and walked back to his cart. Ralph offered a different kind of support as he followed Jim with a 4–wood into the same bunker.

This time Arnie decided to walk. As Jim and Ralph's carts headed down the path on the right side of the fairway, Arnie walked alongside of John.

"That was some heck of a shot," said John. "Just take a look at your ball sitting up on the green. All by itself. Now isn't that a pretty sight?"

"It's an absolutely beautiful sight. One that I rarely get a chance to see."

"It'll come. You just have to put in the time. That's all."

"Yeah, but I'm realistic about where my game is going. I'm never going to hit the ball like you or Jim."

"So what. Look at Ralph's game. Guys like him outplay the big hitters all the time. And they have a lot more fun in the process."

"You're right. It's just so damn hard for me to enjoy this game. To enjoy anything for that matter. A few years back, I had this young woman working for me. She was a student at the time, studying psychology. We used to talk about all kinds of things. Something she once said stayed with me. She told me I had a critical father, and that as an adult, I'd internalized my father's voice. I put myself down just the way he used to do. Ever hear of such a thing?"

"Makes perfect sense," answered John as he pulled the sand wedge from his bag. Walking to his ball, eyeing his target, he added, "I've done the same thing. We all do it, to some extent."

John took an easy chopdown swing at the ball and brought up a good sized divot. He watched his ball hook left of the flag, clear the bunker, and land just off the back, left fringe.

Arnie thought he caught the flash of a grin from Jim, who was in the sand, standing over his ball, studying his next shot.

"You're pretty even tempered on the golf course," said Arnie.

"Take a look at this day," replied John. "Look at this setting. What's to get upset about?"

"What about what you said a few minutes ago, about how all of us are tough on ourselves and put ourselves down? How did you overcome that?"

John looked straight ahead while walking, taking some time before responding. "I didn't. Let's just say I'm working on it."

From the bunker, Jim studied the shot from all angles. He picked the spot he wanted to hit on the green, and the point behind the ball he wanted to blast. Since John had missed the green, Jim was determined to get close to the pin. Getting ready to hit, he forced himself to concentrate. Keep your head down and follow through. As sand flew in all directions, Jim could feel that he hit the ball a little too clean. Heading right at the stick—hit it! hit it!—the ball landed less than a foot from the cup and rolled about twenty feet past, to the back of the green.

"Shit." Jim yelled out. "I played it perfectly, but hit it too solid."

"Just concentrate on making your putt," advised Ralph.

Jim glanced at Ralph, stared hard for a moment, marked his ball, and strode off shaking his head.

Ralph's shot from the sand hit the upper lip of the trap and rolled right back down to his feet. "Well look what we got here."

Ralph let out a big laugh as he looked down at the ball. "My limit's ten. If I'm not out of here in ten, I pick up."

With a quick second swipe at the ball, Ralph got the ball out and in a decent position, about twelve feet from the cup. "Now I'm supposed to say, why couldn't I do that the first time? Well...I'm not going to say it, dammit! Said it too many times in my day. I'm done saying it."

Laughing while struggling to get out of the deep trap, Ralph looked at Arnie. "Hey, Arnie," Ralph asked, "How's it feel to be spending all your time waiting to putt? Watching everybody make damn fools of themselves while you study your damn birdie putt."

"It feels great," replied Arnie. "The pros don't know what it is to play golf. They just hit a couple of shots and putt. That's not golf."

"You're right," agreed Ralph. "They don't know the suffering that comes with playing real golf."

John was last to putt out on the tenth, and he tapped in for his par. Despite coming up well short on his lag, Jim saved bogey by sinking a tricky five-footer. Ralph two-putted for a double, and Arnie added meaning to his memorable approach shot by making par.

The eleventh was the eighteenth handicap hole. A simple, 159 yard, par 3, with no trouble to speak of. It was also the first hole that none of the group managed to par. John made bogey after flying over the green with an 8-iron, and Jim also took a four after three-putting. Ralph saved bogey with a one-putt, and Arnie pulled his infamous 5-iron about thirty yards left of the green, behind an ill-placed tree stump. When all was done, he took a triple.

Play on the twelfth and thirteenth holes was very similar. Long, straight, and relatively open par fours. The 423 yard twelfth featured a tired Ralph's chip–in for a bogey from 30 yards out. Jim and John both made par, while Arnie held his own with a double.

On the thirteenth, Arnie lost his second and third balls of the day. He said goodbye to the first Prostaff off the tee when it sailed into the woods on the right hand side. The second ball—a solidly struck 3–iron—found its way into a stream that Arnie hadn't noticed on the scorecard diagram. His snowman was only one stroke worse than Ralph's seven. Both Jim and John, playing like the talented, young men they were, again parred the hole.

As the carts rolled in to the tee area of the 555 yard par 5, fourteenth, the play had once again backed up.

"Thank you, God," said Ralph, arms extended, looking up at the sky. Slouching back, his cap over his eyes, "Wake me up in twenty minutes, will ya?"

"We're starting to get some backup from the Savage," said John.

Looking at John, Jim asked, "Why would the sixteenth slow things down? Even if you hit in the water, you just drop one and hit again."

"Hitting into the pond is only one way to lose strokes on the Savage. There's woods on the left and a ravine that runs along the right for about a hundred yards. Balls that go down there are tough to find."

"And don't forget," added Arnie. "They have to remove the corpses from the pond. That takes time, you know."

"That's what I've been meaning to ask you," Jim again looked at John. "What is that bullshit all about? Were there really drownings in that pond?"

"Unfortunately, yes," answered John. "One in 1986, and another in '91."

Ralph took the cap from his face and sat up to listen as John began to explain.

"Both drownings were freak occurrences, but you know how the media plays on these things. Actually, the publicity was good for business. You wouldn't believe how many people wanted to play this course after all the publicity."

"What actually happened?" asked Ralph.

"The 1986 incident involved an older fellow who played here all the time. He fell face down into the pond on sixteen. His buddies pulled him out, but he was dead by the time he got to the hospital. Later, they found out that the cause of death was a stroke, not drowning." John walked over to the water fountain and took a long drink before continuing.

"Well," countered Jim, "People die of strokes everyday. This one just happened to occur at the sixteenth hole."

"Just the same," added Ralph. "You boys better keep a close watch on me around that pond. I'm a tired old man, and I could go at any moment."

"Give me a break." Arnie turned around and shouted as he relieved himself from behind a tree, just off the cart path. "You're a horse, Ralph. You're goin' to outlive me. You're a goddamn horse."

"What about the second drowning?" asked Jim.

"The incident in '91 *was* a drowning, but it resulted from an accident. It seems that a couple of young guys got pretty drunk one night and decided to go out and play the sixteenth. No one even knew they were on the island. By that time, we had already shut down the lodging facilities. Well, apparently, these guys camped out with plenty to drink and set out for the sixteenth hole when one of them decided to take a swim. The area was pitch black and the guy just dove in. Parts of the pond are pretty shallow, and unfortunately, he picked one of those spots for his dive. He hit his head, and was knocked unconscious and drowned. His friends couldn't find him. It was too dark."

"And the legend of Wild Links lives on," concluded Jim.

"That it does," added Ralph. "A lot of history made in this place. I told you guys before. This is the third time I've visited this island, and there is something special, yes, maybe even magical about the place. You always leave feeling like you're not quite the same person who came in."

"Still sounds like bullshit to me," said Jim, as he stretched from side to side with Big Boy behind his back.

"Many people agree with you, Ralph," said John.

"Who's got the honors?" shouted Arnie from the tee area. "Those guys must be hitting to the green by now."

"Forget honors," said Ralph. "Go ahead Arnie...hit away."

"Any use in trying to get there in two?" Jim turned to John and asked.

"I wouldn't try it—especially with the ground so soft from the rains. You'll get no roll. I think I'll hit my 1–iron off the tee."

Jim thought about John's comments, but didn't trust them. He'd let John hit first. A lot of things about John just didn't fit. That his old man owned the place and that John was obviously going to own it himself someday. Why did he have to work in a kitchen? Maybe that was bullshit. Jim almost felt sorry for him when he thought about Tina. It was obvious that she was after John's money. And the dumb shit had no idea. Poor guy. He'd be paying the price soon enough.

Arnie hit another good 3–wood. "Way to go," said Jim, quickly shifting his thoughts back to John, who had picked up a stroke on the backside. Right now, they were dead even. And that stroke was a set–up. Jim had to focus on every swing. He had to beat John. If he could par the Savage *and* beat him; now *that* would be something special. Another Savage legend for posterity. Maybe Ralph was right. Maybe something special would happen here.

Ralph hit his driver for the first time all day, a straight, but towering drive that only made it about 125 yards out.

"My first giraffe's ass of the day," joked Ralph as he stood and watched the shot. "Well, at least it's in the fairway."

John finally decided on a 2–iron, and pulled the ball badly into the woods on the left hand side.

"Want me to hit a provisional?" he asked as he turned to face the others.

"Nah," answered Ralph. "We'll find it. And if we don't, you'll drop one out there."

Jim hurried to the tee, placed his ball in the ground before suddenly stepping back, taking a deep breath. He reminded himself to keep steady, to just focus on the shot he was playing. After John's wild tee shot, Jim thought of using his driver, but quickly realized how stupid that would be. John had originally said 1–iron. Right now, that sounded good. Jim rarely hit that club, but had pretty good success with it when he did.

Seconds later, either the length of the club or its difficult loft caused him to open his hips early. Jim pulled the ball into the same place in the woods where John's ball disappeared.

Neither John nor Jim was too hopeful about finding his ball in the dense thicket of trees and ground brush.

"Best chance of finding the ball would probably be to step on it," said John. "I don't know about you, but I'm going to drop one in a couple of minutes. I don't have a lot of patience for this kind of thing."

"We've got time," answered Jim. "When I looked, the foursome in front of us was still hitting to the green. What do you do if you drop one? Take a one stroke penalty?"

"It doesn't matter. Whatever the guys I'm playing with want to do."

"Well, why don't we agree to take one stroke if we drop. Okay?"

"Fine."

Jim continued kicking through the brush half–heartedly. It would take at least a stroke to get out into the fairway anyway.

John re–entered the wooded area and asked, "Any luck?"

"No. I don't think there's any chance. Might as well drop one."

"Well, Arnie and Ralph are both in the woods on the other side," said John. "Looks like we're the ones who are going to back things up on this hole."

John spotted a ball wedged beneath a thick root near the trunk of a pine. A Top–Flite, that apparently had been there for awhile. John looked at the ball carefully, wiped it on his leg and put it in his pocket. Turning to Jim, he said, "While we have a minute, there's something I've been curious about. Hope you don't think I'm getting too personal, but I was wondering about your dad. Did he have any success in his pro career?"

"He won a couple of tournaments his first two years on the mini–tour. But that was it. It never amounted to anything significant. Not like your father. European champion. Now that's an accomplishment."

"Well, maybe. But it wasn't enough for him. He wasn't satisfied, so he came to the States. He felt that if you didn't win on the PGA tour, being a champion didn't mean much."

Jim remained quiet. He wanted to say that his dad had also left when he was a kid—to make it as a golfer. But Jim's dad left with another woman, and he'd never seen him since. John's dad might have left, but he was with his son today, right there for him.

Jim changed the subject. "Tell me, since we're getting personal here, why do you work in a kitchen when your father owns this place? Do you really need the money?"

John laughed. "Yes, I do need the money. But I also work in the kitchen for other reasons."

"Like what? You enjoy washing dishes?"

"It's more complicated than that. Aside from the money, it kind of keeps me in touch with my beginnings. Helps me appreciate what progress I've made. I feel it's necessary for…"

"Hey, John, Jim." Ralph's voice came booming through. "You boys okay?"

As the two young men walked out of the woods, onto the fairway, Ralph said, "There you are. Me and Arnie are sitting on the green in two. Can't believe you missed those great shots."

"Yeah," added Arnie. "I hit my 3–wood 355 yards. I don't know where I got the strength from."

"Actually," continued Arnie, "I hit one in the woods. Chipped into a tree, the ball bounced back and nearly hit me in the head. Then I chipped out and hit the next one into the woods. Lost the ball, too. Ralph here is doing much better, though."

Both men roared with laughter.

"I won't go through the details of my play," said Ralph. "Let's just say that I also had to drop one, and whereas Arnie here's lying six, I'm lying seven."

Jim and John smiled and shook their heads.

When the last putt finally found the bottom of the cup, Arnie scored a ten, Ralph a twelve, and John and Jim both settled for bogeys. Ralph decided to sit out the par 3, 183 yard fifteenth. He figured he needed to save himself for the Savage. He parked the cart in the open sunshine and stretched his legs out while the others attempted to hit the elevated green.

"Man, this is heaven." The words filtered from under his cap. "Don't know why I didn't do this before." Sitting up, looking at Arnie, he added, "You know, the more I think about what Mark Twain had to say, the more I do believe he was right." Stretching out again, cap over his face, Ralph continued, "Yes sir, this is the life. I'll let you boys try and hit that little dance floor out there."

With a slight breeze in their faces—Jim hitting 4–iron, John hitting 5–iron—both men hit the green. Arnie avoided trouble when his topped 5–wood rolled to about thirty yards short of the target.

Heading down the last fairway before the Savage, Jim thought about his play to this point. After fourteen holes, he and John were tied at five over. Jim was proud of the way he had played. He knew John was a player, and he was right there with him. Even if John pretended not to care or even keep score, he wasn't fooled. Jim knew that John understood the situation perfectly.

"Nice chip," shouted Ralph in response to Arnie's pitching wedge to the green.

"Thank you. Thank you." Arnie bowed in Ralph's direction.

"Nice up," said John, stopping to talk to Arnie. "That's the shot I was telling you about. Get that little thirty yarder down, keep hitting the 3–wood, and you'll have a nice game."

"Thanks," answered Arnie.

Walking to his cart to get his putter, Arnie felt good. Sure, he had screwed up any chance for a great score with a couple of terrible holes, but he had also made some great shots. Arnie was happy, at peace with himself. Looking at the cloudless blue sky above the variegated shades of green and brown, he vowed to memorize this moment. When he was back at work or home, with his wife and kids, Arnie would remember how he felt at this very instant. He'd remember, at least, that such moments exist.

CHAPTER 14

The par 4, 458 yard, sixteenth hole at Wild Links, played straight out to a narrow fairway. On the left was thick forest; and 100 yards down on the right, edging all the way up to the pond that sat in front of the green, the ground dropped off to a ravine laden with ground brush. The distance from the tee to the front of the pond was 304 yards. The front of the green was another 150 yards from this historically popular drop zone sight.

The foursome ahead had just finished hitting their tee shots when Arnie, Jim, Ralph, and John approached the Savage. Except for Ralph, who bypassed play on fifteen, each of the men had two–putted the last green. All were ready for the challenge of the moment, for the challenge of their golfing lives.

"God, will you look at that tree," said Arnie, squinting as he stood at the tee and looked down the fairway.

"It's a big, old hairy arm, I tell 'ya," added Ralph. "And wait till you get closer. It's even more of a sight."

"You know, without that tree, this would be a pretty easy hole," said Jim as he also stared down the fairway.

"Yeah, and if my grandmother had wheels...how does that go?" kidded Arnie.

"Well I don't know about that tree," said Ralph. "But this hole plays like a par 5 to me. I'm just going to hit an iron out there, and see if I can't keep it in the fairway. Then I'll worry about the next shot."

"I've got to take the same approach," agreed Arnie. "I already got two pars today. That's two over my usual standard."

"You really hitting three 9–irons?" Jim turned to John and stopped suddenly in his tracks. His brow wrinkled and mouth opened. "What the hell is that?"

John was swiping at the grass off to the side of the tee area with a club that Jim did not recognize.

"This is my 9–iron," answered John.

Unlike most 9–irons, this one had a wood shaft. Polished mahogany. Smooth as satin.

"Where in heaven's name did you find that?" asked Ralph.

"Originally, it belonged to my great grandfather. He gave it to my grandfather, who gave it to me. Well, actually he never gave it to me. I took it after he died. He always told me it would be mine someday. When I was a kid, and my grandfather took me out on the links with him, I saw him hit some incredible shots—impossible shots—with this 9–iron. It was the only club left from the original set of Zeus irons that his father had given him. He told me it had magic in it and I always believed him."

"They certainly don't make 'em like that anymore. I can see why you'd want to keep it in the family," said Jim. "But can you actually hit with it? The head is so small. You've hit a 9–iron today, but it was from your regular set."

"I hit with it when I feel I have to do the impossible. Every once in a while. Like on the Savage. Last few times out I've been using it. I'll admit, though, it's tough to hit. But when you catch it right, it's a thing of beauty."

Jim walked off to the side and started taking some practice swings with Big Boy.

"So, who's got the honors?" asked Ralph.

Although up until now they had not paid careful attention to the rules of honors, Jim was quick to respond. "Technically, it's John. We've tied every hole since the tenth when he made par, and I made bogey."

"No problem," countered John. "I'll be glad to lead the way." Looking out at the fairway, "Let's give those guys a couple of more minutes."

John walked to the tee, bent over and laid down a shiny, gold ball—right on the ground, without a tee.

"What's that?" Jim was first to notice.

As Jim gazed at the gold ball, John bent down, picked it up and threw it to him. "My dad played with this ball three or four times. He stopped using it because he was afraid he might lose it. It's legal. Just a regular golf ball that's gold–plated. I use it whenever I use old Zeus here."

Jim looked closely at the gold sphere. Usual size, and the dimples looked about right. "When did your father give this to you?"

"He never actually gave it to me," replied John. "I just took it."

"You mean you stole it? Does he realize that you have it, that you play with it?"

"Oh yeah, now he knows. But originally I took it without permission."

"Come on, John," cut in Ralph. "Tell us the story of this gold ball. I for one am curious as hell."

Looking at the fairway, John saw that it was still too soon to hit. He turned to the others and began to explain. "When I was a kid, this ball fascinated me. When my dad took off for the States, he left it behind. I was really surprised, because he scored a victory the last time he used it. Anyway, my mother knew how important it was to him, so she locked it up in his trophy case. For years, I wanted to get it out so badly. Just to touch it. When I decided to leave home, I just had to take it with me."

"How did you get it out?" asked Arnie. "Did your mom know you took it?"

"My mom didn't want me to leave, so I couldn't ask her for it."

"Then you stole it," said Jim.

"Yes, I did. I found the key to the case, opened it, and removed the ball. I wasn't proud of what I did, but I did it just the same."

"Now that your dad knows you have it," asked Arnie. "Does he mind?"

"No. He just thinks I'm a fool to play with it."

Jim tossed the gold ball back to John. "I think your old man's right. No way it travels as far as the new designs."

"Probably not," replied John. "But there comes a time when you want more than the right physics and engineering in your game. A time when you need a little magic."

Ralph was quick to agree. "I know what you mean. Superstition. Magic. I believe in that stuff. Hey, Bud is the most superstitious guy you'll ever want to meet. A few years back, he wore the same pair of socks all summer. Believed it made a difference. And you know what? He played the best golf I've ever seen him play. I think John might be on to something here."

Arnie offered his opinion. "I'm not that superstitious. But maybe that's why I can't get a decent game together. Yeah, that's my problem. I haven't been superstitious enough. First thing when I get home, I'm going to hit some garage sales and pick up some lucky golf paraphernalia. Some clubs, balls...hey, maybe some knickers. Yeah, that's what I need. I'd look dynamite in a pair of knickers."

Laughing, John approached the tee box, placed the gold ball on a natural wooden tee, and walked behind the ball to view his target.

He didn't take much time. Took his stance and almost immediately began an easy swing, as if hitting a short approach shot. The ball exploded off the old Zeus 9–iron and headed straight up. Rising, the golden sphere gleamed in the sunlight and appeared to grow larger—a broadening circle of white light. Finally reaching its apex, the gold ball became a second sun in the glorious April sky. As it fell back toward the earth, the scene played in reverse. The explosion of light regained its original form. The gold ball landed in the left center portion of the fairway, about 150 yards from the tee.

"Well, I'll be damned!" shouted Ralph. "That was about the prettiest golf shot I ever saw."

Walking toward John, stopping when face–to–face, Arnie deadpanned, "Do they happen to carry Zeus clubs in the pro shop? If so, I'll take a set."

Jim stood, arms crossed, and calmly muttered, "Two more of those, and you've got your shot at par."

Walking past Jim, John shrugged his broad shoulders and said, "That's much easier said than done."

At the tee, Jim delayed the beginning of his preshot routine. He began to question his decision to hit Big Boy. It seemed stupid after John's impossible 9–iron. Forget it, thought Jim. Play your game. Parring this hole won't be easy, but if he was going to do it, he had to get there in two. At 458 yards, he needed all of his driver. He set up behind his teed up ball and zoned in on the area of the fairway that represented his target. He took a deep breath, checked his alignment, made sure the ball was positioned inside his left heel. See the ball. Come on. Guts, man, guts! Jim was still looking down at the tee, when the ball sailed on its way, straight down the heart of the fairway, coming to rest 100 yards past John's gold ball.

"Whoooooeeeee!" Ralph belted out the loudest, longest scream of the day.

High five from Arnie. "You really are something. You know that? Unbelievable."

"A perfect drive," said John, offering a handshake.

"Clearing that tree is still gonna be a bitch. Right?" answered Jim.

John looked at Jim and nodded. "It's never easy."

After these two spectacular shots, Arnie and Ralph discussed the merits of a two man playoff, but Jim and John encouraged them to go ahead and hit.

Arnie was first. Having found a new love in the form of his Big Bertha 3–wood, he remained faithful to the club off the tee of the Savage. As he stood over his ball, he fidgeted, shifting his feet, buckling his knees several times. He became aware of how tired he was. The brisk morning had modulated into a hot day, and the steady pounding of sunshine was beginning to take its toll. There's no pressure, thought Arnie. No delusions of par. Today's had been one of his most enjoyable rounds of golf ever, and nothing could ruin his sense of well–being at this point. With no particular swing thought in mind, he took a lazy hack at the ball, got his hands around way too late, and push–sliced the ball into the ravine out to the right.

"Take a mulligan," shouted Ralph.

"Go on, hit another if you like," seconded John. "It's doubtful that you're going to find that ball anyway."

"Well, why the hell not." Arnie figured it would take less time to hit another ball than it would take to look for the first. He quickly teed one up, focused on keeping his head still, and hit a decent shot that stayed just out of the woods to the left.

"That's the ticket," said Ralph on his way to the tee. Looking back, he added, "Now, just for your information boys, I fully expect to par this hole. Played the damn thing a half dozen times and never came close. But I got a good feeling about it today."

Ralph hit his 3–iron long, perfectly down the middle. The ball landed about twenty–five yards past John's, but well short of Jim's mammoth drive.

"Hey, the man's back from the dead!" shouted Arnie.

"That's the hardest I've seen you hit a golf ball in two days," added Jim.

"Beautiful shot," said John, shaking Ralph's hand.

"I don't know what you guys are so surprised about. Haven't you ever been hustled by an old man before?"

The men descended the fairway toward the pond and the powerful, old tree. Jim walked with John, while the others tended to the carts. A scene that had been played out several times during the day. Jim glanced anxiously at John, who stared straight ahead, his bag on his left shoulder. He looked no different than he had all day. Jim wondered how much of this mellow demeanor was an act. John had to be feeling the pressure. Jim certainly was.

"Aren't you afraid of losing that gold ball on this hole? I know how important it is to you."

"It's extremely important to me. But the way I figure it, there's always the risk of losing something important when you try to accomplish a feat that's out of the ordinary."

Jim glared at John. "What are you talking about? You can hit a damn Titleist and par the hole."

John turned to Jim and smiled. "Oh yeah? Hasn't happened yet."

John reached his ball, pulled out his 9–iron, laid his bag on the ground, and looked down the fairway. The foursome in front were on the green. John was ready to hit.

"That pond's not far away, don't give it too much," warned Jim.

Ralph and Arnie, with a clear view of the play on the green, waved John on from their carts. Over the tall trees to the left, the sun had begun its retreat from the eastern sky. John's ball was sitting up nicely on flat turf in the heart of his shadow. He took another easy swing, gentler than the first, and the results were just as spectacular. The ball pierced the sky. All heads turned upward and followed the gold sphere's ascent. In awed silence, Arnie, Jim and Ralph watched the ball land ten yards short of the pond.

"Well, I guess your game plan's working," said Jim.

"This is the easy part," replied John slinging his bag over his shoulder and heading out to join the others.

Arnie had little choice but to lay up. Since his ball was only about 130 yards from the front of the pond, he elected to go with an 8–iron.

"Maybe you should give John's 9–iron a whirl," suggested Ralph.

"What for?" answered Arnie. "I don't need any magical gimmicks to hit a golf ball. God–given talent is the magic I rely on."

"Cut the shit, Arnie," said Jim. "Come on, just hit the ball."

Arnie turned, put his hands on his hips, and looked right at his young partner.

Jim stared back.

Finally, Arnie got into his stance, and quickly took an uncharacteristically hard swing. Catching it thin, the ball never elevated. A low, line drive, that hit the turf just before the sight of John's ball. It continued to skip, and took two short hops into the pond.

Arnie, his 8–iron in his right hand, lifted both arms into the air. "I've made my sacrifice to the Savage!" he shouted. "Free at last. No longer bound by the spell of the Savage." Yes, I'm free. Looking straight up, Arnie muttered, "Thank you God. Thank you."

"You're out of your fucking mind," said Jim. "Do you know that?"

John was laughing.

Ralph, laughing and shaking his head, walked up to Arnie and put his arm around his shoulder. "Come on, good buddy. Let's see what the good Lord has in store for me."

Ralph approached his ball which lie about 120 yards from the water. "Learned a long time ago. If you're going to lay up, lay up. I'm goin' with a wedge."

Ralph took a big divot as he chopped down at the ball and sent it upward, landing in excellent position a good twenty–five yards short of the water.

"Did you see that?" said Ralph. "I do believe I put John's shots to shame. Sorry about that Johnny. Man, wasn't that a pretty lay–up?"

"Excellent shot," John said smiling broadly. "You and I are in the same position. We've got a good shot at it."

"You know," said Arnie. "I believe in you, Ralph. I think you're going to par this fucking hole. I can see it now. A big sign right on the trunk of that oak tree. The Savage. Parred for the first and only time by Mr. Ralph Peterson.

"I told you I wasn't here to fool around," said Ralph. "And don't laugh. I think you're right about that sign."

Jim quietly headed in the direction of his ball. He was carrying his 2–iron, 3–iron, and 5–wood. He eyed the giant oak wondering how its trunk managed to support the weight of those widespread, overhanging branches. He knew he couldn't hit under, and doubted he could get it over from this distance. Maybe John was right. But he couldn't lay up from this spot. He'd need to hit a forty foot chip. And then he'd be looking at one–putting for par. No, he had to go for it. He wasn't going to waste that incredible drive. He was going for it, and he knew he had to try something a little different.

"Hey John." Jim turned around to the others. "If I hit the ball left and fade it, do I have a chance?"

"I think so. That's what I tried for the longest time. The problem I had was that I either went too far left and caught the brush off to the left of the green, or I didn't go far enough left and caught a branch. The one time I almost made it, I rolled off the back edge of the green. The pin placement was up front that day, like it is today. But, even if the pin was back, it would have taken a hell of a putt to make par."

Jim continued to eye the giant oak. Finally, he made up his mind. It wouldn't be easy, but it was his only chance. Normally, a right to left player, Jim knew that hitting a fade would be tough, but he practiced the shot at the range on occasion and knew how to execute it. Normally, from this distance, he'd use a 3–iron, but with the added lateral distance and side–spin of the fade, he decided to go with the 2–iron.

Jim took his stance aiming left of the target. He weakened his grip and soled the ball with a slightly open clubface. He settled his feet and looked hard at the area he had targeted to the left of the oak. As he locked into the ball, Jim heard the shrill cry of a crow. Not unusual during a round of golf. He remembered a fall day, one of the rare times his father let him come along while he played. Jim tended the flag, looked for balls, and rode the cart by sitting on the fender and holding on to the seat. Each of his dad's playing partners gave him a buck for helping out. His father had a great round that day. He told Jim that the sound of a crow, just before beginning a swing, meant good luck. Jim had never forgotten that story. Zoning in on the number 1 on his Titleist, Jim felt confident. One more look at the target, then back at the ball. Low and slow. Jim made a perfect swing and got all of it.

"Don't tell me!" Arnie shouted, as he ran to the center of the fairway to get a better look.

"Son of a bitch! I think you pulled it off!" yelled Ralph.

John stood silent and motionless, one hand over his brow, watching the flight of the ball.

Jim walked forward, watched the ball soar straight to a point that was at least thirty yards left of the flag before it slowly began to bend back.

"Come on you fucker, get back, get back," whispered Jim.

The ball headed toward the left, front edge of the big old oak. Rotating, biting the air as it came around the side, it finally cleared the oak's massive girth. Suddenly, without warning, the familiar sound of surlyn hitting wood echoed in the distance, followed by the gulping rush of air displacing water and finally, the splash. Across the pond's surface, ripples orbited the collision sight, covering the entire surface of the large pond. Hundreds of perfectly choreographed ripples. The final proof of destination and outcome.

"How the hell did that happen?" Ralph broke the silence. "That ball cleared the goddamn tree. I swear I saw it in the clear. You see what happened, Jim?"

"I can't figure it," answered Jim weakly. "I thought I made it. I don't know what happened."

"Well, you couldn't have hit it any better than that," consoled Arnie. "That was a spectacular shot."

"Goddamn spectacular. I'm in the water." Jim picked up his clubs and walked back to the cart.

John followed along. "I know how disappointed you are. You hit that shot as well as it could be played. I really thought you had a chance. I think you just caught one of those back branches that aren't visible from this angle."

"What back branches?" asked Jim. "You didn't mention any back branches before."

"Well, I told you how hard it was to fade around the tree. You know that I gave up trying to pull it off."

"Yes, but I didn't know it was impossible. You said it could be done."

"Well, maybe it can be done. Then again, after the great run you made at it, maybe it *is* impossible. I didn't mean to steer you wrong. I just never hit as perfect a shot as you just did."

John walked toward the other men, down near the pond. Jim took a seat behind the wheel of his cart and pulled out a new Titleist from the storage rack. He replayed the shot in his mind. It *was* perfect. Maybe the Savage couldn't be parred after all. If he believed in such nonsense, Jim would almost have to admit that the tree had reached out and whacked his ball into the pond. Like Ralph had said—like a big old, hairy arm. Suddenly, Jim slammed his fist into the cart's vinyl seat. "Shit!," he cried. "Goddamnit!" Bitterly disappointed, he couldn't get the shot out of his mind. He wanted that par. He needed that par. And for all intents and pur-poses—at least in his own mind—he should have made it.

Ralph checked his lie and took a real hard look at the path between the ball and the flagstick. Even from this close range, clearing the tree seemed impossible. "I can barely see the flag through that big, old, ugly tree," he said, turning to the others with a look that asked more for sympathy than for help.

"I figure you're about 165 yards from the stick," said John. It'll be tough to get over that tree. You could try to punch it under, and maybe get it onto that little mound just over the pond, in front of the green."

Ralph looked straight ahead and considered John's suggestion. "Yeah, but then I'll have to chip it in for my par. Probably have one foot in the water while I'm trying to do it too. Nah, it ain't worth it. Getting a bogey on this hole's nothing to celebrate." Ralph again stared into center of the oak's convoluted branches. "Can't get it over, can't get it under, can't get it around. Goddamnit, I'm going through it. Goin' to smash my 3–iron right into the guts of that old fucker."

"That's a very dense tree," replied John. "To find a path through there would take a small miracle."

"Hey, don't count Ralph out," said Arnie. "Ralph, you know my money's on you. Go ahead and blast it. I know you can do it."

Jim, who was just pulling up in the cart, got out and approached the others. "Go ahead Ralph. Smash it right through. You have as good a chance of getting there that way as any other."

Ralph, stroking his chin, was still staring at the flagstick through the thick, tangled branches. He turned and looked at John. "A miracle? Is that what you said it would take? A miracle? Well, that just so happens to be my strategy. To par this baby with a freakin' miracle. Give me room boys. I'm ready."

Ralph went into his stance, aiming right for the flag, and right into the thick of the oak tree. Adrenaline flowing, reminiscent of days when he was younger and stronger, he hit another steaming 3–iron. As planned, the ball entered the mangled web of twisted bark and green foliage. It penetrated the first layer of defense. Leaves flew from its pathway, and twigs snapped from the ball's furious assault.

"Get through there, you son of a bitch," screamed Arnie.

Avoiding the larger branches, the ball continued its radar–like course through the oak's limbs. Finally slowed by the soft resistance of leaves and webbed branches, it lost momentum and dribbled onto the embankment just beyond the water's far edge. Failing to stick in the soft, muddied dirt, the ball rolled down the short hill, finally coming to rest at the pond's edge—half submerged, half dry.

"Holy shit!" Arnie rushed over to Ralph, and pumped his hand. "How in God's name did you do that? You *are* a miracle man."

John offered his hand next. "I never thought you could get it through that far. That was incredible."

Jim waited his turn to shake Ralph's hand. "I think you just gave me my strategy for the next time I go after this hole. That was a great go at it."

Ralph was beaming. "Come on guys, I'll grant you that it was an entertaining shot." Pausing to catch his breath, he put his hand over the left side of his chest and continued. "Entertaining? Shit. If my heart didn't give out on that shot, I'm damn close to immortal." He took a deep breath, removed his cap, and wiped the sweat from his forehead. "Whew! That *was* something. But look here boys. I'm still not making par. There ain't gonna be any sign with my name on it out here."

"Who gives a damn," said Arnie. "That was still an unbelievable shot. And I for one am never going to forget it."

"I agree," added John. "You should be very proud of the way you went after that."

"Wait a minute, Ralph." Jim was standing off to the side, looking at Ralph's ball. "Who says it's over yet. You can knock that ball right in the cup and still make par."

"Well..." Ralph looked at his ball and considered the possibility. "That's kind of a longshot. I mean, we're talking a thousand to one."

"Don't forget the twelfth hole," said Arnie. "You chipped in from thirty there. Why not do it again? Wouldn't that be a hell of a way to par the Savage?"

"It is a longshot," added John. "Your ball's in mud, with an uphill lie. But it isn't impossible."

"All right guys," said Ralph. "I don't need all this pressure. Had enough for one day. Let's just say, I'm happy I hit the damn ball so well and gave it a shot. Actually, now that I think of it, this is the first time I got my ball past that freakin' water. That's right...now that I think of it, first time I've kept my ball dry on this hole." Ralph looked back at the spot of his ball and added, "Well, let's say its the first time I kept my ball half dry."

"Hey, that's what I call progress," said Arnie.

Laughing, having had enough center stage, Ralph looked back, "Hey boys, we better get moving. A foursome just pulled into the tee area. Come on, John, time for you to make history."

John grabbed his 9–iron, headed toward the sight of his ball before Arnie cut in, "Hey, John. Why don't you let me and Jim take our drops and hit first. You've got a big shot coming up. Might as well get our dirty work out of the way."

"Sure, go ahead," John agreed. "Either way, I don't mind."

Arnie dropped a ball right alongside John's, about ten yards from the pond's edge. The rough was short and playable. Arnie studied his shot, turned to the others and announced, "This is just as impossible as the others. I can't hit the ball 150 yards with enough height to get over that monstrosity." Arnie paused, then continued, "Remind me not to come back to this fucking course again. I'm not parring this hole. Today or ever."

"Don't worry about it today," said Jim. "You're already lying about five."

"If you want to punch it out to the left, you can chip it up from there," suggested John. "Or, you can punch it low, and hit out to that mound where Ralph's ball hit."

Ralph's suggestion further complicated Arnie's dilemma. "Hey, Arnie boy, slam that sucker right through the guts. Just like I did. I cleared you a nice little path." Ralph pointed up at the tree, "Don't you see it? Take a careful look now. Right over there. If you hit the ball just right, you can get it through that opening I created."

Arnie shook his head and laughed. "Ralph, you showed me the light. How can I have been so stupid to have not seen it myself. Of course. This is obviously my destiny. Par or not, I'm going to hit that fucking green!"

"Okay, Arnie," said John applauding. "You can do it. Let's go."

Jim added, "All right Arnie, right on the green. Let's go. There's people waiting to hit."

"That's my boy." said Ralph. "What club are you going to hit?"

Together, John and Ralph answered, "Five–iron."

"You got it," laughed Arnie as he went into his setup over the ball.

Arnie peered down at his Prostaff. It occurred to him that he had no plan in his mind. Now that the kidding had ended, he actually had to hit the ball. It had been a long, long day. So many good moments, but here he was, once again pressured to hit a good golf shot. He thought of the great shots he pulled off during the day and was impressed. He was amazed. How did he do it?

Arnie's daring go for it never touched the old oak. It was a very fat shot that traveled thirty yards in the air, then settled into the wide open water.

"Way to go, Arnie," howled Jim, down on one knee, laughing harder than he had all day.

"You are a pisser," said a laughing Ralph. Putting his hand behind Arnie's neck, "Do you know what a pisser you are?"

Patting Arnie on the back, John was smiling, "Those shots happen. We all make them. You've played some great golf today."

Jim, doubling over, exclaimed, "This is my destiny. That was *so* funny!"

Arnie, laughing himself, said, "Look...someone's got to entertain you guys. I tell you, things would be pretty boring around here if you guys had to count on yourselves for laughs."

Arnie backed away and felt, somewhere beneath his laughter, a sick feeling in the pit of his gut. He may have fooled the others, but he couldn't fool himself. He was hurt and humiliated by the shot. Repeatedly, he reminded himself that it was only a game. A game he hadn't been at for very long. Sure, he had the intellectual insight down pat. But his heart hadn't caught up with his head. A pisser. Lots of laughs. Arnie remembered how he was always class clown in elementary school. The kids would be laughing while he marched out the door to the principal's office. "They're laughing at you, not with you," his mother used to explain. Arnie didn't care. He'd take attention any way he could get it. Just like today.

"Okay Jim, your turn to hit away," said Ralph.

Walking toward the cart, Jim answered, "Hey, John, why don't you go and hit first. I want to grab a towel."

"Sure, no problem," answered John.

Jim got to the cart and went through the motions of drying his ball and hands with the towel that was attached to his golf bag. He looked back at John, with his antique 9–iron and gold ball and felt a burst of anger, if not hatred, toward him. Jim didn't have it all worked out, but he knew John was full of shit. Had to be. Always so polite and considerate. And his flower gardens. It was too much. His old man was loaded. That was the bottom line. No one could compare Jim's situation with John's. Not only had Jim not gotten a penny from his old man, Jim didn't even know him. All those years. His father never made any effort to find him. Jim and John's situations were entirely different. As Jim watched John get ready to hit, he prayed that the golden boy would not make par.

"Let's go Johnny boy," cried out Ralph. "One more of those beautiful 9–irons. That's all you need. One more."

"Come on John," Arnie said, clapping his hands. "Over the top, right at the flag."

John went into his stance, taking a little more time than usual.

Because the pin placement on this day was on the right hand side of the lower tier, John's strategy was that much more difficult. He had to get over the top of the tree and down more quickly than when the pin was in the elevated, back portion of the green. After one last look at the target and a hard stare at his ball, there was the sound of a crow. Seemingly unaware of, but in perfect tempo with the black bird's cadence, John took the same easy swing he had taken on the previous two shots.

The gold ball exploded off the clubface with an immediate, upward trajectory—continuing its arc, it caught the sun's radiance. The outward burst of light, the energy captured within, it propelled toward the clear blue sky. Assaulted by the breeze, the oak's tallest branches lifted, lunged at the passing burst of light. Safely out of reach, over the top, the gold ball began its descent—straight down in line with the flag, onto the front edge of the green's upper tier. Finding the downward slope of the swale, rolling back, the golden ball headed right at the cup.

"Go in the hole!" screamed Ralph.

Arnie stepped forward and grabbed John's arm.

John and Jim were silent as they watched the gold ball funnel toward the flag until it finally stopped about a foot short of its target.

"Holy shit!" screamed Ralph. "I don't believe it! What a shot! You parred the Savage!"

Arnie shook John's hand and said, "Who the hell are you? Where are you from? When did your spaceship land?"

Jim stepped in and offered a handshake. "That was a great shot. You've got your par."

"Just a minute, guys," John finally spoke. "I didn't make par yet. I've missed a lot of one-footers in my day. Could we please hold off on the celebration?"

Jim went to his cart to get his 7–iron. It was his turn to hit. He felt like quitting right then. Suddenly, he had played enough golf for a lifetime. This had been a horrible day. If only they hadn't hooked up with John. Jim was off his game. The more he thought about it, the angrier he became. He looked at John—with that dumb smile on his face—holding that family heirloom 9–iron. Jim did not want to attempt the next shot. What the hell for? Nothing good could come of it. Reluctantly, he grabbed his 7–iron, found an old Superflite shag ball in his bag, and headed to the edge of the pond.

"Come on, Jim," encouraged Ralph. "Get it up and down from out here. A bogey would be damn respectable. Keep your round going. No use blowing the whole damn round."

The other men were silent.

Standing over the ball, into his waggle, Jim suddenly stepped out of his shot. He took a few easy practice swings, took a deep breath and again stepped up to his ball. A little bit rushed, he came across the ball but still got it airborne. A pulled shot that cleared the left side of the oak and landed on the embankment about twenty yards left of the green, pin–high.

"Excellent play," said John.

"Good hit," seconded Arnie.

"How the hell do you hit a draw like that?" asked Ralph. "Been playing the game for forty years and I never could understand how a fella could work a ball off the clubface like that."

Although he knew he had unintentionally pulled the ball left, Jim accepted the kind words graciously and headed toward his cart thinking double bogey. There were no objections to Arnie's decision to pick up and enter an eight on the scorecard.

From the green and the area around it, the Savage revealed a surrealistic magnificence. The oak tree seemed larger. Filtered layers of orange haze poured through the mass of pretzeled branches and flapping leaves. From close range, the oak's enormity blocked out wide–angle perspective except for the golden radiance of the pond's front edge, and the piece of blue sky off to the right, above the tree's relatively short and vulnerable branches. Fused within the surreal scene was John's gold ball, which glistened in a patch of sun, one and a half feet behind the white stick with the red flag. On its banner, pointed edge waving straight out, the sky–blue number sixteen marked the Savage.

John spotted his ball while Ralph and Jim grabbed their putters and short game irons, ready to analyze their approaches to the cup. Everyone agreed that it would be best to have John hole out after everyone else had completed play.

With his back foot settled in the mud, his front knee bent under his chin, Ralph had little chance for a chip–in and a shot at immortality. Looking up at John and Arnie who were on the right side of the green, he yelled out, "This is fucking impossible. The ball's half submerged, and I'm sinking fast. Jesus Christ! How can an old man manage to find himself in a situation like this?"

"You better hurry up and hit," shouted back Arnie. "You're getting shorter by the minute."

"Well, here goes nothing.".

Water and mud flew everywhere as the ball popped straight up and landed on the left lower edge of the green, about thirty feet from the stick.

"Holy shit, what a mess!" screamed Ralph as he pulled his right foot out of the mud, and made his way up the short, steep incline.

Walking to the front of the green to meet him, Arnie broke into laughter when he saw Ralph's mud–splattered clothes. "Look at you. What a gamer. A little more to the right and you might have holed it."

"Nice up from that spot," yelled out Jim from the sight of his ball.

Wiping some of the mud off Ralph's shirt, John said, "That was a hell of a play."

"Enough of the bullshit," shot back Ralph. "I'm an asshole to be gettin' myself involved in all this mess. Let's call it like it is. Plain and simple. I'm an asshole and an old fool."

"You love it, and you know it," replied Arnie.

Walking off the green, looking at his mud–stained clothes, and shaking his head, Ralph smiled.

Jim was just about ready to hit. He elected a 6–iron for a pitch–and–run go at it. He had to carry the ball twenty yards on the fly to land it on the green. He needed about thirty yards of roll to reach the cup. Pin–high, adjacent to the green's lower tier, he decided to head the ball straight at the stick. Without breaking his wrists, he kept his head down and swung through the ball with a hard putting motion. Landing on the green, right on target, the ball began an energized run at the cup, until suddenly losing steam. Bearing right, it stopped about ten feet below the hole.

"Nice chip," said Ralph. "Come on, now. Let's knock these putts down and let John have his moment in the sun."

Going through the motions, Jim walked onto the green, pulled out the flagstick, laid his 6–iron across it, and proceeded to begin the study of his putt.

"Now this here putt is for bogey," said Ralph, in a kneeling position, one eye closed, his putter plumbed between his thumb and forefinger.

"That's right," said Arnie. "And who knows. You very well might become the first senior to ever *bogey* the Savage."

"All right, let's stop the chatter," replied Ralph. "I've got me some work here."

Starting the ball well left of the cup, Ralph gave it a good smack, following through nicely. The ball climbed up the swale and rolled back in a perfect line, passing over the left edge of the cup before stopping two feet below the hole.

""Whoa!" screamed Ralph, his back arched, his face contorted by the will expended for the near–miss.

"Great putt," said Jim. "I thought you had it. Perfect read."

"I'll give you that one," added Arnie. "For all the work you put into that hole, you at least deserve a double bogey."

"The hell with that," answered Ralph as he tapped in the short putt. "I deserve a goddamn medal for the way I played that hole. Double bogey my ass."

Jim knelt to study his uphill, ten–foot put. Glancing at his target, he saw John's ball marker, about a foot and a half above the hole. He had a tough putt to save a double and match Ralph for the hole while John waited on his tap–in for par. Jim realized that this could have been *his* moment in the shadow of the giant oak. Temporarily frozen, he became aware of his hands shaking. As Jim composed himself and got ready to make the putt, the anger that had surfaced so many times this day subsided. Walking up to his ball, he noticed John with the gold ball in his hand. No, it wasn't anger Jim was feeling. It was disappointment, and it hurt. It hurt like hell.

No one spoke as Jim's putt came up three feet short. Stepping up quickly, he tapped it in the general direction of the hole with one hand. Missing by a couple of inches, he finally picked up the ball and walked off to the side of the green.

"I gave you that last one," yelled Ralph in Jim's direction. Turning back to face the hole, he added, "Come on, John. Knock that goddamn gold ball in the cup already, willya. I'm getting hungry, not to mention that I got a plane to catch tonight. Too much damn golf. You know there *is* such a thing as too much damn golf."

While Ralph, Arnie and Jim assembled on the green's fringe just off to John's side, John replaced his marker with the gold ball. With only eighteen inches to the cup, it suddenly became apparent that this putt was not a gimme. Downhill, with a slight break to the right, the slightest miscalculation could send the ball rolling three feet past the cup. The men had all missed similar putts in their day and remained quiet as John got into his stance. He took two practice strokes and set the copper blade behind the ball. Flexing his knees and staring intensely at the cup, John took a deep breath and relaxed his grip. A rhythmic back and forth stroke, the putter moved through the ball and froze at the top of its arc. The gold ball rolled left of the target until it found the cup's edge, circled the rim twice and fell straight down.

John looked up and flashed a proud smile as the men surrounded him and offered congratulations.

The Savage had been parred.

CHAPTER 15

The anti–climax of playing out the Savage and John's historic par, had an impact on all four men. Ralph and Arnie sat out the seventeenth and eighteenth holes while Jim continued to struggle with a pair of doubles. Even John's play reflected the letdown. After bogeying seventeen, he lost his tee shot on the final hole, and became an official member of Ralph's "snowman club." Ralph assured John that this was a special honor and ranked right up there with parring the Savage on his list of accomplishments for the day.

John went directly to check in at the pro shop while the others parked their carts in an area off to the side of the clubhouse. Quietly, each of the men went through their personal organizational rituals. Balls and tees transferred from pockets to golf bag; wallets, keys, and watches recovered from their designated, zippered pouches.

Unstrapping his bag from the rear of the cart, Jim broke the silence. "It didn't take John long to run to Tina and dad to break the news."

"What do you expect?" replied Arnie. "He just accomplished something that's never been done. He wants to share it with the people who love him. What the hell's wrong with that?"

"Myself, I'd be at the local television station being interviewed," added Ralph. "Then I'd get on the horn to the wire services. I figure by Monday, it would be a guest spot on the Letterman Show."

"I hear what you guys are saying," said Jim. "I'd be pretty pumped myself. But, I'm talking about John and his whole act. The guy acts like he doesn't care about anything. But he *does* care. That's why he had to run and tell Tina and his old man all about it. Don't you think he puts on an act?"

"I don't know about that," said Ralph. "John's just got one of those steady, even-keeled temperaments. The kind you're born with. You can't teach that. He's laid-back. That's all. He's just laid-back."

"I think it might be more than that," added Arnie. "You make it sound like he had a lobotomy or something. I just think the man's a class act. He's been around for a guy his age, and I think he's learned a few things. And besides, he's marrying Tina. She obviously sees something in him."

"Yeah, his old man's money," answered Jim. "A couple more years and she'll be sitting pretty. The Queen of Wild Links."

Ralph lifted his bag and threw it across his shoulder. "None of us knows the whole truth about any of this. Why can't people be just what they seem to be? John and everyone we met on this island are nice people. Period. Besides, it's none of our damn business. Now, let's get the hell out of here. Just don't turn your back on me. You never know, I could be one of them hatchet murderers. Been waiting all day for this moment just to chop you up in little pieces." Walking ahead, laughing, Ralph yelled out, "Come on, boys. Let's get going."

When they entered the pro shop, a clerk was behind the front counter, making change for a customer. Voices could be heard coming from behind him.

"Where'd we leave our shoes?" asked Arnie.

"Back here," replied Jim.

Before they reached the doorway leading to the locker rooms, Hans Keeler wheeled out. When he saw Jim standing in front of him, he said, "Excuse me, young fellow. I'll get right out of your way."

Jim moved to let him pass.

"Excuse me, Mr. Keeler?" Ralph, his hand outstretched, walked to the man in the wheelchair and introduced himself. "I'm Ralph and this here's Jim and Arnie. We just got through playing with that son of yours. You must be damn proud of that young man's accomplishment."

"Well, how do you do," replied Keeler, wheeling in position to shake the hands of all the men. "It's very nice to meet you all. And yes, I'm very proud of John. And I must add surprised. That hole hasn't been parred in the seventeen years I've been here, and I can't say I expected it to ever happen."

"John made it look easy," added Arnie. "Three 9–irons and a tap in. Looked like he does it all the time."

"If you ask me, I think he did it the hard way," countered Keeler. "With that gold ball and his grandfather's club. I always figured the only chance was with a driver and a long iron fade. But he proved me wrong."

"That's what I tried. A driver and a long iron," said Jim.

"You must be that big hitter who was flirting with par all day," said Keeler. "John said you almost made it yourself. Is this the first time you played the Savage?"

"Yes it was. But I've heard about it since I was a kid, when..."

Before Jim could finish his comment, there was a sudden burst of laughter that grew louder. John and Tina entered the pro shop.

"Well, here's the man of the moment," exclaimed Ralph. "Have you heard from President Bush yet?"

Through the laughter, John replied, "Yeah, he called, but I left word that I'd call back after my shower."

The men laughed and John put his arm around Tina, pressing her close to his side.

"You know guys," said Tina. "I'm not sure I like this. We're getting married tomorrow, and all this excitement is overshadowing our wedding."

"Don't you worry, pretty lady," reassured Ralph. "A man would be a fool to let marrying a beautiful woman like you take a backseat to anything. In fact, that's probably why John parred the darn Savage. He had you and this wedding on his mind. That's it, it was the power of love. I can see the headlines now. 'The Savage Conquered By Love.' Kind of like a modern day King Kong." Ralph turned toward John and added, "No offense there, Johnny."

Once again Ralph's commentary drew chuckles.

"Ralph, you know I like your way of looking at things," said Tina. Looking at John with a little girl smile, she went on, "Don't forget what the man said. I played a very important role in that par today."

"Obviously, honey," replied John, tightening his grip around her.

"Well, as far as I'm concerned, the wedding is the most important thing," said Keeler. "But I don't see why we can't also celebrate the parring of the Savage."

"I have an idea," said Tina. "Why don't you men attend the wedding. That would be a way to bring together both events. It's tomorrow at 3:00 in the flower garden. Just a short service and small reception. Should be over in three hours. It would be very nice to have you there."

"That's a great idea," said Keeler.

"We'd love to have you," added John. "What do you say?"

"That's very kind of you," said Ralph. "And I'd love to be there. Always love a wedding. But I have a flight out of here at 7:30 tonight."

"Jim and I aren't leaving until Sunday," said Arnie. "I think we might be able to make it."

Jim looked sternly at Arnie, his face was reddened, a vein bulged from his neck. "Arnie, are you crazy? How many hours do you think there are in a day? We have a starting time at Sea Trail Plantation tomorrow."

"Yeah, but that's at 7:40 A.M.. We should have plenty of time to make the wedding."

"Let's talk about this later," Jim barked. "After we check into our hotel and get a little more settled."

"Well, you guys don't have to decide right now," broke in John. "If you can make it, great. If not, don't worry about it. We won't expect you, but if you show, we'll be thrilled to see you. Right Tina?"

"Definitely," she replied. "We have plenty of room, and it's going to be a buffet. No head counts or seating to worry about."

"At least let me buy you guys a beer," added John. "Do you have time for a quick one right now?"

"You've got a good idea there, son," said Ralph. "But I really do have to make my way back to my hotel." Looking at his watch, Ralph added, "It's nearly 3:00. I better get back and hook up with Bud. Appreciate the offer, though."

"Well, *we've* got some free time," said Arnie. "And I wouldn't mind a brew along with one of those chili dogs."

"Arnie," said Jim. "Did you forget about our luggage at the airport? We never even checked into our hotel. And, Jesus, I need to take a shower."

"I can help you two out on that score," said Keeler. "If you want to relax for an hour and grab a bite here, I can have your luggage transferred from the Jetport to your hotel for you. And you're more than welcome to use the showers in the locker room."

"That's very generous of you," said Arnie. "But Jim's right. It *would* be a good idea to get settled into our hotel."

"Well, I can still make a call and get your bags transferred for you," suggested Keeler.

"If it's not too much bother, that would be great," Arnie replied.

"Actually," said Jim. "I wouldn't mind grabbing a quick shower right now. It got awfully hot out there today."

"Be my guest," answered Keeler. "There should be plenty of clean towels in the locker room. Now, what hotel are you fellows booked at?"

"Holiday Inn, Downtown," Arnie responded.

"Whose name is the luggage checked in under?"

"Weiss. Arnold Weiss."

"Consider it done," said Keeler. "If you other men would also like to shower, please help yourself."

"You're a very kind man," said Ralph. "But I've really got to get going now. Don't have another moment to spare, so I think I'll say my good–byes to all you good folks right now."

"It's been a pleasure, Ralph." Jim stepped forward and the two men shook hands.

"The pleasure's been mine, son," replied Ralph, holding his grip on Jim's hand. "Watching you whack that ball has been an honest– to–goodness joy."

"Thanks. I just wish I could have held it together at the end today."

"Now, don't you go berating yourself. Just keep that young hot head of yours under wraps and let your God–given ability take charge. You'll be parring a lot of Savages in your day." Extending his hand in Arnie's direction, Ralph continued. "And Arnie, I thoroughly enjoyed…"

"Not so fast," Arnie interrupted. "While Jimbo here steams the muck off, I'll walk you to the dock."

"Don't you want to take a shower yourself?" asked Ralph.

"Why, do I smell that bad? No, my man, no need. I don't sweat when I play golf. It's such a mellow sport."

"Okay, good buddy. I'd love to have the company."

Ralph extended his hand to Hans Keeler. "Mr. Keeler. Thank you for your hospitality. You've got a beautiful course here. I hope the good Lord gives me an opportunity to visit again."

"Thank you, Ralph. I hope you make it back."

"John and Tina." Ralph walked in the direction of the couple. "I want to wish you all the luck in the world. You two make a beautiful pair." He shook John's hand. "And the way you hit that golf ball, young fellow, I must say I'm envious. Yeah, looking at this pretty young lady by your side and thinking about the day you had out on the links, I have to confess I'm good and jealous of you. Can't imagine a more perfect moment in a young man's life."

"Thank you," replied John.

"Excuse me, Ralph," Arnie interrupted. "I thought you were in a rush to get out of here."

"You're right, Arnie," answered Ralph, glancing at his watch. "Talk too much. That's always been my problem. I just can't shut up."

Arnie looked for Jim. He wanted to make plans to meet outside the snack bar.

Jim was already in the showers.

CHAPTER 16

Ralph and Arnie exited the winding path that ran through the forest and connected the dock's beach with the island's interior. The vast ocean surface was calm and radiant, blanketed with golden sparkle from the late afternoon sun.

Squinting, holding his hand across his brow, Ralph said, "I don't see the Serpent."

"I'm sure that money–grubbing Captain will be here any minute," said Arnie. "Let's grab a seat on that bench and wait."

As the men walked down toward the shore, Arnie was suddenly hit with the impact of the moment. Saying goodbye. He had only known Ralph for two days, but had come to care deeply for the man. A good man who made Arnie feel at ease. Who knew the right thing to say. There was so much that Arnie could learn from Ralph. But he wouldn't have the chance. Ralph would be another fleeting memory in Arnie's life. Another loss. This was the part of life that challenged Arnie's faith. Anything that brings pleasure, that's worth having, must be temporary. Michelle always said that you have to be damn lucky to lose something, because it implies that you had something worthwhile to begin with. Arnie understood her point logically. But he just couldn't feel the way she did.

As they took their seats on the bench, Ralph spoke first. "This has really been a pleasure, good buddy. We're going to have to make arrangements to get together one of these days."

"I'd love to. Which reminds me...I never did ask where you and Bud come from."

"Upstate New York. Bud lives in a town called Clifton Park. About fifteen miles north of Albany. I live about twenty miles further north of him in Saratoga Springs."

"That's not far from me at all. As a matter of fact, we've been to a concert or two in the Berkshires. At Tanglewood. That's not too far from you, is it?"

"Sure isn't. The wife and I have been there more than a few times ourselves. That might be a way to hook up right there. And there's also the racetrack and Performing Arts Center in Saratoga. August is horse season in Saratoga. Me and a couple of buddies get out at least once a year. Maybe you'd like to come up in August."

"Sure. It sounds great. Why don't we exchange phone numbers. I think I have a business card here somewhere." Fumbling with his wallet, pulling out credit cards, receipts, and scribbled messages, Arnie felt uneasy remembering how many times he had been in this situation. A warm, intimate moment flush with genuine warmth and good intentions. But, somehow, the good feelings faded. The best of intentions were forgotten. Lost in the routine of unpaid bills and sick kids, the self–absorption of dailiness eventually consumed.

"Don't worry about the card. I've got a pen and some paper right here. You know, Arnie, I'd really like for us to get together some time. You're a good man, with a good heart. And you're funny as hell. I must say, I've had more laughs these last couple of days than I've had in years. Sure, I wish Bud was there today. What with John parring the Savage and all. But then again, if Bud had been there, we wouldn't have played with John. In fact, John might not have played at all. It's funny how things work out, don't you think?"

"It sure is. Make sure to tell Bud that if it wasn't for him, the Savage wouldn't have been parred. Let him know that he played a big part in history. Him and his damn tequila."

"He'll love that. Bud'll definitely be more than happy to take some of the credit."

As the men shared one last laugh, the Serpent could be seen heading toward the shore.

Folding the paper with his phone number on it and handing it over to Ralph, Arnie said, "I really do want to follow through on contacting you. The truth is, I don't always make good on these kind of commitments."

"None of us do, good buddy. Life's too damn busy. And you've got a business to run and a couple of kids in the house. Don't you worry about it. I'm the one who should make the damn call. I'm retired, my kids are grown. Have nothing to do but bang a golf ball around and go shopping with the wife."

The Serpent pulled into the dock, the voice of Captain Ayman could be heard shouting, "Caramus. Next stop, the Mainland."

"Well, Ralph," Arnie extended his hand, his empty eyes peered away from Ralph's. "I guess this is goodbye."

Ralph took Arnie's hand, put his left arm around the younger man's shoulder, and pulled him into a short, strong hug. Ralph backed away, looked Arnie in the eye, and said, "This was special, my friend. I've been around a long time, met a lot of people. Let me tell you, this was something special."

"You fellows coming aboard?" The Captain motioned the men to come forward and get on deck.

Ralph picked up his golf bag and headed toward the boat.

"Send my best to Bud," Arnie shouted out after him. "And, we will be in touch."

Ralph took his seat. Paid his six dollars. As the Serpent backed away from the dock, he turned and waved. The engine roared and the bow lifted. As the Serpent sped into the open water, a seam of white foam split the golden water. Heading straight toward the heart of the giant orange sun that merged boundaries with the edge of the world, the Serpent faded into darkness.

Ralph was gone.

Chapter 17

B y the time Arnie and Jim got to the hotel, their luggage had already arrived. Before leaving Wild Links, Arnie had found time for a quick chili dog and soda, and assured John there was a good chance that he and Jim would make the wedding the next day. Jim, figuring he'd deal with Arnie later, stayed out of it.

The Holiday Inn Downtown was a typical beachfront high–rise on the Grand Strand. Although not as lavish as some, it was clean. Had a pool and a hot tub, and was reasonably priced. As they entered the lobby and approached the registration desk, Jim and Arnie were greeted by a young blond woman with blue eyes and large breasts that were showcased by her snug and low–cut, bright yellow tank top.

"Hey, y'all just checking in?"

"Actually, we should have been here yesterday. That storm held us up." Arnie leaned over the counter and searched for his name on the list the blond was scanning. "The name's Weiss. Weiss and Carlson."

"Oh yeah. I know who y'all are." The blond woman turned, walked through a door into a back room, and quickly returned with Jim's small, gray suitcase. "Your bags were delivered about an hour ago. Three of them. Let's see." Keypunching some information into the computer, she said, "Yup, I've got it now. Weiss and Carlson.

Arrive Thursday April 23, leave Sunday April 26. Room 2405. That's an oceanfront. Want to have your bags sent up?"

"That'll be great," Jim cut in. "Where's your lounge?"

"If you walk straight down this corridor, you'll see the Oasis Lounge. That opens at 4:00 P.M. and closes at 2:00 A.M—weekdays. Closes at midnight on Saturday and remains closed all day Sunday. County law."

Taking a pad and pencil from the desktop, she went on. "Let me write some of this information down for you. First, there's a restaurant adjacent to the lounge, but you'll need reservations. It's very good. And then if you just want a light bite, our snack bar's right opposite the vending machines, just down that hallway." The woman leaned over the counter, spilling out of her tank top, and pointed.

"How about the hot tub?" asked Arnie. "That's what these aching bones really need."

The blond laughed and tossed her hair away from her forehead. "That's what everyone says. Gotta stay relaxed when you're on vacation. Right? Well, if you keep walking down the corridor, past the lounge, you'll see a sign for the pool. Go through that door. The hot tub's alongside the pool." She handed the men their keys and added, "Now is there anything else I can do to make you boys more comfortable?"

"No, I think that about does it," answered Arnie. "Thank you."

"You're very welcome."

Jim and Arnie reached the elevator. As the doors closed, Jim leaned over to Arnie and whispered, "Is there anything I can do? Yeah honey, let me play with your tits for about an hour and a half. Did you see those tits? God, they were perfect."

"Yes, Jim, I saw her tits, but they're already out of my mind. I'm no sooner going to get near them than I'm going to visit Australia in the next two days."

The elevator stopped, the men got out and looked for Room 2405.

Walking down the corridor, Jim continued. "But why, Arnie? Why wouldn't you get near tits like those? You're not too old to lust after a beauty that that. Are you?"

The men found their room, Arnie tried the key and said, "I'm not old, but I'm not a kid anymore either. And then there *is* the simple matter of Michelle, Jim. Remember her? The woman I married about twenty–one years ago?" Pushing the door open, Arnie added, "Her's are the only tits I get to play with. At least in this lifetime."

The room was a standard double–occupancy hotel room. On the small side, but well kept. Two double beds, a small round table with two chairs, and a dresser with a twenty inch color television sitting on it. There was a small refrigerator and bathroom. At the end of the room was a heavy peach and teal drape that covered the sliding glass door leading to the balcony.

Arnie went to the balcony while Jim attempted to decode the workings of the television.

"Jim, come on out here and take a look at this."

Jim backed through the glass doors, arm extended, experimenting with buttons on the remote control, before turning to have a look.

"There's the Atlantic Ocean, my friend," said Arnie.

"Nice view. And check out the view straight down. There's a pool and hot tub. Looks like a couple of babes are heating up, too. Let's go check it out."

"I definitely agree. Especially considering the fact that we'll be playing golf the next two days. The hot tub'll keep us loose."

Over the sound of waves crashing onto the shore, Jim thought he heard a knock on the door.

"Must be our luggage," said Arnie, as he hurried to answer.

"Looks like we didn't lose anything," said Arnie, handing the bellhop two bucks.

"Thank you very much, sir. Is there anything else I can help you with?"

"No thanks. We're just fine."

Arnie threw the suitcases on the two beds and said, "Let's find our suits and get down to that tub. I could also go for some dinner pretty soon. What do you want to eat? Lots of nice restaurants to choose from around here. How about Italian? I could go for some lasagna or veal parmigiana."

Jim pulled his Speedos over his thighs, "Hold on now, Arnie. Let's play it by ear. We'll go to the hot tub, maybe have a cocktail or two, and then if we want to, we can always find a place to eat. What's the big rush to eat? Didn't that chili dog fill you up?"

"I'm not big on prime rib at midnight. And yes...I am getting hungry."

"Will you relax? Don't worry, you're not going to starve to death. Maybe we'll just grab a sandwich or something. Chill out, man. Let's see what goes down."

"What are you talking about? What goes down. What is this...a Spike Lee flick? What the fuck's going down?"

"We're not just going to eat and go to bed at 10:00 are we? My man, stop and think for a minute. We're on vacation. Let's do something a little different. Out of the routine. Let's hear some music, or just check things out. I don't want to have the whole night revolve around a big, expensive meal."

"Well, maybe you're right. I eat at nice restaurants all the time back home. This *is* a vacation. I'll try to keep an open mind."

Jim grabbed two towels from the bathroom, slapped Arnie on the back and opened the door to the corridor. "That's my boy. Now let's go hit that hot tub."

The pool and hot tub were busy after the long, hot day. The circular hot tub, about twelve feet across, was constructed on a slab of concrete no more than fifty feet from the beach, which was lined with palm trees that waved in the tropical breeze against a backdrop of dusk—purple sky and orange wispy clouds. The tub was already occupied by two men and two women.

"Ahhh, that feels nice," Arnie murmured, half submerged in the 104 degree water. "Come on, Jim. This is heaven. Temperature's just right." Arnie slowly sank and settled on a bench, the water up to his chin. He stretched his legs straight out until his toes appeared above the white foam.

Jim placed his watch and wallet by the tub's edge and stepped in.

"Am I right?" Arnie shouted over the roar of the hot tub's jets. "And look at that ocean and those palm trees. You know Jim, I'm starting to really appreciate this golf vacation idea."

Jim's arms were winged along the tub's edge. He held his face up, as if capturing late afternoon sun rays, and closed his eyes. "We definitely agree on this one, Arnie. This *is* nice."

Suddenly, the water stopped swirling, and the sounds of the ocean and of voices from the pool area could be heard.

"That's okay, I'll reset the timer," said the woman sitting opposite Arnie. "We're leaving, anyway."

The two women left the hot tub.

"Thank you," Arnie shouted.

Sliding closer to Arnie, Jim said, "Did you see the ass on that redhead? The other one's a cow, but that redhead had a nice, tight body."

"Actually, I thought they were both pretty damn good."

Jim glanced back toward the hotel and added, "I wonder if they're here alone. Maybe they're married and their husbands are here to play golf."

Arnie sat up straight and turned to face Jim. "Christ, is there a woman you're not interested in? First Tina, then the woman at the front desk, now these two. Man, you really are something."

"What can I tell you, Arnie. I just love women. That's all there is to it. Eight to eighty, blind, crippled, or crazy. I'm a lady's man for sure."

"You're a goddamn sex maniac. That's what you are. Do you happen to like female animals?"

"Only sheep and certain breeds of dog."

Arnie smiled, shook his head, leaned back and closed his eyes.

"Hey, have you guys been to any of the topless places on Restaurant Row?" A voice echoed from across the tub.

One of the two strange men stood and walked toward the center of the hot tub. "If you guys want to see some incredible women, you've got to check out the *Femme Factory* or *Wild Horses*."

"Where are they?" asked Jim.

"Just go east for a few miles on 17, the main drag. Where all the restaurants are. They're only about a mile apart. Both on the left–hand side. You can't miss them."

"And you say the women are good looking?" asked Jim.

The young man smiled at his friend and said, "Frankie, what do you think? Are the women at *Wild Horses* good looking?"

"Unbeeeeleivable!" replied the man identified as Frankie. "And they're all over the damn place. Everywhere you look."

Jim pressed for more details. "What do they do, just dance?"

"Well yeah," answered the first man. "There's a stage. And they'll come and dance at your table. It's pretty standard. You stick a buck in their G–strings and they throw you a wiggle."

"Ah...I've been to those places," said Jim. "I'm usually bored after thirty minutes."

"I usually feel the same way," said Frankie. "But the women are so magnificent at these places, I could stay interested for thirty days. Especially with a few couch dances thrown in."

"What are the couch dances like?" asked Jim.

"That's where the lady of your choice takes you into the VIP Lounge and gives a private performance."

"What do you mean? Is touching allowed?"

"Who knows?" answered Frankie. "I took the standard $20.00 couch dance. I don't know what I could've gotten for a little surcharge."

"Hey, just to look at all those tall, big–breasted, tight–assed babes is worth the experience," added the other man. "Even if you just knock down one beer and leave after a half–hour. I'm telling you, you've never seen anything like it."

The jet's timer ran down again, and the two men left the hot tub. Jim and Arnie decided to stay for one more cycle.

Quiet throughout the conversation about the topless places, Arnie finally spoke. "Shit, I'm not going to that horse factory place. I hate those places. Migraine material. Loud. Smoky. Screaming rednecks. And a strange woman shaking her ass in my face does nothing but make me uncomfortable."

Jim paused a moment before calmly replying. "Arnie. I thought you were going to keep an open mind. Why not stop by one of these places just for a beer or two? Let's check it out. We're on vacation, buddy. Let's live a little. There's more to life than planning your next meal."

"And there's more to life than getting laid."

"You've got to admit, we have hit the high spots on the list."

Arnie shook his head and laughed. "Well we haven't mentioned taking a good shit. At my age, that's starting to rank right up there with sex."

As both men laughed, Jim proposed a compromise. "What do you say, we stop at one of the topless bars for a half–hour or so. Just a couple of beers. And then we'll go and have a nice relaxing dinner. You can choose the restaurant."

"Okay, Jimbo. Fair is fair. You're on."

CHAPTER 18

The taxi pulled into the crowded parking lot of *Wild Horses*, a rambling split log structure that stretched for half a block. Across its roofline, a curvaceous woman atop a red horse blazed a neon invitation to the throng of men which pressed toward the front entrance. White–haired retirees, twenty–five year old jocks, bearded mid–lifers, were lined up for the evening's entertainment. A loud, steady thumping bass slammed through the busy front doors.

"I better drop you off here," the cab driver turned to tell Jim and Arnie.

Jim paid the cabby while Arnie walked toward the entrance to get a better look.

"Hey, you want to buy a re–entry ticket?"

Arnie turned and faced a tall, muscular man wearing an orange tank top, two feather earrings and Mohawk haircut.

"What the heck's a re–entry ticket?"

"It costs eight bucks to get in, man. Give me five and I'll give you my ticket. You can come and go all night with it."

Arnie paused and glanced at front door where women were collecting money as people entered. "I'll give you three bucks."

"Are you fucking crazy?" The muscle beach prototype began walking away, but suddenly stopped and turned to face Arnie. "Ah, what the fuck. Give me the three bucks."

Arnie felt the rush that a great business transaction promoted. No way that young punk was going to get the better of the deal.

"Come on, Arn, let's check it out," said Jim, already closing in on the front door.

"That'll be eight dollars," said one of the women who was wearing a pink T-shirt sporting the neon horse logo.

Jim reached for his wallet, gave the woman a ten, and stuck the change in his front pocket.

"I'm re-entering." Arnie flashed his ticket to the woman who nodded her approval.

"What the fuck!" Jim turned to Arnie, who pushed him forward.

"Just get in there. I've got connections. Come on, let's go."

Once past the second set of doors, there was an explosion of sensory stimulation. Staggered arrays of blue, red, purple, and yellow strobe effects glared through the smoky haze. Hard driving rock and roll was overdubbed by the voice of a disc-jockey who shouted encouragement to the hundreds of pot-bellied, tan, bald, tall, short, beer-drinking men.

And women.

Everywhere, there were gorgeous women wearing stiletto heels and G-strings. On tables, in velvet roped cages high above the floor, dancing on the giant center stage, mixing with the groups of men. Everywhere, women.

"Let's find a place to sit." Jim screamed above the loud music and raucous male voices. Wide-eyed, Arnie pushed through the crowd and followed Jim.

"Excuse me, honey." A luscious brunette with piles of teased chestnut hair and moist red lipstick, put her hands on Arnie's

shoulders as she slid behind him. Turning quickly, Arnie felt her
breasts trace his back.

"Those two are getting up," shouted Jim. "Let's go."

Jim pushed through the crowd and grabbed two seats. Arnie
was right behind him.

"Man, those guys at the pool didn't exaggerate," said Jim. "I
never saw anything like this. And I can't believe we lucked–out
with these two seats. We've got a clear view for the main show,
there on center stage. Now all we need is a waitress to bring us a
couple of brewskis. Shit, Arnie, look at that one over there."

Arnie sat slump shouldered and quiet. He looked toward a
small round table where four men applauded the long–legged,
large breasted blond who danced on their table. She pressed the
palms of her hands against the ceiling as she gyrated her ass to the
shouts of the men.

"She's a fucking Amazon," Jim yelled into Arnie's ear. "What
an incredible body. I think I'm in love."

Arnie didn't respond but continued to watch as the woman on
the table looked down at the men and pushed her breasts together.
Her attention now directed to only one of the men, she squatted
down, ran her finger against her tongue then circled her large,
erect nipple. The targeted man stood up, extended his tongue, and
leaned toward the dancer. She cupped her breast, then moved forward to meet his tongue. A hair's breath away, she pulled back,
tugged off the man's cap, and pulled it over her champagne hair.
Hips thrusting to the throbbing electric beat once again, the
woman smiled at the man and licked her lips. He let out a wild
scream, as his friends pushed him back into his seat.

"Can you believe this place?" shouted Jim.

"I'll admit it's interesting," Arnie shouted back.

"Interesting? Fuck you, interesting. This place is unreal. You
love it, Arnie. Admit it. You love it!"

Arnie continued to look around the room. Christ, he thought. This place was like nothing he'd ever seen before. Alive with music, lights, screaming, and laughter. It was pure energy. And the women. All those lithe, lovely twenty year–old, perfect 10's. Arnie had to admit that they sure looked good. Damn good.

"Jim, look over there." Arnie grabbed Jim's shoulder to get his attention.

At the table behind them, a redhead was pressing her breasts into the face of a stocky man. Arnie and Jim stared at the tapered curve of her back as she bent at the waist. Supple, smoothly muscled legs stretched from her heels to the base of her delicious, firm buttocks. Her thong branched to form an inverted "V" of white silk which gleamed against the tanned firmness of her upper thighs. Suddenly, the redhead threw her right leg over the man's shoulder, rested her hands on his knees, and pumped her crotch in the direction of his face. Then, ending her routine, she kissed the guy's flushed cheek, slid a lacquered red fingernail under the elastic waistband of her thong, and smiled as he stuffed a five dollar bill into the satin pocket.

"Hey, Arnie, you like that one, don't ya."

"What?" Arnie's attention remained fixed on the tall redhead.

Jim laughed and smacked Arnie on the back. "Yeah, she's nice. What's not to like? I knew it would get to you."

"Come on, Jim. I'm just curious, that's all. I wonder how much these women make in a week and...I wonder if any of them are married or shit, if in some cases, their parents know what the hell they're doing."

"Oh, I get it. Forget about those incredible bodies. That's not what turns you on. Earning potential and family history. That's what you're interested in. Of course, that makes perfect sense."

Arnie didn't reply, for his attention had shifted to center stage where a headliner was beginning her act. The driving hard rock beat transformed to the courteous, delicate sounds of the Orient. House lights dimmed, and in the purple shadows, stood a beautiful sloe–eyed girl clad in a gold lame robe. Smiling and serene, her beautiful porcelain face was partially obscured by two large, flower–embroidered fans.

Through the smoky din, a voice blared:

Direct from Hong Kong, featured in Penthouse, our China Doll, Kim Lu. Take your hands out of your pants, boys, and let Kim know she's stateside and welcome!

Arnie turned his chair, and joined in the applause. Staring at Kim Lu, he hadn't noticed that Jim had left his seat and disappeared into the crowd. Arnie, mesmerized by the sight on center–stage, watched as Kim lowered the two fans and slowly parted the folds of gold fabric that draped across her exquisite body.

"Excuse me, Arnie."

Startled by a low throaty whisper, and warm moist lips against his left ear, Arnie leaped from his chair. Backing away, he looked into the face of the flame–haired woman he had just watched perform at the next table. Arnie didn't speak.

She slid his hand into hers and whispered, "I'm Wendy. You have a very generous friend. Come with me."

Arnie offered no resistance and held her hand tightly as he followed the beautiful woman through the crowd. She led the way until they reached the double oak doors marked VIP Lounge.

The redhead placed her hand on the door handle, paused, kissed Arnie on the cheek, and asked, "Are you ready?"

"Ready for what? Where are we going?"

"Relax honey. You'll love it."

Arnie followed her through the doors into the dimly lit VIP Lounge where mauve velvet sofas, set ten feet apart around the room's perimeter, rested on plush burgundy carpet. Behind each couch was a horizontally mounted brass pole. A handful of men and their ladies sat at the bar in the far corner of the room.

Arnie looked around the room and saw a bevy of delectable goddesses—one to a customer—contort their long–limbed bodies. Breathtakingly close, but never quite touching the men who lay sprawled on the couches below, arms above their heads, clasped around the brass poles.

"Would you like a drink before we find a spot?"

Arnie looked at Wendy and felt himself shaking. She was magnificent. He wanted to devour, explore every inch of her body. He wanted to kiss her full mouth and hold her. He wanted to make passionate love to her, spend hours talking with her, and then make love again. He wanted to consume her in a way that he knew was impossible. Agitated by desire, illusion, conflict. Wanting to leave, wanting to stay, Arnie left his self behind.

"Let's just find a couch," he said as he took her hand.

"Arnie." Wendy turned to face Arnie and stroked his chin with her long fingernails. "You're a sweet man. I want you to relax and enjoy yourself. You deserve it."

As Wendy directed Arnie to a vacant couch, he realized that his mouth was dry, his arms and legs tingled, his neck was fire hot. Suddenly, it occurred to him: What if Michelle knew what he was doing? She'd be so hurt, so disappointed. For a moment, Arnie felt heartsick. The kind of pain he experienced when one of his children was hurt. When Lisa fell down the stairs, when Ryan was rejected by a girl.

No way out, Wendy gently nudged Arnie onto the velvet sofa.

"Release that tension, love." Wendy reached behind her, unsnapped her bra, kneeled on one knee and placed her hands on Arnie's knees. She spread his legs and lowered her head. Pressing forward, Wendy rotated her head, her rose–scented hair sprayed

Arnie's thighs and torso. She looked up at Arnie, snapped her
head back, leaned forward and cupped her breasts with her hands.

"Do you like these, Arnie?" Wendy's knees bridged Arnie's legs
as she pushed her breasts inches from his face.

"Very nice. You have a beautiful body."

Wendy smiled as if genuinely flattered and picked up the pace.

Arnie studied Wendy's body carefully. He glanced around, at
the other beautiful women and their audiences of one, yet
attempted to remain dissociated from the sexual energy that
pulsed throughout the room. Legs, breasts, asses, all perfect, all
the same. Arnie knew how these sights could make a man wild,
and as he watched the same scene played out all around him, he
wanted to believe that it was pathetic. Sex without love.
Animalistic passion. That something very real, very human was
missing.

Wendy grabbed Arnie's head and thrust her lower body toward
it. She reached down and slid one red-nailed finger up the center
of her panties and moaned. Arnie stared hard at her white satin
covered mound, inched his head forward until the tip of his nose
practically retraced the path that her finger had just taken. He
shifted on the sofa to alleviate the overcrowded conditions in his
Dockers. Then, he looked up at Wendy's face. She was lost in her
act. In her own world. He glanced at his watch. Eight-thirty-five.
Way past the dinner hour.

Arnie was hungry.

CHAPTER 19

"A deal's a deal," argued Arnie.

"You could have at least given me time to get in a couch dance," countered Jim. "I set you up for the time of your life and suddenly it's time to eat. Well, at least give me some of the details. How was she?"

The oak, leather lined, circular bar at Rizzo's was placed like an island in the center portion of the large Italian eatery. At least 50 tables, with red and white checkered tablecloths—most of them occupied by golf foursomes—filled the low–lit, festively Mediterranean restaurant. Waiters in white shirt and black bow ties, cocktail waitresses with white satin blouses, lacy black dresses, and black fishnet stockings, scurried about to satisfy the loud, laughing, gluttonous patrons.

The bartender placed napkins in front of the men and requested drink orders.

"Absolut martini, very dry, straight up with an olive," requested Arnie. "Do you have large olives?"

The bartender nodded.

"And what can I get for you, sir?"

"Corona with lime," answered Jim.

"I wonder if we can get appetizers served at the bar," said Arnie. "I'm starved. How long did the hostess say we'd have to wait? Forty–five minutes?"

Reaching across the bar, Jim grabbed a bowl of pretzels and dropped them in front of Arnie. "There. That should help you survive for the next twenty minutes. Now will you tell me. What was the couch dance like?"

Arnie grabbed a handful of pretzels, ready to talk.

"It was pretty amazing, Jimbo. Very different than the main room. Private. Classy. And the women there catered to their man and their man only."

The bartender set the drinks on the bar.

"What did she do? Did she take off *all* her clothes? Did she touch you? Did you touch her?"

Arnie smiled and took a sip of his martini, winced, and pulled the toothpick from the glass. He slid the first of two olives into his mouth, placed the other back in the glass.

"Ummm. Love those big olives."

Jim drummed his fingers on the bar and stared. "Arnie. The couch dance?"

"What can I tell you, Jim. It's the kind of experience that can't be described. You have to be there."

"Bullshit. A man with your gift for gab can certainly come up with the words to describe what the experience was like. Come on, just give me a few details. Did you touch her tits? Did she take your dick out? Just tell me what the fuck happened!"

Finishing off the last pretzel in the bowl, Arnie laughed. "Take it easy, Jim. You didn't miss anything that spectacular. It was just more of the same old stuff. A little quieter and a bit more personal, but basically the same old shit."

"Then what's the twenty bucks for? Could you have gotten more if you asked? Maybe you just weren't assertive enough."

"I don't think so, Jim. It's a respectable establishment. I don't think they're looking to lose their license."

"What a tease that is. A woman all to yourself and you can't even touch her."

"What do you expect? You must admit, the women *are* beautiful. And for some men, myself included, that's enough."

"I guess so. But after awhile a man needs to get his rocks off. Women like that can be damn frustrating."

"That's why we get married, my friend."

"I'm not so sure about that. Most of the guys I know who are married don't even get it very often."

"Well," replied Arnie, taking time to spill the last drop of his martini into his throat, "You might want to take a closer look at the guys you know. Maybe they're the ones doing something wrong."

"Holy shit! I can't believe it." Jim's eye were startled open, his jaw dropped, he was a statue, attention fixed on something on the other side of the bar.

"What is it?" asked Arnie.

"Look. With the green and black blouse. It's Tina. What the hell's she doing here? Doesn't she realize she's getting married tomorrow?"

"Where?" Arnie squinted and scanned the darkened bar area.

"Over there. She just sat down. One…two…the third seat from that lady with the red scarf." Jim pointed.

Arnie found the blond. "That's not Tina. Are you crazy?"

"Sure it is. I'd recognize that hair anywhere."

Looking again, Arnie shook his head and smiled. "Good old Dr. Freud would have a field day with you, my friend. That is *definitely* not Tina."

"I think you're wrong." Jim slid off the barstool. "I'm going to get a closer look."

Pushing, excusing himself through the bar's crowded perimeter, by the time he was half the way toward his target, Jim realized that Arnie was right. He paused, the abrupt halt of an adrenaline rush gripped his chest tightly. What to do now.

He had wanted it to be Tina. He already begun to converse with her in his mind. Figured that maybe she and John had feuded, that maybe the wedding plans had been called off. That maybe *he* had a chance. A hard, dry swallow, Jim shrugged off disappointment and walked over toward where the young blond woman was sitting and merged with the crowd behind her. Reaching between her and the woman on her right, Jim motioned to the bartender. He glanced to his left and looked at her profile. God, she did look like Tina. Just as beautiful. Soft, blond curls, a full mouth. He watched as she sipped her scotch.

"Excuse me," Jim got the bartender's attention just as he turned and met the young woman's gaze. She smiled at him. "Could I have a Corona over here, please? With lime." Jim smiled back.

Adept at barroom opportunism, he spoke quickly. "Hi. Pretty crowded tonight. How long have you been waiting?"

"Oh, I'm not eating dinner. I'm just here for a drink or two." The young woman lifted from her seat, gripped the sides of her stool and slid it to her left. "I'm sorry I can't offer you a seat. Here, why don't you squeeze in against the bar. That is, unless you're with someone."

Jim temporarily froze, his mouth open, no words. He couldn't believe what he was hearing. It's *never* that easy.

"I'm not with anyone," he finally muttered. "Well, not with a date. Just a golfing buddy. Hi, my name's Jim." He extended his hand.

"Hi, Jim." She reached out her hand, held Jim's firmly, then gently, then firmly again, and stared directly into his eyes. Beautiful, large, Caribbean Ocean blue–green eyes. "I'm C.C."

"C.C. Does that stand for something?" Jim's voice was shaky. He knew the handshake, his entire body *felt* that handshake.

"My actual name is Carol Catherine. My friends call me C.C."

"I like it," replied Jim, wiping the sweat from his hand against his leg. "It's different."

"Thanks. So what are you doing in golf heaven? As if I need to ask."

"It's a vacation. But I wouldn't call it heaven. I'm getting a little sick of golf."

"Sounds like someone had a tough day out there." C.C displayed the pout of a spoiled little girl. Knowingly cute, sure to get whatever she wanted.

"Actually, not. I played well the last two days. I just get a little bored with golf after awhile. How much can you play?"

The bartender delivered the beer. Jim reached for his Corona, took a sip too quickly, the foam shot up the bottle and fell down the sides, onto his hand.

C.C. passed Jim a napkin without speaking. Her eyes remained fixed on his.

Jim wiped his hand and the bottom of the bottle before placing it back on the cocktail napkin on the bar. "Let me get you another drink," he asked her. "What are you drinking?"

"Thank you. Scotch, rocks. Dewar's."

"Yeah, I got it C.C.," said the bartender who intercepted the request.

"You must be a regular here," noted Jim.

"My old boyfriend was friendly with the owner. I still come around occasionally. It's a nice place. Lots of good people."

"Do you have a new boyfriend?"

"No, I'm free as a bird."

As the bartender placed C.C.'s drink on the bar and borrowed her attention for the moment, Jim checked her out more carefully.

The teal and black paisley silk shirt and sleek black skirt she wore emphasized a perfect bronze tan. As C.C. crossed her black stockinged legs, the slit of her skirt opened to her thigh. Two gold bracelets and a single gold neck chain gleamed against her golden skin. No dizzy glitz. Definitely a class act.

As she turned back to face Jim, he asked, "What are your plans for tonight?"

C.C. sipped her drink, leaving a trace of lipstick on the glass. She rattled the ice, and again looked right at Jim. "That depends."

Jim felt a tingling in his arms and legs. Lightheaded, throat dry, he reached for his beer and took several short and quick sips. "Depends on what?"

Eye contact locked in, C.C. replied, "I'm working tonight. But I can spend some time with you if you're interested."

"That would be great. When are you free?"

"I'm a professional escort, Jim. I can be free anytime you want me to be."

Jim's jaw dropped. He stared blankly and said nothing.

"Come on, Jim. I think you're really cute. I'd like to spend some time with you."

"But only if I pay. Right?"

C.C. finished her scotch. "That's right, Jim. I'm a working girl, got to make a living. But I still think we could really have a good time together."

Jim again grabbed his beer and gulped down most of the remaining contents. He turned from C.C., faced the bar, and acted as if he was waiting for the bartender to take his request for another. He took a deep breath and thought about the hand he had been dealt and whether he should up the action or fold. This was C.C. at work. A real pro. Her smile, words, body language were perfect, and Jim had to admit that he wanted her, that she had gotten to him.

"I don't think so," Jim finally replied curtly. "I don't pay for it. I don't need to."

"I'm sure you don't. You're hot. There are a lot of women who would jump at the chance to go out with you. It's just that sometimes, men don't want all the bullshit that goes along with meeting a woman. They don't want the games. Sometimes, it's easier to just *be* with someone you're attracted to without all the strings attached."

Jim processed C.C.'s sales pitch as he started at his fresh beer. "Just how much would this arrangement cost?"

"One–fifty for an hour."

Jim finished his beer and the conversation.

"Nice to meet you C.C. I wish you lots of success with your wonderful career. Gotta go. I'm meeting a friend for dinner."

C.C.'s smile didn't waver. "Let me know if you change your mind, Jim."

The bar had grown more crowded. Jim pushed his way through, like swimming against a muddled tide, until he found his way, three deep, behind Arnie's stool.

"I still can't believe I hit that 3–wood onto the green from 210 yards out."

Jim heard Arnie's voice before he pushed alongside him and cut in. "Don't believe this guy. It wasn't more than 190."

"Jimbo! I was just telling Ted and Frank about our adventure over at Wild Links. Hey boys, this is one of the fellows I was telling you about."

"Tell them about John," said Jim. "I'm not the one who parred the Savage."

Excusing himself from the others, Arnie turned to face Jim. "Looked like you were doing pretty well for yourself there. I didn't think I'd be seeing you again tonight. What happened? The big push fall through?"

"Actually not. She's interested. And real nice. I just don't know if I feel like going through all the motions. I'm pretty tired. And I hate to admit it, but pretty hungry."

Arnie turned his head off to the side and glared suspiciously at Jim. "Come on, now. Cut the shit. Is she married? A dyke? I know you better than that, Jim. Admit it. She wasn't interested, was she."

Jim caught the bartender's attention. "Dewar's on the rocks." He turned back to face Arnie. "I could have her if I wanted to. Believe me, she was interested. Very interested. I just backed off. I wanted to come over here and think about it. She's not going anywhere. I'm telling you, she's mine if I want her."

"And you don't know if you're interested. Right?"

"I didn't say that. I just don't know if it's worth the hassle."

"So, what are you going to do?"

"Partly, it depends on you."

"On me? This I've got to hear. How so?"

"Thank you." Jim spoke to the bartender and handed him a ten. "I also owe you for a Corona. Keep the change."

Jim lifted his glass and swallowed all the scotch in two gulps. He cast a couple of ice cubes into his mouth, and wiped his chin with the back of his hand.

"So, what do *I* have to do with your little conquest?" Arnie asked.

"Three things. First, I'll have to take off and leave you on your own."

"Yeah, I'm a big boy. I could handle that. What else?"

"You have to keep away from the hotel room until you get the clearance from me."

"Now, wait a minute. I've got to get some sleep tonight. Is she going to spend the night?"

"No, she definitely won't spend the night. How about this? If you don't hear from me by midnight, just go to the room. I'll make sure it's cleared out by then."

Arnie glanced at his watch. 9:55. "Okay, that's reasonable. I'm going to eat dinner anyway. And if the room is clear before that, can you call me here?"

"Yes. Definitely."

Arnie brought his hand up to his mouth, his index finger brushed the area above his lip—an old habit ingrained during the six years after college. His mustache days. "And what's the third favor you need from me?"

"A little cash."

"How much?"

"A hundred."

"A hundred! What are you goin' to do, help her out with her Christmas shopping? Why would you possibly need a hundred bucks?"

"Look, if you don't have the money, forget it. I just wouldn't feel comfortable going out with her without a few bucks in my pocket. She's a class act. I don't know what we'll do if we leave this place. I'll definitely need cab fare, and she might want to eat. I'm a little short on cash, anyhow. Don't forget the money I dished out for your couch dance."

"How could I ever forget my couch dance." Arnie reached into his back pocket, removed his wallet and counted the cash. "I guess I can spare some cash if you really need it."

"Then hand it over." Jim reached for the money while glancing across the bar. "You've got to admit, she is hot."

Arnie took another look. "Tell you the truth, Jim. I think she's as beautiful as Tina. Which reminds me. *Before* I give you the money. What about the wedding tomorrow? You going with me?"

"I can't believe you're going to blackmail me. Arnie, if you don't want to give me the money..."

"Hold on, Jim. You can have the money either way. But, I really would like to go to the wedding and I don't want to go alone. One hand washes the other. Right?"

"Maybe so. But, I really don't need to see John and Tina get married. I've had enough of John, Tina, the old man, the golf course, that whole fucking island for one vacation. For one lifetime."

"Think of it this way, Jim. A beautiful day, a free meal, a chance to check out Tina's friends. And don't forget your hot date tonight. You'll be feeling soooo gooood."

Arnie gestured with his chin in the direction of C.C.

Jim looked long and hard at the blond across the bar. She threw her head back in laughter. Tossed a handful of curls away from her face.

As beautiful as Tina.

"Give me the hundred bucks. I'll go to the fucking wedding."

CHAPTER 20

Before they left Rizzo's, C.C. asked to see Jim's driver's license, asked him who the governor of New York State was, and for payment in advance. She agreed to go to Jim and Arnie's hotel room, and the hour didn't officially begin until they arrived there.

"Place is a mess," said Jim as they entered the room. "We just checked in today and didn't have a chance to get settled in."

"Don't worry about a thing. It's just fine. Which bed is yours?"

"Take your choice."

C.C. pulled down the spread on the bed furthest from the terrace. Taking two of the pillows out from under the blanket, she propped them against the headboard.

She turned to Jim, hand on hip, and smiled. "Why don't you put some music on. The TV should have a radio. I'm going to freshen up. Be right back."

Jim watched C.C. walk toward the bathroom. The tight skirt accentuated her great ass. She walked with a calm confidence—in no hurry, but with a clearly determined purpose. Her hips swaggered in a slow, quiet rhythm, until she reached the bathroom door, turned briefly, without smiling, and closed the door.

Jim pulled the curtains together, turned up the air conditioner, and switched the radio dial to some light rock. He thought about taking off his clothes but decided to see what C.C. had planned.

For a hundred and fifty bucks, he was going to get his money's worth. Let her run the show.

The bathroom door opened. C.C. stepped out in hip–cut, black lace panties and a matching bra that barely contained her full, rounded breasts.

She smiled, said nothing, and walked over to Jim.

"I'm glad you decided to be with me."

C.C. pulled Jim's shirt out of his pants and unbuttoned his shirt. Gently, she glided her fingernails up and down his chest.

"Ooh, that's nice. I like men with just enough hair. Not too much, not too little."

Jim reached out and touched C.C.'s breasts. He fiddled unsuccessfully with the front clasp of her bra.

"Let me help," she said, as she slid the black lace cups toward her waist.

In the shadows, the tips of C.C.'s firm, supple breasts gleamed white against her tan line. Small, hard nipples begged for attention. And Jim was ready. He had seen bigger breasts, but none more perfect. None that excited him more as he tongued their soft, musk–scented contours.

C.C. reached forward and slid her right hand against Jim's crotch.

"Umm, that's quite a handful."

Jim took C.C.'s face in his hands and parted the mass of blonde curls with his fingers. He leaned forward to kiss her.

"Stop." C.C. put her hand over Jim's mouth.

"What's the matter?"

"I can't kiss you."

"You can't get AIDS from kissing, can you?"

"I'm sorry, Jim. No kissing. House rules. Come on, let's check out the bed. How about a massage? I give a great massage."

Before Jim could answer, C.C. had pulled a yellow plastic bottle from her black tote. She squeezed some lotion into her left palm and rubbed her hands together."

"Okay, Jim. Take off your shirt and pants and lay on the bed. Face down. I'm gong to help you relax."

Jim did as he was told. As he rested his head on his folded arms on top of the pillow, he noticed the light blue package of Trojan–enz on the corner of the nightstand. Jim felt C.C.'s body heat against his lower back as she mounted him. She began kneading his shoulders.

"You're tight as a drum. Let me loosen some of those knots."

C.C's touch was very firm. Rhythmic, as she rotated her thumbs against Jim's upper back. She applied more lotion and worked her way down his sides, to his lower back.

"All those golf swings. Those muscles need to relax. Hmm, you've got a great body. Really firm. I'll bet you're a good golfer."

Jim's eyes closed as the tension eased. He felt calmer now and realized just how much he had bottled up during the last two days. A frustrating two days. Arnie and his new found buddies. Arnie could be such a pain in the ass. And John. Jim had his faults and was as selfish as the next guy, but at least he admitted it. John played the part of Mr. Perfect. And people bought it. Even Tina bought it.

"Come on, now. Relax, you're starting to tense up again."

C.C.'s penetrating massage became gentler. Soft, undulating strokes now. The heat from between her legs radiated into the small of his back. She lifted herself gently.

"Time to turn over," she whispered.

Jim turned on his back and saw the blue Trojan–enz package between C.C.'s teeth. She slid his jockeys down his legs, off his feet. After tearing open the package, C.C. slipped her head below Jim's waist. The mane of blonde curls sprayed across his belly as her lips closed around him. A sheathed, cool, dry sensation that was arousing but distant.

C.C. looked up and smiled. "You're so big, Jim. You're really turning me on. I want to feel you inside of me."

Jim groaned softly as C.C. moved upward, straddled his hips, and lowered herself onto him.

Throwing her head back, she closed her eyes and said, "Fuck me, Jimmy. Fuck me."

Jim reached for C.C.'s breasts, put his arms around her waist and pulled her forward. He grabbed her face and forced his mouth on hers.

C.C. pulled back, placed her hands on Jim's chest and gyrated her hips, tightening her muscles, her grip on him.

"I'm sorry Jim," she whispered. "I can't."

Suddenly, C.C. straightened her back and pumped her hips rapidly.

Jim let out a scream of surrender.

From the opening between the drawn drapes, a thin ribbon of moonlight striped the moist bodies.

"That was nice," purred C.C.

"I think I needed that," Jim replied.

"We all do."

C.C. lifted herself off Jim and headed toward the bathroom.

Within seconds, wearing her panties again, C.C. returned with a warm, moist washcloth. Sitting on the edge of the bed, she removed the condom and wiped Jim off.

Jim looked at the beautiful woman who was washing him gently. "No kisses. But I'll fuck." All in a day's work—lover, mother, whore. She could be one or all of these, thought Jim.

C.C. dressed quickly. Jim put on his underwear and pulled the blanket up to his neck.

"That was really fun," said C.C. "You mind if I use your phone?"

"Be my guest."

C.C. informed the person on the other end that everything had gone well, and that she was about to leave. While she talked, she smiled and winked at Jim.

Shoving her pantyhose into the black tote, C.C. slung it over her shoulder and walked to the edge of the bed.

"If you're ever in town again, look me up. We're in the Yellow Pages under Executive Escorts. Just call and ask for C.C. I'd love to see you again."

Jim said goodbye as C.C. gently kissed him on the cheek.

CHAPTER 21

He found the number to Rizzo's, waited for a couple minutes on hold, until he finally heard Arnie's voice.

"Hey, Jimbo. How's it going with Miss America?"

"Great. She just left. You can come to the room anytime you want."

"Hold on. Aren't you going to tell me? How was it? Did you have fun? Did you guys eat? If you didn't and you're hungry, you should come here. The foods terrific."

"No, that's okay. We've got a 7:40 tee–time tomorrow, and I'm beat."

"Everything okay? You sound funny. Kinda down."

"No, everything's fine. I'm just really tired, that's all. I'll tell you about it tomorrow. How'd you do tonight? Get a belly full of good food?"

"An Italian extravaganza, Jim. We wound up getting served at the bar—stuffed shells with tennis ball–sized meatballs. The best I've had in a long time. And we watched the Braves–Dodger's game. I had a blast. And Jesus, guess who we met here? You'll never believe this, Jimbo. Tom Weiskopf. No shit, you know, the pro golfer. Senior Tour. He does a lot of television work now. I got his autograph right here on a cocktail napkin. Isn't that great?"

"Sounds like you had a ball there, Arnie. I'm glad. I don't feel as bad about hanging you up. That's just great, Arnie."

"Well, I'm awfully anxious to hear about your amore adventures with that gorgeous young woman. What was her name?"

"C.C."

"Weird name. What kind of a name is C.C?"

"Look Arnie, I've gotta get to sleep. I'll talk to you tomorrow. You got your key to the room?"

"Let me check. Yeah, here it is."

"Well, keep it down when you get in. I want to get a good night's sleep. I'll see you in the morning."

"Okay, Jimbo. Pleasant dreams. I'll wake you at about a quarter–of–six for breakfast. And don't forget about the wedding tomorrow afternoon."

"No, I haven't forgotten."

"Okay, goodnight."

"Goodnight."

Jim leaned over and shut off the light on the nightstand. He pulled the blanket and sheet up to his neck, kicked out a section of the sheet that remained tucked. C.C.'s scent wafted through the dark stillness, underscoring her absence. Jim stared straight ahead where a beautiful face appeared. A face with blue eyes, framed with golden curls. A face that edged closer and closer. A face whose lips smiled, opened, and kissed him fully on the mouth as he drifted into a deep sleep.

Chapter 22

The restaurant at the hotel began serving full breakfasts at 7:00 A.M., but offered a limited menu at 6:00 for golfers with early tee times.

"So, there's no way I can get sausage with my eggs?" Arnie asked the sleepy–eyed waitress.

"Only bacon sir."

"Okay. Then give me bacon with eggs, easy–over, hash browns and rye toast. I'd like the bacon well–done, please."

"I'm sorry, sir. We only have scrambled eggs. Just what you see on the golfer's breakfast menu."

"That's fine," cut in Jim. "He'll have the scrambled eggs. I'll have the same without the potatoes or bacon, and with whole wheat toast."

The waitress yawned as she reached for their menus. "Two coffees?"

"Yes," answered Jim.

"And a glass of ice water, if you don't mind, please," added Arnie.

Arnie unfolded his napkin, laid it across his lap, sat up straight and leaned toward Jim. "You were snoring good and loud when I got in last night. Looks like that beauty gave you a real workout."

"Not really. I was exhausted, that's all. It was a long day and I needed some sleep. I'm surprised you held together so well. You sounded really up on the phone last night."

"Got my second wind. I met some really nice guys at Rizzo's and had a great meal. And hey, I'm on vacation. No time to get tired. But forget about me. I want to hear about…what's her name again?"

"C.C."

"That's right. C.C. What kind of a name is that? Sounds like a dog or cat. Is she foreign?"

"No, she's not foreign. The initials stand for something. I don't remember what."

"I know. Carol Channing. That must be it. You sure she wasn't Carol Channing? Now that I think of it…the blonde hair and all."

Jim shook his head and smiled. "You never stop, do you? It's six–o–clock in the freakin' morning and already you're wired."

"Life's too short, Jimbo. Got to cram it in while I can. Now, will you stop changing the subject. What happened with Carol Channing?"

"We had sex, that's all."

"You had sex, that's all? That's all?! Jim, you're talking to a man who married the second girl he ever had sex with. And the first one didn't count because it only happened once and I was drunk and had an anxiety attack in the middle of it. Come on, Jim. This dirty old man needs details."

"There's nothing much to say. We really hit it off. There was a strong chemistry between us and we went with it."

The waitress placed the orders on the table and filled the coffee cups.

Arnie paused until she was out of earshot before continuing. "Well, how did she rate? Was she good?"

"Yeah, she was good. She's a beautiful woman and she was horny as hell. What could be bad?"

Arnie placed down his fork and leaned forward. "Did you use a rubber? You know this is exactly how people get themselves in trouble."

"Relax, Arnie. I'm not stupid. Of course I used a rubber."

"Well, good for you." Arnie spread strawberry preserves on a piece of rye toast, covered it with scrambled eggs, folded the bread before putting it in his mouth.

"Did you really meet Tom Weiskopf last night?"

Arnie put his hand up, chewed quickly, and wiped his mouth with his napkin. "It was great, Jim. What a guy. Frankie—he's one of the guys I hooked up with—thought it was Weiskopf, so I finally went over and asked him. He was real friendly. Gave us his autograph. I'll show it to you later. He was with a real attractive young lady himself. Which reminds me. You changed the subject on me again. I want to get back to your lady. Did she sing Hello Dolly for you?"

Jim laughed and then began to cough. He took a sip of Arnie's ice water before responding. "No, she didn't. A little screaming maybe, but no singing."

"Now we're getting down to it," answered Arnie as he balanced the last of his home fries on his fork and finished off his breakfast. "Did you two tear each other's clothes off and get crazy with wild, uncontrollable passion?"

"Something like that. What more can I tell you, Arn? It was good sex."

Arnie pushed his plate away and sipped his coffee. "I don't know, Jim. When you're married as long as I've been, sex is like an old pair of Levis—nice and comfortable. Feels real good, but it's not that crazy rip your clothes off kind of thing."

"I'll bet you wouldn't mind a little crazy, rip your clothes off sex with that redhead from *Wild Horses*. Speaking of details, you never gave me the complete rundown on *that* little encounter."

"Come on, Jim. That wasn't sex. It was a performance. She put on her act, and I was her audience."

"Yeah, Arnie. But suppose she dropped the act. Suppose you *could* be with her. For a night, for a weekend. And you could do anything you want with her. How would you feel about that?"

Arnie got the waitress' attention and pointed at his empty cup. She came right over with refills.

"Could I get you boys anything else?"

"Just the check," said Arnie before turning back at his young partner. "Tell you the truth, Jim, I don't think it could work. Don't think it's possible. Not that I don't think about it. I love a beautiful woman as much as the next guy. But to actually act on a fantasy? I don't think so."

"I'm not asking you if you would actually go through with it. I know you better than that. And I respect you for being faithful to Michelle. But wouldn't you love to be able to make love to a beautiful woman? A strange and different woman. No history, no bullshit, just straight–ahead, unadulterated passion."

"It sounds awfully good, but I think in the end, I'd be disappointed."

"How do you know? You say you desire beautiful women. Why wouldn't it feel great to experience them? Maybe you're just afraid that it might feel *too* good."

"You might be right about that. If it was really great...then what? I'd either spend my days and nights longing for more of the same, or I'd keep going back for more and really screw up my life. I tell 'ya, I couldn't win. If I love it, I'm fucked. And if it's not all that great...it wasn't worth doing in the first place."

"But the experience, Arnie. What about the experience. Do you really want to end up in a nursing home—an old man in a diaper, with drool hanging from your lip—watching pretty, tight–assed nurses and wondering what could have been?"

Arnie shook his head and smiled. "So, you've already got me shitting my drawers at the old age home. Come on, Jim...there's more to life than sex. Surely, even a studmuffin like you can see that. And everyone's life is going to have its share of regrets. Hey, I'll probably never skydive, or visit India, or for that matter, make a hole–in–one. This is life, Jimbo."

"I can live without a trip to India or without jumping out of a plane. But babes, Arnie. Beautiful, soft, luscious, and moist babes. Nothing—and I mean nothing—falls into that category."

"I know what you mean, Jim. I'll be honest with you. When that redhead, Wendy, put her privates in my face, I felt a stirring in my loins, a rush of desire that was as strong as any I've felt in years."

"All right," said Jim, his face lighting up, rubbing his palms together. "I knew she had your number."

"But Jim. Something was missing. It just wouldn't, couldn't work. It's like when I first see any great looking woman. My first reaction is that I want to screw her. Then, when I think it through, I realize I want more. I want to talk to her, get to know her, have her adore me. Shit, when I met Michelle in college, we used to sit up all night and talk about music and politics. Sure, the sex was great, but it was more than that. She laughed at my stupid jokes. Hell, she loved me. Not because she was paid to, but because she thought I was wonderful. I guess I have a big ego, Jim. I need a woman to think I'm something special."

"I understand where you're coming from. I just can't imagine a life with just comfortable sex."

"You're young, Jim. Give it time. Wait till the testosterone begins to plummet. You'll be ready someday."

"Maybe. But right now I want to get ready for some golf. It's a new day, and I want to put Wild Links behind me. Do you have that scorecard to Sea Trail with you? I want to check it out."

Arnie reached into the inside pocket of his jacket and pulled out a folded scorecard. "You can put playing golf at Wild Links behind you, but don't forget about the wedding at 3:00."

Jim grimaced, rubbed the side of his face. "Arnie, why do you have to insist on going to this wedding? We don't know anyone there except John, his old man, and Tina. We don't even have decent clothes to wear."

"Tina said that it was informal, and that a golf shirt and slacks would be fine. And who cares if we don't know anyone. There'll be music and good food. I love weddings. I think this adds a really nice twist to our vacation."

"I guess I can't talk you out of it."

"Right."

"You know I'm a man of my word. But listen, we don't have to be the last to leave. I can see you bullshitting into the wee hours."

"Don't worry, Jim. I just want to check it out. And it's supposed to be over at 6:00 anyhow. Now let's check out this course we're playing today."

Glancing over at the scorecard Arnie was holding, Jim asked, "How many total yards from the white tees?"

"Let's see. 6,332. 3,210 on the front, and 3122 on the backside. This'll be like a walk in the park after Wild Links and the Savage."

"What's the first hole like?"

"Par 4, 295 yards, dogleg right. With water running down the left side of the fairway. Now that I look this over, there's a lot of water on this freakin' course. It comes into play on one, two three...on eight or nine holes. I'd better buy some extra balls.

Show me a water hazard, and I'm in it. Well, I'm glad the course isn't too long. Gives me a fighting chance."

Jim took the scorecard from Arnie's hands. "This course looks pretty nice. Of course, you can't tell from these diagrams, but there are a lot of interesting holes. Looks tight with a lot of blind shots. Good. I'm up for something different. Look at the ninth. The first handicap hole; par 4, 445, severe dogleg left. And look at the fifteenth. The second most difficult hole. Par 5, 555 yards with a trap running down the entire left side. And look how the trap runs across the fairway in front of the green."

Arnie sat, chin in his palm, his face fatigued, as if he had already played the challenging course. "Why do I do this to myself? Play this game. What am I trying to prove? Here I am, ready to frustrate the living hell out of myself. And you know what's really sick? I'm looking forward to it. I must be crazy. Fucking crazy!"

Jim smiled. "No, Arnie...you're a golfer now. That's all. And from what I can see, you'll like this course. Mostly short and tight. With that 3–wood of yours on fire, and your solid short–game, this course was made for you. And look at the par 3s. 160, 170. Here's your hole, Arnie. The third. One–hundred, fifty yards, open and straight."

"Now you're talking. How long are the other fours?"

"The second is 335, the seventh is 375, but it's an island tee area. Not too bad. All very reachable in regulation."

"Sure, they're reachable for you. Probably with your pitching wedge. I'll be using my 5–wood on approach shots."

"Hey, what are you talking about? I heard you bragging about that 3–wood last night. How far did you say you can hit it? Two–ten, two–twenty? That's all you need."

"Shots like that happen about twice a year. I think I've already met my quota."

"Well, I'm up for some golf." Jim threw the scorecard onto the table and leaned forward, closer to Arnie. "C'mon, buddy. You're ready to bring your game to a new level. I can feel it. Think positively, will you? Now, let's get the hell out of here. There still might be time to hit balls and putt."

CHAPTER 23

Jim's round couldn't have gotten off to a worse start at the Maple's designed course at Sea Trail Plantation. After hitting his tee shot at the first hole out of bounds, he three–putted for a triple, and never got it going after that. Arnie managed to keep the ball in play, hit his medium and short iron approach shots well, and flirted with breaking 100 right up until the eighteenth hole.

The two men were paired with a couple of hackers. Narcotic's detectives from Hackensack who started hitting the beer at the third tee and didn't stop until they had torn up every fairway on the course. Ed was the bigger of the two; about six–three, three hundred pounds. His partner, Pinto, was average height with a small frame and beer belly that peeked out from beneath his shirt after he finished his swing. Pinto delivered a steady stream of jokes and vulgarities throughout the round while Ed, a man of few words, was a ready audience for his pal. Ed's booming, baritone laugh drew more than a few looks from other golfers. The men's slow play infuriated Jim, and Arnie was ticked off by the unre-placed divots. And while Jim found no redeeming qualities in the day's playing partners, Arnie enjoyed the cop's streetwise repartee and raw humor.

Along with the jokes, Arnie liked outplaying his competition. The Hackensack boys, who stopped keeping score on the backside, hit shots right, left, straight up, on occasion behind them. Arnie's scorecard showed a solid and legit 101. This tied his best score ever and even came close to matching Jim's 93 for the round. Arnie's shots for the most part were clean and straight. Even his misses were usually topped shots that were straight, with plenty of roll toward the target. Arnie felt like a damn good golfer on this mild, sunny Saturday. More committed to the game than at any other time in his short golf career.

For Jim, his low ninety's score was a disappointment. He hadn't been over 90 in two years, but blew off the round as "one of those days." He played well in spurts, but his pull–hook off the tee cost him a good ten strokes. Without some good recoveries and clutch putts, he would have been dangerously close to being outscored by Arnie. Realizing this, Jim assured his buddy that this would never happen. Eight strokes was as close as Arnie would ever get. At least in this lifetime.

Highlights from the day's round included Big Ed's tee shot on four. Smoked low and left, the ball hit the thick trunk of a maple, dead center, bounced straight back at the tee area, before it rolled to a stop under Jim and Arnie's cart. Ed and Pinto agreed on a drop somewhere between the tee markers; no penalty strokes because the ball was hit so solidly.

Arnie had his only par of the day on fifteen; the long par five with the trap that ran down the left side of the hole and then cut across the fairway in front of the green. Arnie's tee shot was solid but left, and found the sand. His second shot was a 3–wood that held its line and stayed in the lateral hazard, about 165 yards from the green. Next, Arnie found the heel of his 4–iron and only advanced the ball about 50 yards—still in the sand. On his fourth shot, Arnie took a little too much sand with his 8–iron and came up short. His ball settled in the bunker in front of the green. To make par, Arnie blasted out of the trap. The ball just cleared the bunker's front lip, released when it hit the fringe of the green, and rolled straight into the cup. Arnie's feat was rewarded with a hard slap on the back from Big Ed, and a scalp full of sand. Pinto thought Arnie's accomplishment was a hole–in–one of sorts, since the ball, for all intents and purposes, never touched any green from tee to cup.

After the foursome completed the five and a half hour round, Arnie and Jim went back to the hotel. They had a quick lunch, spent fifteen minutes in the hot tub, and swam a few lengths in the pool before taking showers and heading out to the Ayman Hydroshuttle and the wedding at the Wild Links.

CHAPTER 24

Wedding guests congregated on the lawn area by the flower garden, on the north side of the clubhouse. Most of the men wore pastel golf shirts and slacks with sports jackets. No ties. The women, unconstrained by any particular style, walked about in silk slacks, ruffled sun dresses, and figure–hugging jersey minis. Trellises adorned with ivory roses and peach silk ribbon outlined the perimeter of the sculpted grass courtyard. An acoustic guitarist, regal in white tuxedo, provided counterpoint for the guest's conversational chatter and the echoes of the surf breaking offshore.

"I feel like an idiot," said Jim, as he and Arnie hesitated at the base of the small hill that led to the garden. "We have no business being here."

"Calm down, Jim. Just stick with me and you'll be fine. These people are all here to have a good time. Half of 'em are probably drunk already. And don't forget about the ladies. You'll probably be off with one of Tina's bridesmaids before long. Just do me one favor please...don't take her back to the room tonight."

"Don't worry about that. I just want to get out of here and have some time to do *nothing,* to just relax. I'm beat."

"Wait a minute, Jim. Let's not forget that this is a vacation. And our last night at that. Lighten up and enjoy yourself."

Jim responded with a silent smirk and followed Arnie smack into the heart of the activity.

Arnie quickly grabbed two glasses of champagne from a waiter's tray, handed one to Jim, and headed to a table filled with fresh vegetables, cheese, and fruit. As he filled a small plate, Arnie scanned the crowd.

"A lot of seniors here. Looks like old money. I wonder if they're friends or family. What do you think?"

"How the hell would I know? One thing I can already see is that you were wrong about the babes. I don't see any under fifty."

Arnie wiped blue cheese from his chin and finished his champagne. "I don't see John or Tina or even Hans Keeler for that matter. Maybe the young ones are with the wedding party."

Arnie stopped a waitress serving potato puffs and small triangles of broccoli cheese quiche. Jim secured two more glasses of champagne.

"Want one?" asked Jim. "If not, I'll take both."

"Yeah, give me a glass." Arnie drank it down in one gulp. "Umm, I love champagne. And I love weddings. Come on Jim, admit it. Isn't this nice? The decorations, the music, the people, the sun, the blue sky, that ocean breeze."

"Sorry, Arnie. I just don't share your enthusiasm. I feel out of place here. And one bald, skinny guitarist is not my idea of music. What in hell is he playing anyway?"

"Malaguena. It's a classic. What would you suggest, heavy metal? Or some rap, maybe? Oh no, my man, this is class all the way."

"Class, shit. It's about as exciting as Bingo at my grandmother's church."

"Someday, Jim, you'll learn to appreciate the finer things in life."

"Like you, Arn? And your buddies, Ed and Pinto? Yeah. The Hackensack duo would really dig that guy with his guitar."

"Who knows, Jimbo. They might enjoy a touch of the good life. Adapting. That's what it's all about. Adapting to circumstances and getting along with all kinds of people. Cops and quitters, saints and sinners. How do you think I made it in business?"

"Well, I'll stay with Civil Service and the people I feel comfortable with. What can I tell you Arnie? I just can't toss the bullshit around the way you do."

Arnie nodded and refilled his plate. Jim found two more glasses of champagne. The music stopped, and the guests were requested to find seats. The ceremony was about to begin.

Folding chairs, ten rows of eight across, were set up in front of a white archway decorated with ivory and peach roses, laced with white baby's breath. The guests took a few minutes to get seated. Jim and Arnie sat on the right-hand side, in the next to last row.

"Looks like about seventy-five people," whispered Arnie, as he checked out the others in attendance.

"I hope this isn't a long, drawn out ceremony."

"I don't think it will be. I wonder where they'll be coming from. I don't see an aisle."

As the guitarist started playing, necks stretched right, and there was a chorus of "Shhhhs."

"It's starting," said Arnie. "Look, here they come."

The guitarist gently plucked Canon in D, and the guests grew silent. The judge, a middle-aged woman in a white robe, led the procession and took her place under the archway. She smiled broadly. Next, Tina's father walked in, accompanied by a tall, thin stunning young woman. They took their places on opposite sides of the archway, facing each other. Hans Keeler followed in his wheelchair, accompanied by an elderly woman dressed smartly in a white with navy trim dress.

The guests murmured, and the members of the wedding party looked left as Tina and John walked in together. John wore a gray double–breasted suit with a white, collarless shirt—no tie, top button fastened. Tina was breathtaking in a white organza tea length dress. Pink rosettes hemmed the bodice's off–shoulder ruffle and dotted the wide brim of her lace hat. The couple joined hands and faced the judge.

The judge whispered something to the bride and groom, they all shared a private laugh, and then she began to address the guests.

"Dear friends and family. We gather this afternoon to celebrate with Tina and John, their marriage commitment to one another and to witness the ceremony which symbolizes the intimate sharing of two separate lives. It is in this context that Tina and John give themselves in love, but do not give themselves away. Rather, they honor the individuality which brought them together initially and respect the strength of a union forged by love and regard for each other's unique qualities. Tina and John will now read to each other the words they have especially chosen for this day."

John stepped toward Tina, took both her hands, and faced her as he spoke.

> *"Forsaking all others, we are true to all. What we love here, we would not desecrate anywhere. Seed or song, work or sleep, no matter the need, what we let fall, we keep. The dance passes beyond us, our loves loving their loves, and returns, having passed through the breaths and sleeps of the world, the woven circuits of desire, which leaving here arrive here. Love moves in a bright sphere."*

Tina wiped her eyes with her hand, inched closer to John, stared up into his eyes, and began her portion.

"For years now we have loved, now well, now badly, now a love of honey and fire, now of bone and rust, now of pick handles entwined with red roses. Love is work. Love is pleasure. Love is studying. Love is holding and letting go without going away. Love is words mating like falcons a mile high, love is work growing strong and blossoming like an apple tree, love is two rivers that flow together, love is our minds stretching out webs of thought and wonder and argument slung across the flesh or the wires of distance. Love is the name I call you."

As Tina and John stepped apart. Arnie pulled a handkerchief from his pocket and wiped tears from his eyes. Love is work. Love is pleasure. He thought of Michelle, Ryan, and Lisa. Hearing these words, Arnie knew at this moment, that he had it all. All that could make a man happy in this life was his. And he had worked hard to get it and to keep it. No, he wasn't perfect, never would be. But he loved his family and did his best for them. Just as his father had done. Arnie thought for a moment that perhaps his own father also had a good life that he just never appreciated or understood. Arnie knew all too well how this could happen. How, if he himself didn't wake up and begin to *feel* moments—to rise beyond the boundaries of worry and regret—that he like his father, could drift through life without a clue of the joy and wonderment that surrounded him each day. To die without ever being born...the ultimate tragedy? For the moment, at least, Arnie knew that he didn't have to accomplish anything more in his life. That his life already had meaning and purpose.

"Will you, John, take this woman as your wife, to love, honor, and cherish her, keeping yourself only unto her for as long as you both shall live?"

"I will."

"And will you, Tina, take this man as your husband. To love, honor, and cherish him, keeping yourself only unto him for as long as you both shall live?"

"I will."

Tina's father handed the judge a ring.

"John place this ring on Tina's left hand and say after me: With this ring you are consecrated to me."

John echoed the judge's words.

"Tina, repeat after me. In accepting this ring, I pledge you all my love and devotion."

Tina repeated her vows and the young woman standing beside her handed the judge a ring.

"Tina, place this ring on John's left hand and say after me: With this ring you are consecrated to me."

As Tina slid the ring on his finger, John too, pledged his love to the beautiful young woman who would share his life.

"Tina and John have now solemnly declared to each other and to you assembled, their commitment to their marriage, and having done so, I do further declare that they are husband and wife. John, you may kiss the bride."

John grabbed Tina around the waist and kissed her long and hard, as the guests stood and applauded.

Arnie wiped tears from his eyes and turned to Jim. "That was beautiful."

"It was okay. But, I told you, Arn. Weddings don't do much for me."

"Your day will come, Jimbo. You just wait. Let's get some more champagne."

Arnie squeezed through the crowd that was pressing forward to congratulate the bride and groom and found a table with filled glasses of champagne. He picked up two and handed one to Jim.

"We should congratulate the bride and groom now, because it looks like the buffet's about to start. Look at all those chafing dishes. It's going to be a good one, and I'm starved."

"Okay. Let's get this over with."

Arnie and Jim took their places on the receiving line.

When their turn came, Arnie spoke first, to the young woman who served as Tina's maid of honor.

"Hi, my name's Arnie Weiss."

"Nice to meet you. I'm Debra. Tina's sister."

"Is that so?" Arnie turned to Jim, as he shook hands with the young woman.

Arnie spoke again. "We just met John and Tina a couple of days ago. We were with John when he parred the Savage, and they invited us to celebrate with them."

"Oh, the Savage. I'm afraid I know very little about golf, but everyone's been talking about John's triumph."

"You grew up in a golf family. How'd you manage to not get sucked into it?"

"It was dad's and Tina's great passion. I never had any interest."

Before Jim had a chance to speak, he had already studied and summed up his impressions of Debra. Attractive...but darker, taller, thinner, harder, colder than Tina. "Is Tina your older sister?"

"Yes. Fifteen months older." Debra locked her large, almond–shaped, dark brown eyes onto Jim. Her smile broadened to reveal flawless white teeth.

"I don't envy your father." Jim smiled back. "Two beautiful daughters. Must have been tough, with all the guys coming after you two."

Debra blushed and laughed.

"Nice meeting you," said Jim, poking Arnie in the ribs in an effort to move him along.

John and Tina were next. Engaged in conversation and laughter with an elderly couple, Jim and Arnie waited for them. Arnie whispered to Jim, "There's your chance, buddy. That Debra's a knockout. I think she might have a leg up on Tina."

"I don't think so. Not my type."

Before Arnie could protest, John noticed them.

"Arnie, Jim." I'm so glad you could make it." John vigorously pumped the hands of both men. "Tina. Look who's here."

Tina greeted the men. "It's so good to see you two again. We're really happy you made it."

"You look beautiful," said Arnie. "And the ceremony was wonderful. I loved the poems you read to one another. Where are you going on your honeymoon?"

"Bermuda," answered Tina. "We leave first thing tomorrow morning."

"Great place. Michelle and I went there for our fifteenth. Just don't ride those mopeds. I almost killed myself riding one of those."

"We'll be sure to be careful. Thanks again for coming."

"Congratulations, Tina," said Jim, as he moved to take her hand.

"Thanks, Jim."

"Did you guys get out and play this morning?" asked John. "Great day."

"Yes we did," answered Arnie. "At Sea Trail. Ever play there?"

"No, I haven't. But I heard that it's nice. How'd you do?"

"Great," replied Arnie. "You would have been proud of the way I hit my woods."

"Your game's coming along nicely. I'm not surprised." John paused and looked at Jim.

"I'm just trying to forget today's round," said Jim. "What about you? Still pumped about parring the Savage?"

"It's a funny thing. I've wanted to make that par for so long, and now that I have, it doesn't feel like I thought it would. I almost feel let down. Like I'm going to miss having the Savage as a goal."

"What do you expect?" said Arnie. "It happened just yesterday and you got married today. Give it time. You'll feel good about it."

"Maybe you're right. For now, I'm looking forward to a relaxing honeymoon."

"Are you going to play any golf in Bermuda?" Jim cut in.

John smiled. "Of course. The clubs are packed."

The men laughed, and John went to greet other guests. Arnie and Jim offered their congratulations to Mr. Keeler and the elderly woman, his sister, who accompanied him down the aisle. Jim slipped from his place on line, passing on the opportunity to congratulate Tina's father.

Jim and Arnie each took a plate and stood in line for the buffet. Featured was pasta with fresh basil pesto, artichoke hearts au gratin, chicken almond mousse, fruit crepes, three–cheese eggs, and an assortment of salads. The long, peach and ivory skirted buffet table was also garnished with assorted cheeses, fruits and breads.

"This is some spread," said Arnie, as he scooped a portion of eggs onto his plate.

"It looks good," replied Jim. "Just go easy on the three–cheese eggs. At your age, you don't need all that cholesterol."

"One cheese for each type of blood vessel—arteries, veins, and capillaries," laughed Arnie, squeezing pasta into an open corner of his heavily loaded plate. "Come on, let's find a table."

The chatter in the courtyard picked up as sunlight filtered through the tall trees on the western shore of Caramus. The guitarist switched to a more popular song selection and was mid–medley when Jim and Arnie took their seats.

"Embrace me, my sweet embraceable you," sang Arnie. "I love this song. You must know this one, Jim."

"Yeah, I've heard it."

"What's the matter, Jim? Still can't relax?"

Jim breathed deeply as he buttered a sesame roll. "I'm doing okay. It's not that bad, I guess."

"What's not to like? Umm. Did you try the chicken? All the food's great. And I think Tina's sister had a thing for you. Did you see her eyeing you? I thought her face was goin' to split open with that smile she threw your way."

"Not my type, Arn. Too hard–edged and pointy. Not feminine enough…" Jim's words were cut off by the sound of forks clanging glasses, by the sound of a man's voice.

"*Can I have your attention. Ladies and gentleman. I'd like to propose a toast.*"

The chatter fell off and soon, the courtyard was silent.

Hans Keeler held his glass high. "*To my only son, John, and his beautiful wife, Tina, whom I've loved like a daughter for many years now.*" Keeler turned his head and looked at the couple. "*You've made me vary happy. Have made all my dreams come true. May you have a long and healthy life together.*"

Glasses were hoisted as "here–here's" sounded everywhere.

"He's a good man," said Arnie.

"Yeah, I like Mr. Keeler," agreed Jim. "John's the one I have the problem with. Did you hear what he said about being let down after parring the Savage? Give me a break. I can't believe…"

Jim was cut off by the sound of silverware chiming once again.

"Now what," he said, turning to see a gray–haired man with glasses and a green sport jacket propose a second toast.

"I've known Hans and his boy since they've come to this country. I'm very pleased to share this wedding celebration with John and his lovely bride, but something else happened yesterday that deserves a toast, too. John became the first person to ever par the sixteenth hole at Wild Links..."

"You hear that, Jim?" asked Arnie.

Jim listened to the man toast John. The first person ever...the first person ever. Jim heard the words, tightened his grip on the arms of his chair, felt a hollowness in the pit of his stomach.

"To ever par the sixteenth hole." As Jim replayed the sound of those words, his chest tightened, he noticed a clammy breeze pass across his forehead.

"The first person to ever par the sixteenth hole at Wild Links." That voice. Who was this man? His face wasn't familiar. But the voice...He had heard that voice a thousand times before.

Jim sat straight up, leaned forward in his chair, and took a hard look at his father.

CHAPTER 25

Arnie chased Jim down the hill that lead to the front of the clubhouse.

"Jim, hold on," he shouted. "What's wrong? What happened? Wait!"

Arnie ran a few more feet and closed the distance. He grabbed Jim's elbow and finally succeeded in stopping him.

"What's the matter, Jim?" Arnie held Jim's shoulders with both hands, trying to establish eye contact, but Jim looked away.

"Try to calm down, Jimbo. I've never seen you like this. Not since you were a kid and you were scared of something or someone."

Arnie stopped talking and waited.

Jim took a deep breath, stepped back from Arnie and crossed his arms. "That guy who gave the toast. The guy with the green jacket."

"Yeah, what about him."

"That's my old man." Releasing the words seemed to help. Jim breathed deeply, and suddenly appeared calm. He slowly walked over to a bench by the practice putting green and sat down. Arnie followed.

"Are you sure, Jim? You haven't seen him since you were a kid. Are you sure you're not mistaken?"

"I'm sure. He doesn't look anything like I remember him. But the voice is the same. I can't be mistaken. That's definitely my dad."

"He said he knows John and Keeler for years. How can that be? Didn't your old man move to Florida?"

"Yeah. But it all makes sense. You know he always came to Wild Links when I was a kid. He talked about it all the time. That's what got me interested in the place."

"But a once–a–year trip wouldn't build a close relationship. Not one that would include an invitation to the wedding and a toast to the bride and groom."

"But he left in '81—the year Keeler came to the United States. He could have come back here several times a year once he moved to Florida. And they were both professionals. It all makes sense."

Jim closed his eyes, took a deep breath, and put his face into his hands.

"I can't believe it, Jim. It's a million–to–one shot. Think of the incredible coincidences. That *we* were there when the Savage was parred. Because of that, we were invited to the wedding. And you heard the voice because *he* made the toast."

"My dad always obsessed about parring that damn hole. Well, at least *he* didn't do it. For the first time, I'm glad that John parred the fucking hole. Anybody, but that bastard."

Arnie studied Jim's face carefully, not sure of what to say. Arnie remembered times when Jim was ten or eleven. When Jim's mother had asked Arnie to talk to him about some problem. When she thought that it would be better if he spoke to a man. Jim looked like that little boy now. Bent over, head in hands, too proud to sob. Arnie recalled how he handled the situation years before.

"This is a tough situation, Jim." Arnie reached over and put his arm around Jim's shoulder. "No easy answers. But we'll work it out."

"I don't know what to do, Arn."

"I know...I know, Jimbo. It's tough."

"I've got to get out of here. I can't run into him. What would I say? What the fuck would he say? Happy to run into you? Been a long time, son. I was planning on calling you next week. Shit, I never expected to see him again. Ever. This is so crazy."

"You're right, Jim. It is crazy. But maybe you *should* talk to him. Introduce yourself. *He's* the one who'll be uncomfortable. You didn't do anything wrong. You didn't leave. He did."

"I know that. But what the hell am I supposed to say? Missed you at my birthday parties, Christmas, and graduation. By the way, mom sends her bests. Gee dad, when did you get so fucking old?"

"This is one of those times where you can't predict what will happen. John didn't see his father for years and look at them now."

"Come on, Arnie. That's a totally different situation. Keeler wants John to be a part of his life."

"Well, you don't know what your father wants."

"The hell I don't! I know he doesn't want to run into me. Shit, if I had parred the Savage, he would have heard about it. I can just imagine the expression on his face when he heard that Jim Carlson parred the Savage. If only...God, I came so close."

"You still have a chance to surprise him. You're a great golfer, Jim. And you've got a college education and a damn good job. Don't you want him to see all that you've accomplished?"

"It wouldn't work, Arnie. You're a great father. You're talking from your point of view. My old man wouldn't see it that way."

"You'll never know if you let this opportunity pass. You'll always regret it if you don't take the risk. You'll always wonder what might have happened."

"I can't, Arnie. You might be right, but I can't face him. Please, let's just get back to the hotel. I've had enough."

Arnie waited before responding. Then he grabbed Jim by the shoulders and said, "Suppose I talk to him. Suppose I tell him that you're here and see what his reaction is. If he's really interested in seeing you, he'll come to you. If not, I'll come back alone, and we'll go to the hotel."

"I know you, Arnie. You'll talk him into it. You'll get him here, even if it's the last thing he wants to do."

"I won't, Jim. That wouldn't be fair to you. I'll know what he's thinking. If I'm not convinced that he really wants to see you, I won't push it. You've got my word."

Jim shuddered, stirred in his seat. "But, even if he wants to see me, I don't know if I want to see him. Why would I? I have nothing to say to him."

Arnie put his hands on Jim's knees and waited until he looked up. "You don't need a reason, Jim. Do it just to find out what happens. Do it to show, to *know* you have more courage than he has. Your father couldn't face his life. Show him *and* yourself that you're not too scared to face the truth."

Jim bit his lower lip, then looked down at his shoes. "Only if he wants to come. No pressure?"

"No pressure."

Jim lifted his head and looked into Arnie's eyes. "Okay. I'll wait here."

CHAPTER 26

Arnie searched the crowd for the man in the green jacket. No sign. The party had settled into a post–feast mood. Scattered conversations, jackets hung on chair backs, one table of four who sang along with the guitar player. Arnie spotted John and Tina talking with a man who appeared to be the caterer. They stood by a table that held a four–tiered wedding cake, presumably to prepare for the cake–cutting ritual. Arnie approached the three.

"Excuse me, John. Can I talk to you for a minute. I'm sorry to interrupt, Tina. It won't be long…promise."

"Sure, go ahead," Tina replied. "No rush."

"Thanks."

John followed Arnie to a private spot behind the buffet table.

"What's up?" asked John.

"Who was the man with the green jacket who gave the toast about you parring the Savage?"

"That's Bob. He's an old friend of my father. Why?"

"Bob Carlson? Is his name Bob Carlson?"

"Yes, it is. What's the matter, Arnie. Do you know him?"

"I don't. But Jim does. Bob Carlson is Jim's father."

John, wide–eyed, remained silent.

Arnie continued to explain. "Jim hasn't seen him since he was eight–years–old. Until moments ago. When he gave that toast."

"I can't believe it, Arnie. I knew Bob had a family up north, but I didn't know any of the details. Where is Jim now?"

"By the clubhouse. He's very upset."

"My God, who can blame him?"

"He's agreed to talk to his father, but I want to talk to Carlson first. Do you know where he is?"

John turned around and scanned the guests. "There he is." John pointed to a table that seated three couples. "With his wife, Gloria. Did Jim realize he was remarried?"

"I'm afraid not," Arnie replied, still unable to spot Jim's father. "Oh, I see him. I'm going to talk to him. Thanks, John."

John grabbed Arnie by the arm. "Arnie, wait a minute. Is there anything I can do?"

"I don't think so."

"Well, do me a favor. Tell Jim that if there is anything he needs, I'd be glad to help. Tell him I've been in the same situation. And tell him that I hope it all works out."

"I'll tell him, John. I think he'll appreciate it."

Arnie cut through the center of the courtyard, stood behind Mr. Carlson, until a lull in the conversation provided the opportunity to interrupt.

"Excuse me. Mr. Carlson. My name is Arnie Weiss."

Jim's father stood up and offered his hand. "Pleased to meet you."

Arnie shook Carlson's hand and said, "Can I have a minute of your time please? I have a personal matter to discuss with you."

Jim's father's expression turned to one of concern. "Uh, sure, Mr. Weiss." Turning to the others. "Excuse me, please. I'll be right back."

Arnie led the way to the spot where he and John talked.

"What's this about? Is anything the matter?"

"I guess there's no way to say this without it being a shock. So I might as well…"

"What's wrong? Is anyone hurt?"

"No one's been hurt. But I do have news about your son."

"Jim? What happened to Jim?"

"He's here."

"Here? At Caramus? At this wedding?"

"Yes."

"Why? What's he doing here?"

"Let's grab a couple of chairs and I'll explain."

Arnie found two folding chairs and opened them, opposite each other, behind the buffet table. The two men sat down and Arnie spoke first.

"I've known Jim since he was a kid. Since right after you left for Florida. Your ex–wife came to work for me then, and has been with me ever since."

"Sure…Arnie. I know who you are. Susie's told me about you."

"Who's Susie?"

"She's my sister. Lives in Massapeuqua. She keeps me up to date about family matters. But what are you doing here, today? Did you know I'd be here?"

"No, we didn't. Total coincidence. Actually, an amazing coincidence. Jim and I are on a golf vacation together. We happened to play with Keeler's son yesterday, when he parred the Savage. That's why we were invited to the wedding."

"You mean you had no idea? None whatsoever?"

"Mr. Carlson. I can assure you that right now, no one is more shocked than your son."

"Where is he?"

"That's why I came to talk to you. He's at the bench by the putting green. He didn't think you'd want to see him."

Carlson didn't answer. Behind his gold–framed glasses, his eyes darted nervously. His hands rubbed up and down his thighs.

Arnie broke the silence. "Is he right? Would you rather not see him?"

Clasping his hands, he leaned forward, and looked Arnie in the eye. "Listen, Mr. Weiss."

"Arnie."

"Okay, Arnie. For some time now I've thought a lot about that boy. Thought a lot about this very moment. Don't you think I want to see Jim? To have him be a part of my life? It breaks my heart to be at this wedding and see the joy Hans has gotten from *his* son. To know that I have a son out there, who's not a part of my life…well, it hurts. It hurts like hell."

"Well, Mr. Carlson, this could be your chance to do something about it. It might be the only chance you'll ever get."

"I'm not sure you understand, Arnie. It's been so many years. I can't just walk back into his life and expect things to be all right."

"You're right about that. It'll take time. Lots of time and a lot of work."

"But is he willing? What does Jim say about seeing me? Susie tells me that he's good and angry. That he hates me. Why would he want to see me? Just to tell me what a son–of–a–bitch I've been?"

"No, because, you're his father. Why do you think we came to Wild Links? Because you always talked about it. He's been obsessed with this place for years. And do you know why? Because it connected him to you. And I'll tell you something else. He's turned into a hell of a young man. And an excellent golfer. He played right along with John all day yesterday."

"Is that so? I know he graduated from college and has a good job. I didn't realize he's stayed with the golf."

"For as long as I've known Jim, he's talked about the driving range you operated. And the cutdown 7–iron you made for him. His fondest memories are of the times you took him out on the course with you."

"Christ, I fucked up good, Arnie. Do you know what it is to hurt the people you love, who need you? I fucked up good."

As he looked at the beaten man whose history had finally caught up with him, Arnie hoped that he never had to know.

"Let's go. Jim's waiting for you."

CHAPTER 27

Bob Carlson stopped and stared down the hill at his son. Frozen, unable to advance any further, pausing the moment that enabled the last opportunity for delusion. For re–inventing the truth about his relationship with his son. For living a life put together with the promise and hope afforded by the ambiguity of an unfocused reality.

"I'll give you guys some time alone," said Arnie.

"Thank you. I appreciate all you've done. And I don't mean just today."

Arnie looked at the man he shook hands with and saw the face of fear and regret. Arnie's usual self–deprecating perspective was gone. He felt strong, powerful…a big hitter, a warrior.

"I've been glad to help. I regard Jim and his mother as good friends."

"Thanks, just the same."

Arnie left and Carlson took a deep breath and began walking toward his son. He moved slowly, carefully studying the young man who sat on the bench. He was still ten yards away when Jim turned suddenly and saw his father approaching. He stood quickly and walked toward the man he hadn't seen in seventeen years.

"Hi." Jim spoke first. "I didn't think you were coming. It took quite a while."

"I was talking to Arnie."

"Yeah. Arnie can really talk. Where is he now?"

"He went to get some dessert. He said he won't be long."

"It figures. Arnie can't miss any of the eats."

"We had quite a conversation. He told me about your golf game. Said you're very good."

"Not that great. Not pro caliber."

"Not many of us are. Heard you were with John when he parred the Savage yesterday. Must have been something."

"Yeah, it was spectacular."

Jim turned away and walked back to the bench and sat down. His father followed and sat beside him.

"Look, Jim. I don't know what to say. I had no idea I'd be seeing you. I feel pretty uncomfortable."

Jim stood and walked toward the putting green, away from his father. The champagne had given him a headache. His mouth was dry. And already he'd had enough of this conversation.

You feel uncomfortable, thought Jim. What about me, for Christ's sake! But then, how the hell would you know how I feel? You *never* knew. And you're still the same egotistical asshole you were when you left us seventeen years ago.

"Always the weakest part of my game," said Carlson, pointing at the putting green. "If I could have missed a few less three footers, I might have..."

"Might have what?" Jim cut him off.

"Oh, I don't know. Nothing, I guess. Would have been a hell of a lot less frustrated, that's for sure."

The two men, silent, walked across the putting surface. Jim lifted one of the numbered sticks from its cup and examined the bottom of it.

Finally, the elder Carlson spoke. "Arnie said that you had always wanted to play Wild Links."

"Yeah. I heard so much about it. You came down here every year. I guess it just kind of stuck in my mind."

"What'd you think of it? Nice course, huh?"

"Real nice. And long. The Savage could be a par five based on distance alone. And that oak tree's impossible."

"I heard John went over the top with his 9–iron. How'd you play it?"

"Driver and faded 2–iron. Just missed clearing it."

"Is that so? You must have hit the ball a good distance. Most fellows I've played with have to get there in three. Like you said, it could very well be a par five."

"How do *you* play the Savage?"

Jim's father laughed. I don't anymore. I still play the course, but I can't hit the ball far enough to think of parring the Savage. When I was younger, I tried all kinds of approaches. The closest I ever came was with a driver and long iron. It was a 3–iron and I played it like you tried to do. A pull–fade. The ball appeared to clear the tree. But...it wasn't meant to be. No, my days for parring that hole are over. It's too late for me."

Jim listened to his father as he talked about the glory days. Those golden years when Bob Carlson was a hot–shot young pro, burning to make par and the headlines. Shit, thought Jim, the bastard left his family to play golf and chase women, and his biggest regret was not making par on a fucking golf hole. Arnie was right. Jim had nothing to be ashamed of. His father was a loser. But, it wasn't Jim's fault. Maybe it *was* time for Jim to make peace with that eight–year old kid whose biggest thrill was riding the fender of his old man's golf cart.

"How long are you and Arnie staying?"

"We fly back tomorrow night."

"Got a tee–time for tomorrow?"

"Yeah, we do. At Caledonia. Ever play there?"

"It's a new one. Haven't seen it yet. Hear it's real nice, though."

"That's what I heard." Jim peered beyond his father's shoulder and walked around him. "Here comes Arnie." Jim motioned for Arnie to come and join them.

"Listen, Jim, I have an idea. We're playing Wild Links tomorrow. Early. We're going off as a twosome. Why don't you and Arnie join us?"

"No, I don't think so. We paid in advance for tomorrow's round and besides, I've had all I can take of Wild Links for now."

"What's this I hear about playing Wild Links tomorrow?" asked Arnie, as he approached the others.

"Nothing," said Jim. "You didn't hear anything."

Carlson addressed Arnie. "I invited you and Jim to join Gloria and me for a round here tomorrow."

"Who's Gloria?" asked Jim.

Carlson and Arnie looked at each other before Jim's father answered the question.

"Gloria's my wife, Jim. We've been married for a little over four years now."

"Lots of changes in your life," replied Jim.

"So," broke in Arnie. "How about another shot at the Savage tomorrow, Jimbo? I wouldn't mind taking a shot at it again, especially after the way my drives smoked today. I think I just might become the second to par that hole."

"You're out of your mind, Arn. We already paid for tomorrow's round, and we have a flight out tomorrow night."

"Listen boys," Carlson interrupted. "You'll be my guests. And Jim, I'll certainly understand if you don't want to get stuck with me on a golf course for five hours. Can't say that I blame you. But, I'd love to see you play. To see what kind of game you have."

Jim looked at Arnie. Once again, Jim's heart raced, his palms grew sweaty. He knew the feeling. Was becoming too familiar with it. It was fear. Fear of screwing up in front of his old man. Of being rejected...again. Of facing the truth.

Jim walked toward his father, looked him straight in the eye, and asked, "What time do we tee off?"

CHAPTER 28

"I'm proud of you, Jim," shouted Arnie over the roar of the hot tub's jets and the whirling, sudsy water.

"It's no big deal. What difference does it make where we play? Tomorrow, at this time, we'll be flying home. Nothing's going to change."

Arnie looked at Jim and wondered what he was really thinking and feeling. So much had happened in such a short time. Arnie prayed that Bob Carlson would come through for his son this time around.

"Where we going to eat tonight?" asked Jim.

"Are you kidding? *You're* asking about food?"

"I'm hungry. I didn't get to eat much at the wedding."

"Anywhere you'd like, Jimbo. And if you want to stop off at one of those topless joints, we'll do it. Tonight, you call the shots. And don't forget, I still owe you a couch dance."

"Nah. Not tonight, Arn. I think I'd just like to eat here at the hotel and maybe watch a movie in the room. They have Spectravision. We can see a recent one."

"Sounds good to me. And we can always have a few at the Oasis Lounge. Maybe there'll be some live entertainment. It's Saturday night."

"I don't think I could drink tonight. The champagne did a number on me. I *hate* champagne. Always gives me a headache. I don't know why the hell I downed 'em so quickly."

"Good enough, Jimbo. Dinner and a movie it is."

Arnie leaned back and relaxed in the warm water. Jim's choices were not necessarily his. But he wasn't going to argue. Not this time. The kid had a big day tomorrow. Maybe the biggest day of his life. Let him get his rest. And let him have the golf round of his life.

"Hey, Jim. Any ideas how you'll play the Savage tomorrow?"

"I've been thinking about it, Arn." Suddenly, Jim sat up, bursting through the blanket of foam, and turned to Arnie. "I don't think I can get there in two. I probably hit that 2–iron yesterday as well as I ever could. And it still didn't make it. That tree makes it impossible."

"Why don't you lay up? Go John's route."

"That's what I was thinking. But I couldn't do it with 9–irons. No, I was thinking that I'd hit a medium iron—maybe a five or a six—off the tee, and then lay up with a wedge—more control over the distance that way. Then I could try my 7–iron from the edge of the pond."

"Can you get over the oak with your seven?"

"I think so. Yesterday, when I hit the 7–iron left, I thought it had the height. Of course, this time I'll go straight at the flag. Shit, I hope the pin'll be placed on the upper tier tomorrow. It'll be easier to hit it a little long. I just better not come up short, though. No way I'm one–putting up that swale. Jesus, what a fucking hole."

"I think you've got a good shot at it, Jim. And I can just see the expression on your old man's face when you do it. Wouldn't that be something?"

"I don't give a shit about him. I just want to play good, steady golf. You know, you were right about him. He's pathetic. A complete loser. And I can't believe how old he looks."

"How old is he?"

"Let's see. He was thirty–eight when he left...he's fifty–five. Shit, he looks more like seventy–five. Don't you think?"

"I don't know, Jim. Age is a tricky thing to read. His hair's all gray and thinned. That could add years to your appearance right there. But, fifty–five? He definitely looks older than that."

"He's also so small. I remember this big, strong guy. And, I'm not imagining it. We have pictures. He was a pretty solid dude. Now he looks like a strong breeze could knock him over."

"Aging does that," said Arnie looking at his outstretched hands. "Yeah, none of us can beat Father Time's cruel justice."

"But Arnie. You look like *you* could be his son. And I could be his grandson."

"Yeah, today I could be his son. Give it time. Did you ever think that maybe your father is not well? That maybe he's been sick?"

"How sick can he be? He's still getting around Wild Links. I wouldn't be surprised if the old man's hustling me with that 'days are gone' number, and plans on kicking my ass out there tomorrow. No. That wouldn't surprise me at all."

"I don't think so Jim. No way is he gonna kick your ass."

For the moment, hearing Arnie's vote of confidence, Jim felt a calm rush of utter competence. The kind he felt when he was in the midst of a good round, or after he had played exceptionally well. During such moments, Jim felt capable, worthwhile, as if there was nothing that he couldn't overcome or deal with.

But, the moment didn't last. Jim visualized the first tee and his pulse pounded, vibrated in his head. His stomach rumbled and his hands began to shake. He quickly stood up and walked to the center of the tub.

"I only wish that his wife wasn't coming along. I can just imagine what she's like. Anyone who'd marry a man like that must be desperate. Unless he made some bucks. It's possible, you know. No way me or my mom would have heard, let alone seen any of it. I wonder how old this new wife is. I wouldn't be surprised if she was my age, or even younger. He always did like the young ones."

"I saw her briefly, Jim. She can't be much younger than your dad."

"Well, that's a switch. Maybe the old guy can't get it up anymore. Damn, I wish she wasn't playing. Women on the course usually screw up my concentration. A second stop at the lady's tee, the slow play, pink balls. I hate that shit."

"Now wait a minute, Jimbo. I've been outplayed by a lot of women in my brief golf history. And I'll bet Gloria is a player. She's married to an ex–pro for one thing. And she *is* going out on a very tough course. No, I'll be surprised if *Gloria* doesn't kick ass. Might kick all our asses. Who knows?"

"Goddamnit, that's all I need." Jim stooped in the water and waved his arms against the whirling force. "I just have to play my game. Stay focused and play my game. That's all."

"You'll do fine. Just fine. You know, we better get out of this tub. I'm turning into a prune. What do you say we grab a shower and some dinner."

Jim didn't respond. He turned from Arnie and walked across the tub, staring at the swaying palms that lined the oceanfront, until the hot tub timer expired. Suddenly, the motor stopped. There was no sound. Jim submerged his head in the water, jumped up, and wiped the hair back from his face. He stared straight up at the luminous blue sky—placid, unprovoked by a single cloud. The sun tucked itself into the curve of the far horizon. The day faded to twilight.

Arnie sat quietly, scooping up and squeezing handfuls of foam.

Finally, Jim walked over to Arnie and said, "You know, I was thinking. About what Ralph said. That crazy theory of his. About how you never leave this place the same person. That something always happens that changes you. Forever. It sounded like such bullshit then. But now, I'm not so sure. This trip has been crazy. I can't believe how much has happened."

Arnie walked to the tub's padded steps, grabbed the railing and turned.

"And it's not over yet, Jimbo. It's not over yet."

CHAPTER 29

The high pressure system that moved in after Thursday's storm had settled and stalled over the southeast. The forecast for Sunday promised blue skies and lots of sunshine—low to mid–80's.

Arnie and Jim packed before breakfast. They settled their bill at the front desk and arranged to have their luggage sent to the Jetport. Having done this, they'd have plenty of time to accommodate a lengthy round, a shower, and a quick bite—still with enough time to make their 6:50 P.M. flight to La Guardia.

Tee time was 8:42. Jim and Arnie caught the 7:20 Hydroshuttle and arrived at the course with almost an hour to spare. The pro shop was busy on this Sunday morning. Many of the wedding guests had spent the night and were going to cap off their trip with a round at Wild Links.

"I can't deal with all these people," Jim said to Arnie. "I'm going to practice putting. You get us signed in."

"Hey, there's Tina's sister," said Arnie. "What's her name again?"

"Debra. I'll meet you outside."

"Okay, Jim. I'm going to say hello."

Arnie lifted and moved a Taylor–Made bag that contained demo 300 Series drivers and avoided pushing through the crowd.

"Hi, Debra. Arnie Weiss. We met at the wedding."

"Oh, sure. Hi, Arnie. Playing golf? Great day for it."

"I'm going to try. You're not playing. Are you?"

"Oh no. This course is way out of my league. I'm waiting for my sister. Then, I'm going to the Jetport with her and John."

"So, the bride and groom haven't left yet?"

"They have a flight to Bermuda later this morning." Debra's face perked up as she waved into the crowd behind Arnie. "Oh, there they are. I've got to go. It was nice to see you again, Arnie. Good luck today."

Arnie left the pro shop. He leaned on the wooden rack out front, designed for resting golf bags, and breathed the clean, early morning air. Arnie listened to the ocean, noticed a flock of geese in V formation, quietly float across the immaculate blue sky. He looked at the deep emerald forest that framed the first tee. Wild Links. Once you've entered those woods, you're never the same. Three days ago, when Ralph first made that comment, Arnie hadn't given it any thought. But, when Jim repeated it again, Arnie realized that it just might be true.

Arnie didn't believe in magic or witchcraft, but he did believe in some kind of higher force that ran the show. A plan that nobody was afforded the luxury and comfort of being privy to. That no one of mortal status could alter. And while he hadn't experienced the drama that Jim had over the past day, Arnie realized that he too had been changed—in some subtle manner that he would not be able to conceptualize, let alone put into words, for months, maybe years, perhaps forever. He *would* see Ralph again. He *would* teach Ryan to play golf. Promises. Commitments to self. A determination to break free of the gravitational tug of routine and habit.

Arnie thought about Michelle. He pictured her laughing as a young woman, when he first met her. She was still just as beautiful to him. After all these years, Michelle was still the one he wanted to spend his life with. He'd never realized it more than during the past few days. Why was it so easy to feel this love when he was not with her? Why did he have to be so grumpy when they were together? Arnie wasn't old yet, but time *was* running out. Precious time. Had the experience of Wild Links changed him? Arnie wanted desperately to believe so. Yet, he couldn't help but feel skeptical. He couldn't risk the disappointment that came with unrealistic expectations.

"Arnie. I was hoping I'd find you. How's Jim doing?"

Arnie turned to face the voice and was struck by the broad presence of John. "How ya' doing buddy? Didn't think I'd see you again. Jim's okay. We're playing with his father and his wife this morning."

"I know. I heard. Bob Carlson had a long talk with my dad last night. Apparently, he was pretty shaken by running into Jim after all these years."

"Well, how do you think Jim feels?"

"I can only guess."

"I'll tell 'ya, John. I don't know what's going to happen out there today. Jim bottles up a lot. You never know when it might come out."

"Well, I think it's a good thing that they're getting out there. Things can't be any worse than they've been. Right?"

"I agree."

"I know you had a lot to do with making this happen."

"Yeah, I've been known to do some meddling in my day."

"You're a good man, Arnie. A rare breed. I have a lot of respect for what you did."

"Thanks, John. I appreciate the kind words."

"You deserve them. Where's Jim now? I'd like to say goodbye."

"He's putting." Arnie pointed down the hill, off to the right.

"Thanks, Arnie." The men shook hands. "Come back if you can. And look us up. Tina and I will be here. And most important, work on that thirty to forty yard pitch, and the 3–wood off the tee. You've got a nice game that's coming along. Next time we play, you'll be scoring in the 80s."

Arnie laughed. "First, let's see if I can break 100. But, thanks just the same. You guys have a great honeymoon."

At the practice green, Jim followed through on a six–foot putt and heard it drop in the cup. No need to see it fall. Head down, putter level to the ground. Follow through to the target. A nice, smooth and rhythmic stroke. It was the six–footers and shorter, that Jim wanted to make sure he didn't miss. Par savers. Jim lined up another. Cling. Dead center. He was ready.

"Jim."

Jim knew the voice. No way out. He looked up. "Hi, John. I thought you would have left by this time."

"No, we leave later this morning."

"Nice wedding. Great food. We had a good time."

"Thanks. We're very happy with the way things went." John's smile faded into a more serious look of concern. "Jim, if you don't mind, I wanted to talk to you for a minute about your dad."

Jim retrieved his two balls from the cup, and walked off the putting surface. "Yeah, what about him?"

"I had no idea Bob Carlson was your father."

"I know that."

"I don't know Mr. Carlson…, your father, very well at all. He and my dad have been friends for quite some time now."

"That's okay." Jim slid his putter back in his golf bag before continuing. "I don't have a problem with you. Even if you were his best friend. So what. He's the one who abandoned me and my mom."

"Jim, it might not be any of my business, but…I think I under-stand how you feel."

"I'm sorry, John. I really don't know what you're talking about."

"I know what it feels like to grow up without a father."

John held his ground, waiting for Jim's reaction.

No response.

"My dad and I hadn't seen each other for thirteen years. Then, five years ago, we started over."

"You're very lucky to have become so close after missing all those years. It doesn't always work out so smoothly."

"I just hope you'll give him a chance."

"And him? Did you have this same speech with him? Look John, I know what you're trying to do. But maybe you should stay out of it. I'm very happy for you and your old man. But our father's are very different people. Yours wants to be with you. You don't even know my dad."

"You're right, Jim. I don't. But I just wanted to tell you that I really hope things work out. One thing I do know for certain is that you're going to blow your dad away with your golf game. You're one of the best players I've seen around here. I mean it. Even if you guys don't work it out, go out there and hit the hell out of the ball."

"Thanks, John." The men shook hands. "And congratulations to you and Tina. Enjoy that Bermuda sun and surf."

Jim watched John walk away and immediately proceeded to forget their conversation. There was golf to be played. Jim looked at his watch. 8:18. He couldn't wait to get off that first tee. No question in his mind that he would smoke one down the middle. Jim smiled as he anticipated bending over to pick up his tee and seeing the expression on his old man's face. Jim was definitely ready, familiar with his current mindset. Alert, relaxed, confident. Pumped.

He picked up his bag, slung it over his shoulder, and made his way toward the clubhouse. Looking at the powerfully built structure sitting in the bright early morning sun, Jim felt a rush of pure joy erupt within him. Hurling up his back, resonating and tingling in the back of his neck, detonating within his psyche, with the loud and very clear message that today was to be a day of greatness. A day that rightfully belonged to him.

CHAPTER 30

Jim and Arnie arrived at the first tee at 8:30. A foursome had just hit, and another—two men and two women—was next in line. Bob and Gloria Carlson hadn't arrived yet.

Jim and Arnie got out of their cart and began to loosen up.

"So, how you feeling, Jimbo? Ready to tear it up?"

Stretching side–to–side with Big Boy locked inside his elbows, behind his back, Jim replied, "I'm ready. Having already played the course twice helps. I have some idea of what I want to do."

"That local knowledge bullshit doesn't do a thing for me. I just want to hit clean, reasonably straight shots."

Jim stepped a few feet away from his partner and took a few full swings with his driver. "Play might be slow today. Looks like there's a lot of wedding guests playing. And that means plenty of women. This foursome in front of us will probably take their own sweet time."

"Now don't get bent out of shape before we even begin. Slow play is part of the game. It's like bad weather. You have to deal with it."

"You're right. I just gotta' take it one shot at a time."

The two men in the next foursome hit off just as Bob and Gloria Carlson parked their cart behind Jim and Arnie's.

"Sorry to cut it so close," said Bob. "Ran into too many damn people this morning. Didn't even have a chance to putt."

Bob and his wife walked over to Jim and Arnie.

"Jim, Arnie. I'd like you to meet Gloria."

"Hi, Gloria," said Arnie as he shook her hand.

"Hello," followed Jim, also shaking Gloria's hand.

"It's a pleasure to meet you both. Thank you so much for playing with us today."

Jim backed away and did some more unnecessary stretching. He looked at Gloria. The woman looked nothing like he would have imagined. Mid–fifties, average height, about fifteen pounds overweight. She wore a white blouse accented by narrow purple and green stripes on the sleeves and green denim culottes. A white "PGA Tour Partners" visor capped her straight, shoulder–length auburn hair, and dark green tortoise shelled sunglasses perched across the bridge of her slightly upturned nose. Her most distinctive feature was her smile and its broad display of very large, very white teeth.

"Hey, look at that woman strike the ball," said Bob in response to a straight 175 yard drive by a member of the foursome in front of them.

"You think I'll ever hit it like that, hon?" Gloria looked at her husband.

"Why not? You're doing fine. Making good progress."

"Are you a beginner?" asked Arnie.

"Well, actually I've played on and off for twenty years, but I started taking the game more seriously when I met Bob."

"Don't worry about a thing," said Arnie. "I've only been at it for a couple of years. I'll bet you're better than I am."

"I don't think so. But that doesn't matter. I just love getting out here—playing the game. Especially when the weather cooperates like today."

As Arnie and Gloria continued their conversation, Jim and Bob stretched and took practice swings. Jim paused for a minute to look at his father. Tan slacks with a deep plum Nike shirt, white and burgundy, saddle golf shoes, and a white cap with red stitching that read Wilson. The old man looked in decent shape. Better than he had looked the day before. His arms were still muscular, and he appeared limber as he bent from the waist to touch his toes. His practice swings appeared professional. Easy, nice turn, good clubhead speed, balanced finish. Jim could see that his father still had it.

"I think we can hit now," said Arnie. "Who wants to lead the way?"

No response.

"Well, might as well get this over with," offered Arnie.

Arnie pulled the 3–wood out of his bag and walked to the tee area. "Dogleg left. Right?"

"That's correct," answered Bob. "You want to keep it right if you can."

Jim watched and listened as his father leaned over and whispered something into his wife's ear. They both laughed. Shit, thought Jim, his dad was so relaxed, so confident. He had played this course a hundred times before, and he was a seasoned professional. Jim wished he had never agreed to play. Right now, he and Arnie could have been at Caledonia, playing with a couple of people they'd never see again. Why had he let Arnie talk him into playing here today? When would he stop listening to people so much and do what *he* wanted to do? Never again, thought Jim. I'm going to get this round over with, hop on a plane, and not look back.

"All right, Arnie. Way to put out it there," said Bob in response to Arnie's well–struck fade that made it 180 yards out.

"I'm happy," said Arnie. "Take those all day."

"Jim, why don't you hit next?" Bob suggested.

"That's okay. You go ahead."

Bob Carlson walked up and placed a tee and new Top Flight Hot XL between the white tee markers. He stood behind the ball and looked at the target. Took a couple of easy swings with his Titleist persimmon driver before he stepped in, left foot first. Once in his stance, he lined the clubface behind the ball, hovering above the short grass. He looked up at the target, then down at the ball and pressed his hips slightly left just before he brought the club-head back. He finished high, his hands frozen at the top of his swing, pointed in the direction of the ball's flight.

"Nice hit," yelled Arnie as he watched the ball dart toward the right rough, before drawing back and landing in the right side of the fairway.

"Thank you," said Bob, who picked up his tee and examined it before putting it in his pocket and heading back to his cart.

Gloria smiled at her husband.

"Good drive," said Jim, as he passed by his father.

As Jim spotted his ball in the ground, he looked at the two balls in the fairway. His dad's ball was about 50 yards past Arnie's. That meant he hit it about 230. And he got it all. It won't be any problem to outdrive him, but Jim had to keep it straight—to stay out of trouble. No use trying to impress with big drives. Jim figured his father was deadly around the greens. He knew that the old man was going to be tough to beat.

Jim began his waggle. His third time playing this hole in four days. The last two times, he had hit perfect drives. One more. Come on. Just one more.

As soon as Jim hit, he knew he had missed it. Off the heel, the ball skied left on the fairway about twenty yards short of Arnie's ball.

"That'll play," shouted Arnie.

"Good shot," added Gloria.

"It's a par five," said Jim's dad. "You've got a stroke to play with."

The two carts drove about 50 yards down a short hill to the lady's tee area. Gloria took a blue–headed, blue–shafted, blue–gripped 3–wood out of her paisley bag and walked to the area between the red tee markers.

"Don't expect much," she said, curtseying down to place her pink Pinnacle.

Gloria took a couple of choppy practice swings.

"I know what you're thinking. Don't say a word," Arnie advised Jim. "Myself, I like pink balls. Think they're kind of pretty."

Gloria swung at the ball, catching the top third of it, sending the little pink sphere rolling about thirty yards into the rough, just in front of the fairway.

"Come on, honey. Keep your head down. You lifted on that one. Remember, no peeking."

"Give me a fucking break," Jim whispered to Arnie. "We're goin' to be here all goddamn day. How can we expect to get a rhythm going?"

"Jim. Focus. Remember? Complaining's not going to help."

"Yeah, but I already fucked up my drive. Got to lay up on my next shot. May not be able to reach the green in three. And the old man is in perfect position. Watch the bastard pull out a wood and roll it right to the fringe. I bet those fairway woods are automatic for him."

"Listen to me, Jim. You're driving yourself crazy. We have eighteen holes of golf to play. You flubbed one shot. Your old man hit the ball as well as he can, and still, he barely outdrove you. Come on, man. One shot at a time. Okay?"

Jim nodded.

Gloria's second shot with the same wood got airborne and traveled about 100 yards before landing in the rough—off the right side of the fairway. It rolled just past Arnie's ball.

"Sorry, guys," she said, getting back into the cart.

"What's to be sorry about? That was a nice shot. Very nice," Arnie replied.

Jim grabbed a 5–iron, and walked to his ball. Shit, he couldn't see the green from this angle. He wanted to stay in the fairway and leave himself no more than 180 yards for his approach shot. The 5–iron should do it.

Jim bore down on the ball, swung smoothly, and hit it cleanly. Running right, he saw his ball roll to a stop in the fairway, about 175 yards from the green.

"Nice play," yelled Bob, as he passed behind them in the cart on the way to Gloria's ball.

Arnie flashed a big smile at Jim, put out his hand for five, and said, "That's my man. Didn't take you long to get it back."

Expressionless, Jim replied, "Like you said, we've got a long day of golf ahead. One shot doesn't mean much."

"Fuck you," kidded Arnie. "You're going to break my balls today, aren't you? You're going to bust my fucking balls."

Jim laughed as Arnie went to his ball, 5–iron in hand.

"Right alongside yours, Jimbo. Want to aim this sucker right at your ball."

Arnie slid right on his backswing, lost his balance, and chopped down behind the ball. Taking a gopher–sized divot, the ball traveled about thirty yards, still short of Bob's drive.

"There we go," shouted Arnie. "Now, my game's back. I was wondering where it went. Was hitting the ball much too well lately."

Arnie shook his head, replaced the divot, and walked up to his ball with the same club. Plenty of wide fairway to aim for, still miles to the barely visible flagstick. Arnie kept his head still, swung smoothly, and ate up 150 yards of straight–ahead turf.

"Very nice shot, Arnie." Bob nodded his head in the direction of Arnie.

"Perfect," added Gloria.

Arnie returned to the cart and slapped Jim's palm. "You're not the only one on a mission today, Jimbo. I want to have a good taste in my mouth when we board that plane tonight."

"That was a good hit. You're right by my ball. We both have good shots at the green."

"Shhh. Gloria's hitting."

"Oh shit. I can't watch this."

With the same blue–headed wood, Gloria went into her long, awkward swing. The ball popped in the air and landed about twenty yards to her right, behind a small pine bush.

Exasperated, Gloria looked back at her husband.

"Come on, hon. Chip it out. Right in the middle of the fairway."

"I can't deal with this," Jim moaned. "I've played with poor players before, but she's totally inept. She has no right playing on a course like this."

"Like it or not, she's here. I'll admit, she doesn't look too good out there. But, we've still got to play our games."

Gloria, hitting her wood again, barely knocked the ball out from behind the bush onto the fairway.

"All right, Gloria," coached Bob. "Don't lift on it. Put it out there. Nice and easy."

Gloria took two practice swings before hitting her ball. She swung too hard, lifted her head, but still managed about 100 yards of roll.

"If you're going to miss it, that's the way to do it," said Bob, holding a 4–wood by his ball. "See. You followed through and the ball went straight."

"Give me a fucking break," said Jim. "Does he believe what he's saying? I've never seen an uglier swing."

"Let's see how his game holds together," countered Arnie. "He's certainly not getting bent out of shape the way you are."

"I knew it. A wood. Watch, right on the green."

Bob stood behind his ball and glared at the target. Stepped in, left foot first. Slightly bent at the waist, knees flexed, two waggles, and *boom*! The ball exploded off the clubface—started low but picked up height—straight at the stick. When the ball stopped rolling, it was still about 80 yards short of the green.

"Great shot, Bob," yelled Arnie.

"Nicely done," added Jim.

Again, Gloria smiled at her husband, but said nothing.

"Shit. He's got a beautiful swing," said Arnie.

"Yeah," agreed Jim. "But you know, I'm surprised. The ball flies out of there, but doesn't get the distance you'd expect. It seems to quickly lose power. I thought that would get closer to the green."

"He's not a kid anymore, Jim. Doesn't have your strength. Now, let's see you put this next shot on the green."

Jim went with his 5, Arnie a 3–iron for their approach shots. Gloria was still away and next to hit.

Hurrying to her ball, hitting quickly, Gloria topped another that was good for about another 100 yards of roll. Her ball settled right alongside Bob's.

Arnie caught his 3–iron cleanly, but was late with his hands. The ball faded and found the right–hand trap.

"It could be worse," said Arnie as he replaced his divot. "Lying four in a greenside bunker on a tough par five. It could be a lot worse. Let's go Jimbo."

Jim was looking at a shot he made all the time. One–seventy–five to a flat green. No trouble in sight. The pin was placed off–center to the right. Jim wanted to hit the fucking stick. The hell with par. Jim was thinking of birdie.

Jim saw nothing except the black number 1 on his ball. He heard nothing except his inner voice. Low and slow. Low and slow. No conscious effort, a smooth easy swing, Jim never saw the ball's flight. Still, he knew it was good. Damn good.

"Get in the cup!" screamed Arnie.

"What a beautiful shot," yelled Gloria.

"Slow down, now. Slow down," said Bob.

The ball landed about two feet left of the stick, took one hop and settled about twelve feet behind the hole.

"Excellent line on that one," said Bob. "You were all over the stick."

"Great shot," added Gloria.

A high five from Arnie.

Jim would have liked to have gotten it closer to the pin, but he knew he had accomplished what he needed to with that shot. He beared down, remained calm, hit it clean, and gave his old man something to think about.

CHAPTER 31

"I'll give you that one," said Bob.

The twelve foot birdie putt didn't break as much as Jim had expected. Rolling a couple inches high of the hole, the ball settled one foot away from the cup. Jim deferred the offer of a gimme and tapped in for his par.

"Nice five," said Arnie who was next to putt. Unable to repeat his miraculous escape from the sand on the previous day, Arnie's second shot from the trap just managed to clear the bunker's lip and find the edge of the green. His thirty foot uphill put was about ten feet short.

"Gotta' hit it. Gotta hit it," muttered Arnie as he got ready to putt again.

"Too hard," said Bob, as soon as Arnie stroked his next putt. The ball appeared to roll right over the top of the cup, catching the edge of the cylinder, and settling twelve feet beyond its targeted destination.

"Good thing the cup slowed it down," said Bob.

"Jesus," exclaimed Arnie. "The old compensate–overcompensate game. When will I learn?"

Still away, Arnie babied his next putt half–way to the hole.

"Anyone have a calculator?" asked Arnie. "I've lost track of my score on this hole. I'm going to hole out if you don't mind."

Straddling Gloria's line, Arnie hit the ball too hard, but still managed to sink it.

"Whew. A slam–dunk," he said, shaking his head. "Hey, Jim, when does our plane leave? Don't you think we should get going? It's getting kind of late."

Gloria looked at Arnie and laughed.

Bob, who would putt after his wife, spotted his ball and began to study the five–foot par putt.

"You're away, hon," said Bob, in a squatting position.

"Okay, Bob. What do you think? Looks pretty straight to me."

"Right at the cup," he answered.

Gloria demonstrated a smooth stroke as she rolled the putt an inch short of the hole.

"Beautiful roll," exclaimed Bob.

"She's been holding out on us," said Arnie. "Now we know the truth about you, Gloria. You hustle us with those precision putts. Hey, what'd you end up scoring on that hole?"

"Let's see," answered Gloria. "On in seven, two putts. A nine."

"See what I mean, Jim? I got a ten. I've got my eye on you, Gloria. All side bets are off."

Gloria smiled at Arnie, then turned to watch her husband get ready to putt. Bob used a pitching wedge off an uphill lie for his approach shot. The ball hooked and caught the leftside bunker—pin–high. A beautiful out from the trap got him in position for a relatively easy par putt.

Bob took his time, studied the putt from all angles, before stroking it right into the center of the cup.

"Nice save," said Jim.

"Easy game. Huh, Bob?" said Arnie. "Come on, Gloria. Let's you and I get out of here. Have a couple of beers, shoot the breeze. Let these guys play their game."

"Sounds good to me," laughed Gloria.

Jim met Arnie with the cart. Driving toward the second tee, Jim said, "You two seem to have hit it off."

"She's a nice lady, Jim. Besides, I've got to have some fun today. Might I remind Par Man that your buddy just took a ten on the first hole. It could be a long day if I don't entertain myself. And you guys. Man, the intensity level is unreal. If I don't chill and find me a few laughs, I'll have an ulcer starting up by the turn."

Jim did not appear to hear Arnie. "I can't believe he saved par on that hole. He fucked up his approach and gets it to five feet out of the sand."

"Think of the positive, Jimbo. He fucked up his approach. And he'll fuck up a lot more shots before the day is through."

The carts pulled under the big oak that hung over the path near the tee area. Despite the early hour, there was little breeze, and the air was comfortably warm. The foursome ahead had just hit their tee shots. There would be some time to kill, as two of their balls sailed into the wooded area on the right.

Jim got out of the cart and looked down the fairway. Bob joined him.

"You've got to keep it right on this hole," whispered Bob. "There's a crest…"

"Yeah, I know." Jim interrupted him. "I birdied this hole on Friday."

"Is that so? This is a very tough hole. How'd you do it?"

"On in two, sunk a twelve–foot putt. Got there with my driver and 6–iron."

Bob nodded.

"What are you playing with these days?" asked Bob, as he walked to the back of Jim and Arnie's cart.

Jim pulled out his 7–iron and said, "Hogan Apex."

"I'm surprised a young player like yourself wouldn't be taking advantage of the new technology. Let me show you something."

Bob got the Ram FX 4–iron from his bag and handed it to Jim. "Cavity backs. They're weighted around the perimeter of the clubface. If you hit it off–center, you still get some of the sweet spot. Those old forged clubs are all right for some of the pros. The ones who like the feel, who want to play a lot of draws and fades. But for a player like yourself, you'd do a lot better with the new cast designs."

"I like these clubs. Mom got them as a gift for opening a bank account when I was eighteen. I've played with them ever since. I think they've done okay for me so far. Excuse me, I'm gonna' go take a leak."

Jim found the path behind the tee area that he had discovered on Friday. As he relieved himself, he recalled his earlier visit to the spot. Like today, he had parred the first hole. John had just joined them. The high pressure system that had moved in before the weekend was beginning to gather some humidity today. It was noticeably warmer. Jim looked up at the tall branches. No movement. Less windy today. Jim thought about his father's advice a few moments ago. Get new golf clubs. Who the fuck did he think he was? Jim wanted badly to beat his father. Wanted to burn up the course. Jim had shown he could play on that first hole, and he'd have to keep it up to impress Bob Carlson. The man was so tough to please. Fuck him, thought Jim. He could play the best golf he was capable of and still hear nothing positive from his father.

Before Jim got back up the hill, he heard the exploding sound of his father's drive.

"You nailed that one," said Arnie.

"Just what I wanted to do," said Bob. "I think I cleared the crest. Should get the good roll."

"Go ahead, Jim," said Arnie. "You've got the honors."

"You hit first, Arn. I'm not ready."

Arnie decided to play it safe with his 5-iron, and got the ball out in great shape.

"You're a smart player, Arnie," said Bob. "Know your game. Know your limitations. I can't tell you how many players try and do too much."

"I have no delusions along those lines. Now women, that's a different story. They've always been after this body. Fight' em off with a club. But sports? Nah. I'm very realistic about my athletic abilities."

Bob and Gloria both laughed at Arnie's comments as Jim stood behind his teed up ball and tried to focus on the shot.

He had to keep it right and he had to get all of it. Jim recalled that it took a full 250 yards to get the necessary roll. He figured his father's shot might have stuck in the downward sloping backside of the crest. This could be a great opportunity to take advantage.

Jim completed his routine, was prepared to hit. The ball. See the ball. Low and slow. *Crack!* He couldn't have hit it any better. Jim held his breath, frozen in his follow-through position, watching the ball's flight. The precision and power of the swing sent the ball soaring, speeding down the middle of the fairway. And while he appreciated the artistry of the ball's flight, he relished the fact that behind him stood his father, observing the very same picture.

Jim's last thought before exhaling was that he wished life could always feel the way it did right at that instant.

CHAPTER 32

Life's not fair. Neither is golf. Jim's drive outdistanced his father's by a good seventy yards. Bob was 240 from the green with a difficult downhill lie. His 4–wood approach sliced and settled in the right–hand rough, barely managing to bounce past a lanky maple tree that would have forced a chip out. He still had ninety yards to get to the green of the long par 4 in three strokes.

Jim's mammoth tee shot left him with a wide open 165 yards to the green. On his second shot, he hit his 6–iron beautifully, but the ball hit a sprinkler head on the front edge and caromed right, settling into a fried egg lie in a deep greenside bunker.

Arnie topped his third consecutive 5–iron, but the ball rolled onto the green, leaving him a twenty–five foot putt for par.

Gloria, taking advantage of the hole's shortened length from the lady's tees, topped and rolled three wood shots—the final one settling right in front of the green.

All four players scored bogeys on the hole.

The next six holes played slow but steady. There had been no birdies. The closest anyone came was on four. Jim's 2–iron tee shot on the par 3, 207 yard hole settled at ten feet from the pin. His putt came up three feet short and he had to settle for par. Arnie's highlight came on the par 3, 199 yard, eighth hole—the "mule train" hole. Arnie had considered opting for Gloria's 135 yard lady's tee shot, but was dissuaded by Bob's persuasive vote of confidence. Despite three–putting for bogey, Arnie avoided the descent into the canyon when his cleanly struck 3–wood flied high and straight onto the front edge of the green.

Jim took thirty–five strokes on the first eight holes—three over par. His father was right there with him at four over. Arnie's numbers totaled forty–nine for the eight holes—respectable in light of his ten on the first hole. Arnie figured that twelve over par for the last seven holes was better than his usual double bogey pace. No one knew Gloria's exact score, but with two balls in the water on three, and at least another three in the woods on five and seven, it was probably somewhere in the low seventies.

The par 4, 408 yard, ninth hole played uphill, with woods off to the right. The wide and open fairway invited big hitters to blast their tee shots. As long as the ball stayed left, it was clear sailing on this one.

"This is your kind of hole, Jimbo," said Arnie. "You and Big Boy can go to work."

"I parred it on Thursday, but took a bogey on Friday," answered Jim, scratching the dirt from the grooves of his driver with a tee. "Hooked the damn shot on Friday. Way left. Made the hole too long. I've got to keep those trees on the right out of my mind."

"This is a par 5 for me. I'd have to hit two perfect shots with my 3–wood to get close. Might as well go with an iron off the tee."

"Don't be so quick to sell yourself short," cut in Bob. "Look what you did on that last hole. You can reach this green with two good woods."

"You sure do have a lot of confidence in my game," said Arnie, double clutching with his 5–iron. "Oh, what the hell. Maybe you're right."

"Get up there and go for it," said Jim.

"Might as well," replied Arnie, pulling the head cover off of his 3–wood.

Arnie teed up his ball and proceeded to swing so hard that he finished on his heels and fell back several steps. The ball hit off the heel of the clubface, and rolled left, just short of the lady's tees.

Arnie, his balance restored, stood motionless before he turned and said, "Thank you, Bob. Remind me to ignore every piece of advice you give me for the rest of the day."

"You tried to kill it," replied Bob. "Gotta stay within yourself."

"Don't listen to anyone's advice," said Gloria. "Do whatever you're comfortable with."

"Now you tell me, Gloria," exclaimed Arnie. "A minute ago, when your husband was sabotaging my game, I heard nothing. Where were you when I needed you?"

Bob hit next. Following the same preshot routine he used for all shots, he took what appeared to be a rhythmic swing and sent a high–flying rocket that began to fade, and finally slice. The ball landed in the right rough and rolled into the trees on the right side. Possibly, a lost ball.

"Want to hit a provisional?" asked Jim.

Bob picked up his tee. "No need to. I'll find that one."

"Are you sure?" asked Jim.

"It's in play," repeated Bob.

"Okay. If you say so," said Jim, teeing up his ball just inside the right tee marker.

Jim had his chance. Even if that ball wasn't lost, it was in pretty deep rough. Already a stroke ahead, this was the hole where Jim could open up a two, maybe three stroke lead. Plenty of wide open fairway. Just put it in play. Don't kill it.

Jim's drive wasn't his best effort, but it was good enough. Skied, pulled a bit left, the ball settled on the edge of the fairway, just short of the 150 yard stake.

"Way to go, Jim," yelled Arnie.

"Another good shot," said Gloria.

"Nice job," added Bob, in the cart, already heading toward the lady's tee area.

Arnie's ball was buried in thick rough. With the top of the ball barely visible, he still managed to rip his 5–iron through the grass and get the ball well out into the fairway.

Gloria's tee shot was easily her best of the day. One–hundred–fifty yards on the fly, it settled right alongside of Arnie's ball.

"Hey, that's my girl," shouted Bob.

"Nice shot," said Jim.

"Gloria," shouted Arnie. "You're obviously beginning to warm up. Great shot."

Gloria blushed and flashed a big, toothy smile.

Arnie and Gloria's next shots were decent. Gloria, who Arnie calculated was away by two inches, hit first. Another topped, blue–headed wood shot that rolled for about 100 yards. Arnie decided to play it safe with his old, reliable 5–iron, and the solidly struck, high flying fade left him with a forty yard chip to the green.

Jim walked up to the sight of his ball and looked across the fairway at his father, still searching for his ball. Jim took a few easy practice swings with his 6–iron and looked at the flag. Easy shot. Pin placement left–center, no trouble in sight. Jim waited. Shit, how long was his old man going to look for that damn ball? Stubborn bastard.

Jim stared across the fairway at the figure crouched among the trees and suddenly became transfixed in a different time. Another place. Kneeling by the trees in the backyard, pulling out weeds, where six–year–old Jim tried to get his father's attention as he rode a red two–wheeler—for the first time without training wheels.

"I've got it," shouted Bob, motioning with his hand.

Jim watched his father hit a hot flyer out of the rough, the ball pulled low, hard, and left. He watched the old man run out from the deep rough to follow the ball's flight. Jim looked at the flag, lying still in the distance, then looked down at his ball. He woke up, mentally rehearsed the details of his present reality.

The dream had already faded.

CHAPTER 33

"Gloria, you're a woman after my own heart," said Arnie.

"Well, I'm not playing eighteen holes without taking a break for lunch," she replied.

After Jim made his par on nine and Bob scampered to save bogey, both men wanted to play through without breaking. Gloria's first assertive request of the day, however, was not to be denied.

"I love these chili dogs," said Arnie, third in line behind Gloria and Bob.

"Eat light. Too much food'll sap your energy," said Bob.

"Energy?" responded Arnie. "What's that? Now, hunger's a different story. I know what that is."

Gloria ordered a B.L.T. on toast—light on the mayo—and a cup of decaf. Bob went with turkey and lettuce on whole wheat and a large orange juice. Arnie stayed with the chili dogs. Two of them, with fries and a large Diet Coke. Jim grabbed a cellophane–wrapped ham salad and iced tea. He informed the others that he'd be waiting outside by the courtyard.

Gloria, Bob, and Arnie found a table.

Arnie opened a napkin, laid it across his lap, and looked around the half–filled snack bar.

"So, you've been coming to Wild Links for years," he stated, chili dog aimed and ready for consumption.

"Since 1974," answered Bob. "Well before Hans took over."

Arnie chewed quickly, wiped his mouth, before asking the next question. "What's with this place? I know it's a nice golf course. But what keeps you coming back here for so many years?"

Bob sipped his orange juice. "At first, it was the challenge. I always figured that if I played well here, I could play well anywhere. I don't have to tell you about the Savage. The ultimate challenge. More recently, I've had other reasons for coming. For one thing, Hans and I are good friends. I enjoy coming to see him. Of course, it was more fun in the old days, when we got out and played the course together."

"What about Mr. Keeler?" asked Arnie. "Why's he in a wheelchair?"

"M.S.," answered Bob. "A real sad thing. It started coming on in the mid 80's. He's been confined to that wheelchair for a few years now." Bob finished half of his sandwich before continuing. "Yeah, I think that's right. I know he wasn't in the wheelchair yet when John arrived."

"It's also very peaceful here," added Gloria. "This is my fourth trip down with Bob, and I enjoy it very much. Find it very relaxing."

Arnie buried his fries in ketchup and looked around the room again. "We met a couple of men here on Thursday. Ralph and Bud. Real nice guys. Ralph, who had been here a couple of times before, said that the place has magic to it. That something special always seems to happen when you come here. I didn't think much of it when he said it, but now...when I think of the past three days...I'm tempted to believe there just might be something to it."

Bob smiled. "I can't say that every trip down has been special or unusual, but I do know that I've learned a lot here. Yeah, this place has been an important part of my life."

"And now, you've met Jim here," said Gloria.

"That's true. That *is* true." Bob froze for a moment, his sandwich in hand, staring off to nowhere in particular.

Gloria finished her sandwich and said, "If you guys will excuse me. I'm going to take my coffee outside. I'll meet you there."

"Sure thing, babe."

Arnie, his mouth full, managed a smile, a nod, and a wave of the hand.

The men finished their lunches quietly until Bob broke the silence.

"He's a tough kid, isn't he?"

"Jim? Yeah, he's tough."

"I can see that he likes to win. He's very intense."

"Like his old man. I wouldn't want to bet against either one of you."

"Well, you'd be better off putting your nickel down on Jim. I can't hit the ball like he does anymore. Of course, in my prime...But now, forget it. That was some drive he hit on the second hole...wasn't it?"

"Oh yeah, he crushed that one. Nothing special to me, though. I see him do it all the time."

Bob finished his orange juice and banged the cup down. "I guess it's time to move on."

"I'm ready when you are."

Carlson started to rise from his seat and then sat back down. "Arnie. Before we go, could I ask you something?"

Arnie nodded.

"He hates me, doesn't he. He wants to kick my ass out there today, and then forget that he ever saw me."

Arnie took his time before responding.

"Bob, I'm not sure what he thinks. Sure, he's angry. But, can you blame him? But he's not just out there to kick your ass. That may be part of it, but there's more. And it's not my place to tell you what it's about."

"Arnie, the boy won't let me in. He's stubborn as hell. I think it's too late."

"Maybe it is too late. But you'll have to find that out for yourself."

Outside, Gloria had joined Jim at one of the wedding tables that hadn't yet been dissembled and removed from the courtyard.

"It was a pretty wedding," she said. "I love outdoor weddings."

"Yeah, it was nice."

"You've been to Wild Links before, have you?"

"Nope. This is my first time."

"What do you think?"

"It's nice. Great golf course."

Gloria stood and walked across the courtyard to the table that had been used for the buffet. She felt the peach satin ribbon that skirted the table, turned away, folded her arms and sighed.

"What a beautiful day. What time's your flight tonight?"

"I don't know. About seven. Arnie takes care of all those details."

"He's a nice man. I really like him. You know, Jim, I'm glad you decided to join us today. I never expected to have the opportunity to meet you. I'm glad I did."

Jim stirred in his seat, but didn't respond.

"Your father's impressed with your golf game. I think you really surprised him."

"What's the big surprise? So I play golf. Lots of good golfers around."

"But Jim, he can appreciate your talent. You know what the game means to him."

"Yeah, I know how much the game means to him. It's his whole life. At least it used to be." Before Gloria had a chance to respond, Jim got up from his chair.

"Let's go," he said. "They should be finished by now."

CHAPTER 34

The two carts followed the path that ran along the western shoreline to the tenth tee. The sun was directly overhead. The ocean waters were calm, the air warm.

"This is just about it, Jimbo," said Arnie. "Tomorrow at this time, we'll be home and back into our routines. It's been a great vacation. I don't think I'd mind coming back again, either. How about you?"

"I don't know," answered Jim, looking at the trail that cut through the woods, to the tenth tee. "Right now, I just want to focus on the back nine. I can't think about next year or even tomorrow for that matter."

"Lighten up, Jim. You've got two strokes on your old man. You broke forty on the frontside, and you're pounding the tar out of the ball."

"Don't count him out yet. A two stroke lead—that's nothing. Especially with his tournament experience. He's not gonna fall apart."

"Neither are you, Jim."

"Not if I bear down. Take it one shot at a time. But you never know. One lost tee shot, one fluky triple. He could blow right past me."

"He's not expecting you to fold. Thinks you're a good player and a tough competitor. You've gotten to him, Jim. He doesn't think he can beat you."

Jim turned to look at Arnie. "Did he say that?"

"Yes he did. Couldn't get over that drive you hit on two."

"Yeah, I really hit that one...need a few more of those."

"You'll get 'em. And, the way things have been going, I wouldn't be surprised to see you par the Savage. I know it's a longshot, Jim, but I've got a feeling about it."

Jim turned the cart left, onto the path, toward the tenth tee. He parked the cart, looked out at the fairway of the par 4, 361 yard hole and said, "First, I've got to make it over those trees. Got to cut that fucking dogleg. Just like John did."

Jim pulled the 5–wood out of his bag and walked up to the tee area about the same time that Bob and Gloria's cart rolled in.

"Are you sure you want to take the chance?" yelled Arnie.

His ball already teed up, taking easy practice swings, Jim replied, "I'm goin' for it and I'm making it."

"You going to try and cut the corner?" Bob cut in.

"That's right," answered Jim, still facing the fairway.

"Better think about that decision," said Bob. "I've *never* tried it. Those trees are awfully tall. What's that, a 3–wood you're hitting?"

"No, a 5–wood."

"I don't know, Jim. Lay it out to the corner and you're looking at a pretty easy par opportunity."

"I'm hitting now," said Jim who turned and glared at his father. "If that's all right with you."

Jim looked at the trees he had to clear, and then down at his ball. John had cleared it without much problem. But then again, John cleared the oak at sixteen with a 9–iron. His old man had never tried it. Maybe he *should* lay up. Jim stepped out to consider his father's words, but it was too late. He had to go for it.

The ball teed up high. Jim set up. One last look at the deep forest he was aiming at. Easy. Don't try and kill it. Jim locked into the ball. Low and slow.

The ball flew high off the clubface, dead on target. Everyone was quiet. Listening for the dismal thwack of a ball striking bark. Looking into a blinding, sun–drenched sky and not hearing it—still, no one could be sure that the ball had made it over the top.

Arnie broke the silence. "I think you did it."

"I don't know," said Bob. "It had to be awfully close."

"We'll see when we get there," said Jim. "I think I cleared it."

Arnie and Bob hit effective tee shots. Gloria took two strokes to reach the corner of the dogleg. When the carts pulled up to the clearing, Jim's ball was immediately visible, in the middle of the fairway—no more than 100 yards from the green.

"Shit, I can't believe you made it," said Bob, shaking his head. "That was a hell of a shot."

"What a great shot, Jim," added Gloria.

Arnie put his arm around Jim's shoulder and whispered, "Buddy, you're magic today. The Savage is yours for the taking. I'm telling you…this is your day."

Jim smiled and said, "Come on, Arn. This is your shot. Three–wood right on the green."

"You're right, Jimbo. This is my par hole."

Arnie hit his shot pretty solidly, but sliced it into the right hand bunker. Two out of the sand and a three putt resulted in a triple for the hole. Bob hit a 4–iron onto the back portion of the undulated green. His first three–putt of the day resulted in a bogey. Gloria scored a double off a good approach shot. Lying four, 140 from the green, she hit her wood cleanly—high and straight at the stick. She got it down with two putts from twelve feet away.

Jim didn't waste his terrific tee shot. He hit a full sand–wedge that was all over the stick. It settled five feet above the hole. His birdie putt broke about six inches left and fell straight into the heart of the cup.

Jim parred the next three holes and picked up another stroke on his father, who bogeyed thirteen. With five holes left to play, Jim's lead had swelled to five strokes. Arnie, weary from all the golf swings taken over the past four days, was buying time with scrambling doubles and triples.

As the carts pulled up to the tee area of the par 5, 555 yard, fourteenth tee, play was backed up for the first time on the backside.

"This is where the backup from the Savage starts," said Jim.

"Oh yeah, now I remember," added Arnie. "This is where I got my ten the other day. And Ralph had a twelve. Man, we had a good time on this hole. I miss Ralph. He was such a pisser."

"Sorry you're not having as much fun today," said Jim.

"What are you talking about, Jimbo? I'm having a ball." Arnie turned and looked at Gloria. "I've got Gloria today. Right, Gloria? Aren't we having a good time?"

"We sure are, Arnie," she answered. It's been a great day."

"This seems more jammed up than usual," said Bob.

"With five holes left to play, I don't mind the break," said Arnie. "And don't forget, we still have the Savage. Playing that hole is so damn draining. Maybe I'll use Ralph's strategy and sit out fifteen. He came back with a vengeance on the Savage. Remember, Jimbo?"

"Yeah, he crushed the ball twice. Almost got through the oak with his second shot. That was pretty amazing."

"What do you mean he almost got *through* the oak?" asked Bob.

"He hit a 3–iron right into the center of the tree and almost got it through," explained Arnie. "The ball actually cleared the pond."

"Was that his intention?" asked Bob. "To hit through the tree. I've never seen anyone try that."

"Yes, he did it intentionally," cut in Jim. "And he did get through. The ball just didn't have enough heat to carry to the green."

"That's impossible," argued Bob. "That tree is so dense."

"That's the second time today you've said something was impossible that wasn't," said Jim. "Didn't you say I couldn't cut the dogleg on ten?"

"Yeah. That surprised me," answered Bob. "I still think it's a bad play, though. Try that ten times and you'll wind up with a lost ball eight of those times."

"Well, it did work today, Jimbo," said Arnie. "And a beautiful shot it was. I love to see you big hitters go for broke. Makes the game more interesting."

Jim walked away and watched the ladies in the foursome ahead hit their tee shots. What an asshole, thought Jim. I made the goddamn shot, but it's still a "bad" shot. Jim remembered being at his dad's driving range, hitting ball after ball, waiting for some positive words from his father. Words that never came. Maybe being separated from his father all these years hadn't been such a bad thing. And maybe Jim wouldn't be the golfer he was today if his father had been around to put him down. In fact, Jim might never have stuck with the game at all. Well, fuck him, thought Jim. I'm kicking his ass. Managed to develop a pretty damn good game without his help. Mom and I did it all without his help. And today, the evidence is right in front of the old man's face. Jim was glad he had decided to play. Glad for himself and glad for his mother.

"You've got the honors, Jim," called out Arnie.

"What are you hitting?" asked Bob.

"Last time I went with a 1–iron and pulled it left. I think I'll go with my driver. Know I can't get there in two, but I'm hitting it well today."

"Dangerous play," said Bob. "When you miss, you tend to miss left. And you've got those woods there."

Jim ignored his father's comment and quietly teed his ball up and took a practice swing with Big Boy. Maybe he *would* get there in two. The ground's pretty hard. If he hit it solidly, there'd be plenty of roll. Why not? Anything was possible today. Jim began his waggle and swung at the ball. Another clean, crunching hit— this one pulled left, high above the trees, hooking, until it disappeared into the thick forest—well left of the white stakes that marked out of bounds.

"Jesus, did that ball sail on you," said Arnie.

"I think you aimed up that way," added Bob. "Go ahead, hit another. Right out in the fairway."

For the first time all day, Jim experienced the sinking feeling that golfers know so well. Fuck up just once and you can do it again. And again. Visceral knowing stomach, arms, and legs— every part of the mind and body is affected. The thoughtless, effortless swing of zoned–in play is only a memory. The shoulders and grip tighten, and there's a tendency to hurry. To breathe more quickly, to haphazardly grab for clubs, to quicken the takeaway. Suddenly, footwork, ball position, the bend of the knees, wind conditions, the lie of the ball conspire to form an overwhelming bombardment of the senses. And time flies by. There is no time for methodically going through the checklist. One bad shot and the simple golf swing becomes an incredibly complex execution of infinite details.

Jim considered switching to an iron. Stroke and distance. He was now lying two. His five stroke lead could be gone in a flash.

Shit! Overconfidence. How could Jim have let it happen. No, he was going with his driver again. He had to.

Jim's struggle to regain a suitable rhythm failed. His timing was completely off. Although not as far left as his first shot, the ball still rolled into the edge of the woods, barely short of the O.B. sticks.

No comments from the others.

Bob was next to hit. He chose a 3–wood, which he hit perfectly, straight down the middle of the fairway. Arnie topped his 3–wood, but the low liner rolled for about 160 yards. Gloria's tee shot popped straight in the air, narrowly missed hitting her in the head, landing back on the lady's tee area.

"Go ahead, hit another," said Bob.

Gloria whiffed on her second swing before popping her third shot up and out about 50 yards.

Jim and Arnie got into their cart and held up at the sight of Gloria's ball. Bob walked with her over to where her ball was lying.

"Keep that left arm a little bit straighter," said Bob. "See…just like this."

Bob stood behind Gloria and guided her through a fundamentally correct golf swing.

"See how that feels?" he said. "Turn your shoulders, bring the club back low, and just unwind. Your body will naturally uncoil, if you make a good turn on the takeaway."

Gloria's next shot was a ground ball that scooted on a forty–five degree angle to her right.

"That obnoxious dick," said Jim. "How does she stand it? She'd do a lot better if he just left her alone. And what's the point, anyway? She's never going to be much of a golfer."

"Maybe not," said Arnie. "But, I have to give your old man credit. Shit, I could never have the patience he has. If I tried to

teach Michelle golf, the result would be divorce, if not murder. I
know I'm goin' to have my hands full with Ryan. No, I give your
dad credit."

"You don't know him at all, Arnie. He just loves to hear the
sound of his own voice. That's not patience. It's arrogance. And
notice his timing. I'm lying three in the woods, he's in the fairway.
Coincidence, you think?"

"I'm not a goddamn psychologist, Jim. I've got to go hit."

Arnie took a couple of clubs from his bag, while Jim took the
cart to go look for his ball. The ball had rolled into the same spot
in the woods where Jim and John had lost balls on Friday. Jim
knew it wouldn't be easy to find this one. He could be lying four
with 350 yards left between him and the green. Jim looked around
and realized he was alone. He could drop one anywhere. No one
would know. A nice lie on the edge of the woods, get to the green
in two, save bogey. Why not? Jim knew he could get away with it.
But then he thought of what Arnie had said. About being better
than the old man. No, he couldn't do it. He wanted to win, but he
wanted an unblemished victory.

Jim was about to give up the search when his father joined him.

"Let's give it a couple more minutes," he said. "No one's pushing us from behind. Let's see. It entered about here and rolled
under this broken branch. Should be here somewhere. Might be
against one of these trees."

Bob poked through the weeds surrounding the trees before
finding a ball wedged against the base of a large tree stump. He
leaned down, lifted his glasses, and asked, "You playing Titlesit
1?"

"That's it. Let me have a look."

Jim didn't like what he found. His ball was not only flush
against the tree, it was on the right side. Jim would have to chip it
out left-handed. He had an opening to the fairway, but he could

very easily knock the ball against another tree and wind up in even more trouble.

Jim took a 5–iron, and executed a few practice swings—left–handed, with the back of the clubface. He had attempted this type of shot before, with mixed results.

"You don't have to hit that ball lefty," said Bob. "If you look carefully, the ball is *behind* the tree. You can whack it right–handed and have the control to place it out on the fairway."

"I have it under control."

Jim tried to settle into a comfortable stance, took a couple of awkward, left–handed practice swings, and felt ready to hit.

"I don't think that's a good play," said Bob.

Jim stepped away and dropped his club to the ground.

"I don't give a shit what you think. I've been doing pretty damn good without your help. Where do you get off thinking everyone wants your advice? Just save it for Gloria. Okay?"

Jim turned away and picked up his club.

"I know you have a problem with me, Jim. You haven't exactly tried to hide it. But *I have* been trying to help. And I've been try-ing to be friendly. You don't make it easy, though."

Jim's face reddened. A vein bulged in his forehead.

"Easy! I'm supposed to make it easy? Why the hell should I? What have you ever done for me? Except run away with your girl-friend. I knew this was a mistake. I never should have agreed to play with you."

Jim turned away again, but Bob grabbed his elbow. Jim pulled it away.

"Just listen to me for a second. Let me say what I have to and then I'll keep my goddamn mouth shut for the rest of the day."

Jim stood still, stared unflinchingly into his father's face. Bob relaxed his stance, breathed deeply, and continued.

"There's a lot you don't know. It's not as simple as you think. Your mom and I had problems. Big problems. Now, maybe I didn't handle them the right way, but it wasn't all me. Listen Jim, I'm not looking to badmouth your mother, so don't take this the wrong way. She was not an easy person to live with. She never accepted my golf. She didn't believe it was a real job. She wanted me to sell the driving range and get what she considered to be a real job."

"Did you ever think that maybe she was right? You were married with a kid. And, you never did make it as a pro."

"But Jim, if I hadn't given it a shot, I never would have known. I would have spent the rest of my days thinking that maybe, just maybe, I had what it took to be one of the great ones. And I would have resented her for the rest of my life. Would have blamed her for preventing me from finding out. And besides, I did all right with golf. Maybe not as a big name on the Tour, but I made some good money with my pro shop and lessons. Right now, I even own part of a country club. A nice one. Yeah, I did all right with the golf."

"You ran away when I was eight. Ran away from mom *and* me—and you never looked back—not once. And you say you did all right with golf. You must have, because country clubs don't come cheap. Mom and I sure as hell didn't see any of your profits."

"I know *now* that running away with that woman was the wrong choice. The relationship didn't last. But Jim, I was young. That woman—stupid as it might sound—believed in me. And I needed that back then."

"What about us? What mom and I needed?"

"I did send money, Jim. Regularly. And I paid your college tuition."

Jim was silent. His mother had never told him.

"Okay, let's say you did you send money. Why? To buy me off? To ease your conscience? How come I never heard from you? Never got a phone call or a fucking birthday card for Christ sakes."

Bob stood quietly for a minute. Jim searched his face. The old man looked frightened. Like a kid who got caught in a lie. Jim stared into those deep–set blue eyes. Clear, icy centers, surrounded by dark blue rings. And once again, memory eclipsed time as he remembered finding his six–year–old reflection in those same eyes.

"I don't have a good answer, Jim. The more time that passed, the harder it was to make contact."

"That's it? It was hard to make contact? Enough said. Come on, we're holding up play here."

Jim went back to the sight of his ball, took two left–handed practice swings and proceeded to hit the ball cleanly into the center of the fairway.

CHAPTER 35

Jim and his father were careful to avoid any more heated confrontations. Aside from the usual ritualistic golf etiquette—nice shot, good roll—the men did not speak to one another. Jim took an eight on fourteen and lost three strokes to his dad. The two stroke differential was maintained when both men bogeyed the par 3, 183 yard, fifteenth hole. Arnie followed Ralph's pre–Savage strategy and sat out fifteen. Gloria was more than happy to join him.

It was just past one o'clock—a few cottony clouds had moved into the western horizon—when they pulled up to the tee area of the Savage. The foursome ahead had already hit and were busy looking for a ball in the ravine off to the right of the fairway.

"What a sight," said Arnie, looking down the fairway. "Already, I had forgotten how huge that tree is."

"I've been to this spot so many times," said Bob. "I don't think I'll ever get used to the sight of that giant oak leaning over that pond."

"It is a beautiful spot," said Arnie. "It's a shame we can't pull up some folding chairs, drink some lemonade, and just look at it."

"I agree," said Gloria. "It seems like we always pass this spot too quickly."

"That's cause we're so uptight when we go by," added Arnie. "There *is* the business of trying to hit a golf ball down the fairway and over, around, or through that tree."

"Well, if nobody minds, I'm going to sit this hole out," said Gloria. "I'd just as soon watch you guys play."

"No problem," said Arnie. "I'm tempted to join you. But I can't resist taking a whack at it."

Arnie and Gloria continued their conversation. Bob walked over to Jim, who was swinging at dandelions with his 5–iron.

"Laying up?" asked Bob.

Jim took a couple of more swings without answering.

"You said you almost got there in two the other day."

Jim turned to his father, stared for a moment, and finally responded. "I thought I'd try something different today. This is only the second time I've played this hole. I'm not expecting to make par."

"Well, it's a smart play just the same. What club you hitting?"

"Five–iron."

"Good choice. You'll have a wedge to the pond, and then a medium–short iron over the top. That your strategy?"

"That's what I'll try. But, I already told you, I'm not expecting to make par."

"I still can't believe this hole was parred. That must have been something to witness."

"Yes, very impressive."

"Han's boy is a big, strong kid. To hit a 9–iron that far and that high takes some kind of power."

"John's a good player."

"You're a good player too, Jim. You've got a real nice game."

"I've only got two strokes on you."

"We're not as close as the score would indicate. With a little better management of your game, you'd have run away from me."

"Well, what can I tell you? This *is* my game. This is how I play."

"Bob," Arnie called from the tee. "It's clear for you to hit."

"Okay," Carlson answered, as he grabbed the driver from his bag.

"Hey," said Arnie. "You're goin' with the heavy artillery?"

"Might as well. Don't have a club in my bag that'll get me over the top of that tree."

Bob's drive traveled 240 yards, down the middle.

Jim motioned for Arnie to hit next. Arnie hit his 3-wood solidly, but the shot sailed right, and found the ground brush, just before the ravine.

"Give me a break!" exclaimed Arnie. "This hole should be illegal. I hit that ball damn well and it's buried, if not lost."

"You'll have a play from there," said Bob.

"If you can find it for me I might. For God's sake, I can lose a ball in the fairway, let alone in that thick stuff."

It now was Jim's turn to tee-off. He walked up with his 5-iron, set his Titleist in place, and stood behind the ball, in line with his target. He ignored the sight of the spectacular oak, instead, previewing in his mind's eye, the anticipated flight of the ball. Had to be straight. Distance was not important. He could hit it a little fat or thin—it didn't matter. As long as the ball stayed reasonably straight.

Jim stayed down, followed through nicely, and watched his ball sail. Starting a little right, the ball climbed and began to draw left just at the top of its arc. One-hundred, seventy-five yards from the tee, the ball landed in the left-center portion of the striped fairway.

"You're the man!" screamed Arnie.

"That was really pretty," said Gloria.

"Perfect play," added Bob.

The carts pulled out and began their descent down the fairway toward the giant oak tree.

"You're goin' to do it, Jimbo," said Arnie. "I know it."

"Don't count on it. My game's starting to fall apart. That four-teenth hole was pretty ugly. I just don't want to screw up and get another triple here. I've got to keep my ball dry."

"How many strokes do you have on him now?"

"Two. But if he's going for it, he'll probably end up in the drink."

"Unless he makes it."

Jim stopped the cart in the area of Arnie's ball, turned and looked at his friend. "Don't say that. Don't even think that. After trying to par this fucking hole for twenty years, my luck and today will be the day he finally makes it. What a nightmare that would be."

"Forget it. It's too late for him. He's not making it. Come on, help me find my ball."

After five minutes, Arnie's ball still could not to be found. Dog tired and plumb out of miracles, Arnie decided to join Gloria in the ranks of spectator. Behind the wheel of his cart, he raced by Bob and Gloria's cart and yelled, "You're a smart woman, Gloria. I finally got smart and picked up. This is great. No pressure. We'll just watch these guys break their backs and their hearts."

Gloria laughed.

Jim was out of the cart before it came to a full stop and grabbed the pitching wedge out from his bag. As he strolled toward his ball in the fairway, he thought that he had to be careful in this situation. About 130 to the pond. If he sculled the shot, it could fly into the water. He set up to his ball and double–checked his alignment. He wanted to stay on the left side of the fairway, and he had to stay down, not lift the club through impact. Two practice swings and Jim was ready.

Jim never saw the ball. He continued to stare at the spot where the ball had sat for seconds after impact.

"That's the one," shouted Arnie. "Looks like one of John's 9–irons."

"Nice lay–up," said Bob. "Very nicely done."

"What a great shot," said Gloria.

While Bob walked up to his ball, Jim sat in the cart with Arnie. "You're gonna do it, buddy."

Jim stared ahead, ignoring his friend's encouragement. "Let's see what club he uses. Probably a 2–iron. I don't think he could get there with a 3."

"Relax, Jim. Take a moment and just relax. Come on. You've got a big shot coming up."

"You're right," said Jim, as he sat back and took a deep, cleansing breath.

"That last shot was a beauty," said Arnie.

"Yeah, it was. I liked it."

"It really did look like one of John's shots on Friday."

"It didn't carry nearly as much as his did."

"Wonder what would happen if you had his gold ball."

"I wouldn't use it. That things twenty–years old. It can't possibly get the distance that the new designs get."

"John went the distance with it."

"Good for John. I'd have no use for it."

Suddenly Jim leaned forward. "Shit, it looks like he's using his 1–iron."

"Doesn't matter. He's not getting past that tree."

Bob soled his 1–iron behind the ball. He had a slight downhill lie. He opened the clubface and aimed left of the tree. The ball sat just inside his left heel. After a deep breath, a focus on the target, and forward press, he swung the long club back and exploded through the ball.

It smoked out low and left before rising into a second level of flight. Jim and Arnie leaned forward from their cart. Gloria took two steps toward her husband, who stood frozen at the finish of his swing. The ball continued to climb the tree's height, fading right, heading toward the hidden green. Just as Jim's shot had on Friday, the ball cleared the frontside of the oak before starting to bend. And, just like that shot, nobody saw the ball hit the tree and drop straight into the pond.

Again, it was the sound of surlyn against wood; the gulping splash that told the story.

"Jesus!" screamed Arnie. "Just like Jim's. That ball was there."

"That was one hell of a 1–iron," added Jim.

Gloria smiled and shrugged.

"Well, that's my best go at it," said Bob. "Can't hit it any better than that. Come on, Jim. Your turn. Let's see you knock it dead at the stick."

Jim was already holding his 7–iron. He walked up to his ball and looked into the heart of the giant oak that stood like a sentry guarding the Savage. How the hell did John hit over from this spot? And, could *he* possibly make it? The ball would have to rise fast and come down just as quickly. One advantage today was the upper tier pin placement. Jim had a little more distance to work with. But he also knew that if his ball rolled down to the lower tier, he'd never make it back up into the cup with one putt.

Jim took a final practice swing before standing in. He had wanted par badly on Friday, but today his old man was here to see him go for it. He should want it even more. But funny as it seemed to him, he really didn't care all that much. For the first time all day, making a shot was not that important to Jim.

Jim stared at the number on his ball, and just before he began his backswing, he heard in the distance the sound of a crow. The swing played out in slow motion. The way a life presumably

flashes by right before the instant of death, he was a young child
who adored his mother and worshipped his father, he was an
angry teen who already flirted with par and successfully seduced
any girl he desired. Jim was outside of his body watching himself
swing. And as soon as he felt the club make contact with the ball,
he knew it was good.

"Holy shit!" screamed Arnie. "It's going to make it."

The ball flew straight over the top of the oak tree and landed on
the back edge of the green. The ball's backspin created roll back
toward the flagstick. The ball stopped its motion two feet from
the cup, leaving Jim a routine, almost gimme, par putt.

"That was one heck of a shot," exclaimed Bob, shaking his
son's hand.

"That was spectacular, Jim," said Gloria. "I'm so happy for
you."

"Did I tell ya? Did I tell ya?" Arnie grabbed Jim around the
neck and slapped him on the chest. "I knew you were going to do
it. I told you it was your day!"

"I still have to make the putt, Arn." Jim attempted to remain
low–key and realistic, but his big smile betrayed his efforts.

He looked back at the green. "I should be able to nail that putt.
I'd better nail it. Come on, let's get going. I don't want to have to
think about it for too long."

Arnie motioned with his chin toward Bob and Gloria, and
whispered. "Hold on a minute. Your old man still has to drop and
hit up."

Bob walked from one side of the fairway to the other, looking
for an angle that would give him a decent path over the water and
under or around the oak. He turned to the others and mumbled,
"I could use your help right about here, Jim. Don't have a club in
my bag that could get the height to clear that tree." Finally dropping the ball in the center of the fairway, he continued in a barely

audible whisper, "You sure did hit one beauty of a shot there. A real beauty."

Arnie nudged Jim with his elbow, trying to get his attention, to get him to smile. Jim remained expressionless, arms crossed, watching his father get ready to play his fourth shot on the Savage.

Five–iron in hand, Bob Carlson aligned his stance left of the tree, and hit a three–quarter punch shot—the kind you might hit to advance the ball out from a wooded area. When you needed to keep the ball low.

The ball was hit cleanly, a good forty yards left of the flagstick, and settled just beyond pin–high, on the mounded area off to the side of the green. It was approximately the same spot where Jim's ball settled after his own disappointing plummet into the pond just two days earlier.

"Seems like I'm always settling for that play," said Carlson, shaking his head as he reached down to pick up and replace the large divot created by his shot. He tapped the turf with his right foot, took a moment to study the repair job, and proceeded to walk to his cart, still shaking his head.

Jim stared at his father, watching a film of himself. A replay of the desire, effort, disappointment, self–disdain that were a part of so much of his own time spent on the golf course. The old man's face was fraught with fear, his eyes glistened with moisture, and Jim heard unabashed sobbing, cries for help, ringing out from somewhere deep within himself. It was a visceral feeling, seemingly experienced in his stomach, like the queasiness that comes with a stomach bug. Jim couldn't quite recognize the source, but still he sensed that it came from a place beyond the confines of his physical being. Jim continued to study his father, and the putt that he would momentarily face, the putt of a lifetime, suddenly seemed meaningless. Jim watched his father climb into his cart, alongside his wife. When Gloria placed her hand on Bob Carlson's shoulder, Jim had to swallow hard in order to redirect the impulse to cry away from his eyes, down deep into a black empty place.

"You coming, Jim?"

Arnie's voice rocked Jim out of his trance. Like waking from a deep sleep, he had to lay out the events of the moment, of the past few days, of his entire life. Reality check. Perspective. He squinted up toward the oak and spotted his white ball sitting in the shadow of the Savage's red flag. Jim trotted to the cart, threw his 7–iron in his bag, grabbed his putter, jumped into the seat alongside Arnie.

"You okay, Jimbo? You look pale. You're not getting sick on me now...are you?"

Jim breathed deeply, felt a calmness working its way up his back, into his shoulders, down his arms, and into the hands that held his Titleist Bullseye. He looked down at the putter, licked his finger and scraped off a white smudge on its shiny black head, before looking up and meeting his friend's concerned gaze.

"Will you step on it please, Arn? I have a par putt to tap in."

CHAPTER 36

The carts circled the road that ran around the pond's perimeter and broke out into the clearing alongside the Savage's two–tiered green. Despite the clear blue skies, and brilliant, early afternoon sunshine, the giant oak's entangled mass of dense branches and thicket of deep green foliage which covered the limbs, almost entirely screened the sky's luminescence. Aside from mottled patches of light—shifting with the quiet, gentle breeze— the green's large surface was mostly dark. Jim's ball sat in line with the flagstick's pencil–shaped shadow, on the green's upper tier, no more than 18 inches above the hole. The bright white ball, sitting in relative darkness, appeared as a pale shade of gray.

When Jim and Arnie parked their cart on the path, just down the hill from the green, Bob was already surveying the sight and lie of his ball. Holding his sand–wedge, 7–iron, and putter, Carlson squatted like a baseball catcher, as he alternated glances at the thick rough that had entangled his ball, and then up at the path to the flagstick.

"Will you look at that guy," said Jim. "He never lets up. Probably figures he can hole this chip and still save bogey."

"And what's so bad about that, Jim? You've got to give the guy credit. He bears down on every shot. And it's not like he's grumpy when he misses. I think he's got a pretty classy demeanor out here."

"Well, if he does, it came late in life. When I was a kid, my mother and I couldn't go near him when he didn't play well. That much I *do* remember. And who knows what he's really thinking? For all we know, he'll take it out on Gloria when he's done."

"I don't think so, Jim. He just doesn't strike me that way. No, I think your old man's mellowed a bit. Mellowed a lot."

"Well, I've had enough of the psychobabble. It's his problem...not mine. His and Gloria's. I'm goin' to mark my ball."

Jim got out of the cart and circled an unnecessarily long path around the lower–tier, front edge of the green. He didn't want to interfere with his father's chip shot. He was hoping to avoid any interaction with his father until that putt hit the bottom of the cup. As he walked up the green, toward his ball, dime marker in hand, Jim suddenly stopped and turned to face his father who had just shouted something in his direction.

"What did you say?" asked Jim.

"I said you can take it away. That's good." Bob had elected to go with his sand–wedge, and was standing behind his ball, eyeing his target, clipping the high–cut rough with the lofted blade.

Jim remained frozen, his left hand on his hip, his right gripping his putter and holding it like a cane. "You're giving me a par putt? A par putt on the Savage?"

Bob smiled and made a sweeping motion with his right hand. "Come on, get that thing out of there. Great par."

Arnie and Gloria quietly approached from the carts, toward the fringe of the green.

Jim's jaw dropped, his brow curled as his gaze on his father intensified.

"Come on, Jim. Don't look a gift horse..."

Before Carlson could finish his sentence, Jim cut him off. "Do you think you're going to deny me the moment of sinking that putt?"

"That's not what I had in mind. That putt's a legitimate gimme. You made the par. You want to putt out...go ahead. I didn't mean anything by it."

This time Jim said nothing. He walked up to his ball, placed a shiny Roosevelt dime, heads up, just behind his Titlesist, picked up the ball, pocketed it, and back–stepped away from the spot, already beginning to study the line of the one–and–a–half footer.

Bob looked at his son for a moment longer, appeared ready to speak, but remained silent. Shaking his head, he stepped into the stance for his chip, his cheeks puffed out as he exhaled, and he took a full swipe at the ball with his wedge. The blade of the club came up covered with grass like a machete, but he stayed with the shot and the ball flopped straight up into the air, right on line with the pin. The ball landed, carving a dent in the green's surface just a few feet below the hole. It checked up nicely, leaving Carlson with a straight–ahead, uphill, eight foot putt.

"Beautiful shot from that lie," said Arnie, as he walked into the center area of the green. "What a touch. I was just thinking before you hit that, how easy it would've been to shank that into the pond. Would have been an easy play for me."

"Nice shot, hon," said Gloria, resuming her customary position in the gallery, at Arnie's side.

"Thanks." Carlson wore a serious expression as he walked over to mark his ball, pull out the pin, place it gently on the green, and lie his two irons across it. He went behind his ball, squatted, took less time than usual to study the putt, and replaced the marker with his ball. Two practice strokes, he placed his putter behind the ball, and took a smooth rhythmic stroke. Head down, blade following through to the target, the uphill putt was struck hard, hit the back of the cup, bounced up an inch, and dropped dead–center.

"Great up and in," said Arnie. "That was as impressive a golf display as I've seen all day. What an up and in."

Gloria kissed her husband on the cheek and winked at him. Bob did not smile and whispered, "Let's move aside and let Jim make this putt."

Jim was squatting behind his ball marker, his putter laid flat on the ground along the line from himself to the hole. Even though there was no discernible sunshine in his field of vision, his left hand was across his brow. Although he gave the appearance of studying the green, Jim had not yet begun formal study of the putt.

As impressive a display as Arnie had seen all day. Leave it to his old man, thought Jim. How in hell did he get down in two from where he was? Jim thought about it, and as much as he hated to admit it, he had to give the old man credit. What concentration. What intensity and desire.

Jim walked around to the other side of the hole, the spot where his father had just putted from, and began to seriously consider his putt. From this side, the green's downward slope was more apparent. Shit, he'd almost rather have his father's eight–footer going up the hill than his little downhill teaser. Jim felt a small legion of butterflies hatch in his gut. Blood flow redirected toward his body's core, he felt a rubbery kind of numbness in his arms and legs. Needing to move, he stood and walked back to the other side of he hole.

One–and–a–half feet. Eighteen inches. Eighteen fucking inches that suddenly appeared longer than the walk from the driving range to the first tee. It was downhill all right, downhill with a slight right–to–left break. Jim figured he should either knock it stiff into the center of the cup, or nudge it gently to the right edge.

Only eighteen inches...no need to get too cute reading break. Can't read any more than right edge. But, if he struck it too firmly, it could hit the cup's right edge, rim the hole and pop out. Jim had experienced his share of those heartbreaking rim jobs.

He had to make a choice. Either firm–center, or ease–up–right–edge. The grain was not a factor in that it ran straight down along the putt's path, toward the pond. But this could only make the putt that much quicker. If he aimed right edge and the ball slid by the hole, it would probably end up right about at the spot his father putted from. A good eight feet away. But what did that matter? If he didn't make par, he might as well make a double. Who cares?

Jim began his preshot routine. Three pendulum strokes while he stood behind the ball before he stepped into the putt. Firm and dead–center it would be. If there was any break, he'd hit right through it. Jim looked up and saw Arnie, his father, and Gloria standing and watching. No movement, like statues. He glanced to their left and saw the sun's golden rays gleaming across the surface of the Savage's pond. He was on a giant stage, encased by earth, sky, and foliage, against a backdrop of the sounds of rioting birds, crickets, the intermittent wheezy swirl of the breeze, as it passed through the mass of branches that surrounded him.

Jim stepped up to his ball, left foot first, then right, took a deep breath, let the air out of his knees. His head was directly over the ball, and he realized for the first time ever, that when a putt was this close, there was no need to shift his glance from the ball to the target. The ball was close enough so that both places were within his peripheral field of vision. A gimme, thought Jim, as he placed the putter's black blade just behind his ball. As much as he wished this putt was already in the cup, no way could he have picked up and rightfully accepted par. *Especially* not on the Savage, *especially* not from his father. No, he'd make par and he'd do it on his own. The way he'd been forced to do everything where his old man was involved.

As Jim brought the putter back, he suddenly became aware of his body. The contracted muscles within the sockets of his eyes, his neck serving as support for his head, over the ball, away from his body. His arms hanging from his shoulders, his hands joining and extending down through his putter to form a "Y." For a brief moment, exactly at that instant of the indiscernible pause—when the putter finishes the backward portion of the stroke, before it begins its movement toward the ball—Jim experienced a sudden sense of confusion, a lack of focus, a rush of uncertainty. He wanted to abort the stroke, to step out of the putt and begin his routine again. But it was too late. As his putter followed–through the ball, he knew he had hit it sweet. Too sweet. The ball flew off the putter's blade, briefly peeked into the right side of the cup, and blew past its intended point of destination by a good six feet.

Jim never heard Gloria's gasp, or Arnie exclaim "Oh, no." He never saw his father stare quietly down at his feet. Never looking up, no expressed reaction of frustration or disgust, Jim walked to the other side of the hole, where his ball now sat, and quickly stroked it into the heart of the cup. He bent over, retrieved his ball, replaced the flagstick, and walked over to his father and handed him his 7–iron and wedge.

"Tough break," said Bob.

Jim shrugged. "It happens. I'll live."

"I'm so sorry, Jim," said Gloria. "I thought you had that putt."

Jim shrugged again, turned, and walked toward the carts.

Arnie followed closely behind.

CHAPTER 37

About thirty minutes after Jim's momentous miss, the carts made their final trek of the weekend up the hill from the green at 18 toward the magnificent castle of a clubhouse at Wild Links. A small cluster of gray–white, wispy cirrus streaked the otherwise sun–filled blue sky that framed the massive red–topped, tan brick structure. The final two holes of the day's round were played in strained silence. Jim's usually powerful swing was reduced to a lazy wave at the ball. He pushed his tee–shot OB on 17, taking a triple on the hole, and finished off the weekend's golf by teeing off on the lengthy home hole with his 5–iron. He sunk a twenty–foot putt to end the day with a double.

Bob Carlson played out like a golfing robot. Fairways and greens, two natural pars, he finished the day scoring two strokes better than his son. Arnie and Gloria, their scorecards already containing several Xs denoting holes that were not completed, did not pick up a club on the final two holes.

As both carts pulled into the parking area, near the bag storage rack, Arnie turned to his young partner and asked, "What do you say we grab a bite. We still have some time to kill before we have to be at the airport. What do you say, Jimbo?"

Jim, hands on the cart's steering wheel, looked left at his father and Gloria. She was removing some trash from the cart, while Bob was busy unstrapping their bags and propping them up onto the rack. "I don't know, Arn," he whispered. "I really don't want to have to hang with them anymore. Maybe we should just head out. Grab a bite at the airport."

Just then, Bob cut in. "If you fellas want to have a bite, go on ahead. Gloria and I won't be able to join you. We have plans for an early dinner, and I have to track down Hans and talk to him about some business matters."

Gloria offered a tight-lipped smile, her eyes in a half-closed peer that was laden with regret.

Arnie looked at Jim. "What do you say. Hungry?"

Jim froze, then suddenly jumped out of the cart. "Maybe just something cold to drink." He put his hand out in the direction of Gloria and said, "Nice playing with you."

Gloria shook his hand and replied, "It was such an unexpected pleasure to finally have a chance to meet you, Jim."

"Good round today." Jim offered his hand to his father.

"Just one moment, Jim. Could I have a minute of your time? There's a couple of things I want to say before we head off."

Jim looked around and stammered, "Well, I know you've got things to do...and we *do* have a plane to catch." Jim glanced at his watch, looked at Arnie, then back at his dad. "I suppose I have a minute. What do you want to talk about?"

"Not here." Bob put his hand on Jim's shoulder and looked at Gloria, "See if you can track down Hans. Tell him I'll meet him at his office in about fifteen minutes. Jim, let's go have a seat on that bench." Bob pointed to the wooden bench by the putting green. The sight of the two men's reunion just one day earlier. Most of the golfers who would tee it up at Wild Links on this day were already well into their rounds and the putting green was unoccupied.

Jim followed his father down a short and narrow dirt path that had been burned into the rich green grass that surrounded the clubhouse. Bob took a seat on one end of the bench. Jim elected to remain standing, his arms crossed, waiting for his father to speak first.

Bob Carlson looked down at his hands, rubbed a callous beneath his wedding band with his right thumb. He looked up at his son, his chest rose and fell as he breathed deeply. "I don't exactly know what I want to say, Jim. I don't have to tell you that I'm not the world's greatest communicator."

Jim maintained a silent stare, arms still crossed, his right foot slid in and out of his untied white and black saddle DryJoy.

"Jim, I still can't believe that I ran into you here. I think it still hasn't really hit me. Like I'm in a some kind of a state of shock or something."

"You don't have to tell me how weird it's been." Jim watched his father. A bundle of nerves. Clearing his throat. Playing with his ring. Rubbing the side of his neck. Straightening his collar. He could have said something to help him out. To make the conversation flow more smoothly. But, he found that looking down at his father, watching him squirm, hearing him stumble for the right words was calming, if not empowering. It was as if all the nervous energy that radiated from Bob Carlson was sucked up by Jim—like smoke toward an air vent—and converted into some kind of magical tranquilizing vapor. The more agitated his father became, the calmer Jim felt.

Bob placed both his palms flat against the bench at his sides. Finally, he stopped stirring, and looked up at his son. "Is there any way I can ever hope to see you again?"

Jim broke out of his relaxed posture, whirled around, with both hands pushed the sides of his hair back. "Jeez. What the hell do you want from me?"

Bob left his seat and walked up to face Jim's back. "I don't want anything *from* you, Jim. The last thing I want to do is to hurt you.

Anymore than I already have. It's just that I've thought so much about you, for so long, and now that I've seen you..." Bob backed away, turned around so that the men were now back to back.

Jim was the first to turn. His father's arms were wrapped around his torso, his head was down, his back hunched over. The man with the tanned and still toned arms, with the beautiful, athletic golf swing gave the appearance of a weak, frail, beaten old man. Jim thought about his father's question. Can he see me again? What would *that* be like? This man isn't my father. He's a stranger. So much had happened since I was a kid. For God sakes, *I grew up!* Mom and I went through so much while he was trying to get a golf career going.

Bob turned and spoke again. This time more slowly, calmly. "I know it won't be easy, Jim. I know how damn uncomfortable you've been around me today. And who can blame you? But maybe if we gave it some time. Maybe it would get easier."

"But, what's the point? I don't know you. Why put the effort into something that's not going to mean anything anyway. I've got mom, I've got Arnie, I've got a few friends. I can live without a father. Shit, I'm an expert at it. One thing I can do damn well is not have a father."

"You do a lot of things well, Jim. You're a college graduate, you've got yourself a professional career. And Jim, I've got to say that you're one hell of a golfer. I might not have made it as a touring pro, but I've been around the game my whole life and I know the golf swing. And yours is one of the prettiest, most fundamentally solid swings I've seen...amateur or professional."

Jim sighed and walked to the edge of the practice putting surface, stopped and turned. "I know I can hit a golf ball. So what? I hit thousands and thousands of balls as a young kid. I kept hitting balls after you left. Played on the middle school and high school teams. But it's just a game. Just a goddamn game. I wasn't good enough to get a Division I scholarship. And I definitely wasn't going to do what you did. Spend my life chasing some stupid dream."

Carlson walked closer to his son. "I'm sorry you think my dream was stupid. I don't know...maybe you're right. Maybe is was stupid. But, it was something that seemed so right at the time." Bob shook his head and mockingly laughed. "I now know that leaving you and your mom was a mistake. Big time mistake. But Jim, don't be so quick to put down your golf game. Sure, it's a game. But I watched you out there today. I watched you do some incredible things. Pull off some amazing shots, pull out pars when it didn't seem possible. And I could see that you know it takes something special, something beyond just whacking a ball to make those things happen."

"I blew the only par that really meant something. Think that was special?"

"We've all done those kind of things, Jim. It just seems big to you because it happened on the Savage. As far as I'm concerned, you parred that damn hole. You made the tough shots, some impossible shots. Shots that I've *never* been able to pull off. So you yipped a gimme. I still say you parred that hole. You wouldn't take the putt from me, but like it or not, I gave it to you and in *my mind*, you made that par. Yes sir, in my mind, you parred the Savage."

Jim watched his father get worked up. To react more excitedly than he had all day. For a moment, Jim felt like a little kid. A child who backs down when his parent asserts their authority. Jim looked into his father's eyes. Those blue eyes. The one constant, the one piece of physical evidence that traversed time. When Jim let himself go, when he allowed himself to dissociate from the moment, from the context of his entire life, this man could be his father. This man *was* his father.

"Give yourself some credit, Jim. Don't be like me. Always down on yourself. Always looking at the negative. Be proud of who you are. God knows you deserve to be." Bob's voice faded, as if his battery was winding down. "So what do you say, Jim. Is there a chance we can keep in touch? Here..." Carlson reached into his back pocket and pulled out his wallet. He unfolded it, reached into one of its pockets, pulled out a business card and handed it to his son.

Jim read the navy blue lettering on the gray linen card. *Bob Carlson...Director of Golf & Head Professional...Omni Windham Resort...West Palm Beach...Lessons by appointment.* He looked up and said, "What do you want me to do with this. Call for a tee–time?"

"If you want to...I'd love to have you came down as my guest. You and Arnie, or anyone you want to bring along."

Jim fanned the card, scraping it against it his left palm. He turned away, walked to the bench, and sat down. Jim thought of saying yes, or at least maybe. But then he thought it through more carefully. Suppose he was to go down for a visit. Does he really want to spend time with the man who broke his mother's heart, the man he had hated for seventeen years? It was so tense, such a drag playing just one round of golf with him and Gloria. Yes, and Gloria. Where did she fit into all of this? Jim considered leaving it up in the air. Of telling his old man that he had to think about it, and just ripping up the damn card and forgetting the whole deal. It was, after all, a pretty good bet that his father would never fol-low things up from his end. Never did before, why should now be any different?

Jim felt the butterflies from the 16th green awaken in his stom-ach. The butterflies that signaled dread, that marked indecision. Jim remembered that 18 inch putt. Right–edge–soft or dead–cen-ter–firm. Jim figured it was his lack of resolution that cost him that putt. He vacillated between two strategies and paid the price. Indecision. A common malady in the mental side of golf. And, thought Jim, in the head game of life. Jim jumped up from the bench. His father stood facing him, just a few feet away.

He handed Bob Carlson back his business card and boldly stated, "Thanks for the offer, but I'm going to pass."

CHAPTER 38

Arnie was about to reach the climactic moment in his story about the time he could've, should've broken 100 for the first time, when he noticed, just over Gloria's left shoulder, Bob walking up the hill. Alone.

"Oh, here comes your husband." Arnie looked both ways and spotted Jim about to enter the snack bar. "I wonder how things went."

Gloria raised her shoulders and brow in a silent gesture that said, "Who knows?"

Arnie approached and met Bob. "How's Jim doing?" He glanced back at the snack bar entrance. No sign of Jim.

"He said he'll meet you inside," said a weary Carlson. "You know, Arnie...that kid is one tough nut to crack. Real stubborn."

"It's like I said, Bob..."

Before Arnie could finish, Carlson finished for him. "I know, Arnie. He's a lot like me. I know."

Gloria walked up behind her husband, put her hand on his back, attempted to establish eye contact. "You okay, hon? You look upset. Did your talk make matters worse?"

Bob pulled away from Gloria, settled alongside his golf bag, and began to undo his shoes. "Nah, how could things be any worse than they were, than they are. The kid hates my guts and who the hell can blame him. He basically wants nothing to do with me."

"Don't be so quick to conclude anything," cut in Arnie. "I know Jim...better than you do. He needs time to take it all in. Look how much has happened in only a couple of days. For Christ sakes, what do you expect? Give him time. You never know. Maybe he'll come around with time."

Carlson stared at Arnie for a few seconds before responding. "I'd love to believe that. But, to tell you the truth, I don't think so. He wouldn't even take my card." Bob found the business card his son had rejected in his right pocket, pulled it out, and looked at it. "I tried to give him this and he wouldn't even take it. At least if he had my address and phone number..."

"He can find you if he wants to," said Arnie. "Trust me...it's not impossible. I'll keep after him about it."

Carlson looked up to meet Arnie's gaze, the pace of his speech quickened. "Would you do that, Arnie? It would mean so much to me if you did."

"Just don't forget that it works both ways. One of Jim's biggest peeves is that you never tried to contact him. It wouldn't kill you to call him, or maybe write to him on occasion. Yeah, I'll try to help on my end, but there's a lot you can do as well."

Bob opened his mouth as if ready to protest, but stopped himself, sighed, and turned away. "You're right, Arnie. But you know what? The thought of giving him a call scares the hell out of me. Some father, huh?"

"But you *can* drop him a note from time to time," said Gloria. "Or a card at Christmas or on his birthday."

"You're right. You and Arnie both. And Arnie..." Bob extended his hand to Arnie who accepted it firmly. "I don't know how I can ever repay you for all you've done. For Carol, but mostly for Jim. I know how you've been there. Have known it for years. You've been more of a father to my son than I have. God bless you, Arnie."

Arnie held onto Bob's hand. "I've only done what I wanted to. I'm not as unselfish as you might think, Bob. I got plenty out of my side of the deal. Believe me." Arnie again glanced in the direction of the snack bar. "I better go join Jim." Arnie released Carlson's hand and extended it in the direction of his wife. "Gloria…"

"It's been such a pleasure, Arnie. I don't know how I would have gotten through the day without you. I think I better stick to courses that are a little less challenging. More my speed."

"What are you saying, Gloria? That you're grateful for the companionship of a golfer as inept as myself? Is that what you're saying?"

"Well…misery does love company." Gloria suppressed her grin before breaking into a laugh. "Come on, Arnie. You're a beginner, I've played all my life. You'll be a solid player in a year or two. For me…well, for me it's hopeless. What I meant to say was that it was a pleasure to play with a gentleman such as yourself. Someone who can enjoy the game *when things don't go according to plan*." Gloria sneered at her husband, who also broke down and laughed.

"Whatever, Gloria. I think I know what you mean." Arnie offered Gloria his most skeptical facial gesture, then peeked at his watch. "Better get moving. Time to see how Mr. Intensity, Jr. is holding up."

CHAPTER 39

Arnie spotted Jim seated alone at a table for two by the far wall. He was eating an oversized chocolate chip cookie, on the table in front of him was a large iced tea. The snack bar was emptier than it had been at any time during the weekend. It felt stuffy, as if the air conditioning had been turned off. Despite the grill's inactivity, the snack bar's signature odor of grease, fat, and smoke was as strong as ever.

Arnie went directly to Jim who looked up and said, "This might break your heart, Arn. But they're out of chili dogs. Nothing left but some cellophane–wrapped sandwiches. I wouldn't touch them. They look like they've been sitting there for days."

Arnie looked back at the service counter. "Not even any pizza?"

Jim smiled. "Sorry, Arn. You *could* have a bite of my cookie."

Arnie was back in a flash with a turkey and cheese sandwich, two packets of spicy mustard, a large Diet Coke, and a shiny, red Macintosh apple. He removed the food from his tray and bit open one of the mustard packets. "So, how you doing, Jimbo? Had enough golf?"

"That's for sure." Jim looked at and rubbed a blister that had formed under the pinkie of his left hand. "Think I could put the sticks away for awhile. I'm feeling pretty golfed out at the moment."

Arnie shoved half of a half of his sandwich into his mouth, wiped some mustard off his lip with a napkin, and took a long and hard sip of his soda. Hurrying to finish chewing the contents in his mouth, he swallowed and said, "I haven't had a chance to talk to you about the Savage. I didn't want to bother you out there. Wanted to give you time to recover. Can only imagine how you felt. So, how you doing with it all?"

"What...with missing that putt? I guess I'm kind of disappointed. But you know, Arnie...it's not as bad as you'd think. I don't know why, but it doesn't make all that much difference to me. So, I missed a putt. And even if I did make it...what then? It's not like I'd be financially independent. Or, like I'd be happy all the time. My life wouldn't be all that different. So I'd be able to say...*I parred the Savage.* Sure, it'd be nice, but it's just not as big a deal as I thought it would be. No, Arn, I'm not all that upset."

Arnie already polished off his sandwich and was rolling the Macintosh in his hands. "Jim, I'm proud of you. To come that close, miss, and take it in stride. I must say that I'm really impressed. You've come a long way, my man. Really matured."

"Thanks, Arn. But it's no big deal. It's just the way I feel."

"Well, it's still good to see you realize that you're more than your golf game."

Jim smiled and stood up. "I'm getting a refill on the iced tea. Want anything?"

"No thanks. I'm set."

Arnie sat back and took a bite of the sweet and juicy apple. He thought about how calm Jim appeared. Then he thought about his own golf game. How up and down *he* became in response to this wonderful, crazy, sometimes cruel game. Arnie turned, looked at Jim by the service counter, and studied his lean, well–proportioned physique. Jim was a golfer, an athlete. So was Bob. Arnie could play the game for twenty years, could practice all the time, and

he'd never be a great player. Never *was* much of an athlete. Arnie
looked down and saw the roll of flab that swelled over his belt. He
pinched it. He knew that he wasn't in terrible shape for his age, but
Arnie never felt good about his body.

Somehow golf had entered his life with the promise of renewed
hope. When he hit the ball straight and sweet, he was effective,
competent, a stud. But on the downside, when he flubbed one fat,
and the vibrations flew from the earth, through the shaft of his
club, and into his hands and arms, it sent shockwaves of shame to
the core of his being. "Good to see you realize you're more than
your golf game." Arnie replayed the comment he just made to Jim
and recognized the hypocrisy. It appeared that student was outdis-
tancing teacher, and Arnie realized that he better get with the pro-
gram. More than your golf game. Damn straight, thought Arnie.
Wake up and get a fucking life. Wake up and see the wonderful
life that is yours already. A life that's flying by with no regard for
your childish whining and foolish self–pity.

When Jim returned, Arnie tossed his half eaten apple onto a
paper plate, and asked, "And what about the little talk you had
with your father. What was that like?"

"He wants to see me again."

"Yeah, and..."

"Come on, Arnie. Why would I want to see him again? He's a
stranger. No, actually he's more than a stranger. He's a person
who shafted me and my mother. Why should I suddenly play
father and son with him? So *he* can feel better about himself? I
don't think so."

Arnie sucked on his straw until he was slurping ice water and
air. He stirred the ice around in the cup and poured a couple of
cubes into his mouth. "I understand how you feel, Jim. And even
though I don't think your father's a bad guy, I can't say that I
blame you for not wanting to see him."

Jim nodded, crossed his arms, leaned back, and peered out the window that he last looked through during Thursday's thunderstorm.

Arnie looked at Jim and was again reminded of the child he used to know. So many days that Jim obediently sat in his office, doing his homework, waiting for his mother to finish for the day. Back then, Arnie was not much older than Jim is now. Ryan was just a baby. Arnie remembered feeling sorry for Jim, sorry that he had to grow up without a father. Arnie always took comfort in the fact that he would continue to be there for his own son. But was he?

Arnie's father never strayed, was home each and every night. But all Arnie remembered of those days, was his father picking fights with his mother, of the old man in tee–shirt and boxers, snoring on the sofa. Arnie didn't know his father. In fact, Arnie's most vivid memory of the man was the process of his dying. In the hospital, helping his mother change his clammy bedshirt, feeling his frail, bony frame resting limply against him. Was it any different with Ryan, thought Arnie? Arnie always assumed he was a good dad because he worked hard and financially supported his family. In his heart, Arnie knew he would never abandon them. But, was that enough? It started with Michelle. She was a warm, loving, even–tempered woman. Arnie loved her, but didn't always let her know it. So often, he'd be driving home from work, thinking about how lucky he was to have her, about how much he loved her. He would feel like buying her something. A bracelet, a blouse, one perfect, long–stemmed, red rose. But something would happen when he stepped foot in the door. He would get snappy, feel annoyed, be critical. Just like my dad, thought Arnie. Just like my dad.

It was easy with Lisa. A pretty, loving, little girl who was intensely attached to her mother. She was more than satisfied with her daily allotment of time with her dad. "Look at my Barbie's new outfit." "I'm going to draw you a picture." "My teacher's going to have a baby." All that was required of Arnie was a smile, a hug, any acknowledgment that he was her dad and was interested in what she had to say.

But then there was Ryan. He always looked to Arnie for a kind of approval that Arnie somehow could not deliver. There was a wall there, and before this moment, Arnie never saw the similarities between the relationship with *his* father and his relationship with his son. The wall between Bob Carlson and Jim was easy to identify and explain. But, thought Arnie, such a wall—although less apparent—can also be built and remain destructively present between a father and son living under the same roof.

Bud and Ralph said to get him into golf while he's young, and Arnie was going to do it. Ryan was going to know he had a father. Already well into adolescence and rapidly separating from his parents into a world of peer relations, cars, the hope and the promise of love, Arnie swallowed hard, his eyes moistened as he realized that there still was time. Arnie couldn't give himself the credit, but by the grace of God, he knew what he had to do. And miracle of miracles, there was still time to get it done.

"Did he say anything to you?"

Arnie was jolted awake by the sound of Jim's voice. "Who, your father?"

Jim nodded and said, "Yeah, my dad."

"No, not really. Just that he was hoping he could see you again. That's all."

"And what did you say?"

"What could I have said, Jim? I told him that maybe with some time, things might change."

"Why did you say that?"

"Well, it *is* possible. Don't you think? I mean…anything's possible, isn't it?"

Jim did not answer the question. Elbow on the table, chin resting on his fist, his trance–like gaze floated from Arnie to somewhere beyond.

Arnie picked up his apple. Areas he had bitten had already turned brown. He moved it toward his mouth, then threw it back onto the plate. He looked at his watch. "Shit, it's past 3:30 already. I want to wash up, we've still got to catch the shuttle, should be at the airport within a couple of hours."

"We've got plenty of time, Arn. Don't get neurotic on me now. The shuttle comes at twenty past the hour. We can take the 4:20 and make it with time to spare. You'll even have time to buy your kids something at the airport gift shop."

"Good idea, Jim. Tell you what. I'm going to make a call. Haven't spoken to the family in a couple of days. I want to make sure they realize when I'll be home tonight. Where should we meet?"

Jim looked out the window. "It's such a beautiful day. I think I'll just go outside and relax. Get one last dose of this ocean air." Jim looked at his watch, pulled his chair away from the table. "Meet you by the golf bags, outside the pro shop, at 4:00?"

Arnie was already up, cleaning the trash from the table.

"See you then, Jimbo. See you then."

CHAPTER 40

Jim wandered out of the snack bar, behind the clubhouse, into the courtyard. This was the place. The place where John and Tina were married, the place where he had seen his father for the first time in seventeen years. Twenty–four hours ago, when he and Arnie arrived for the wedding, his father had been a vague, bitter memory. Now, only a day later, his father was a part of his reality. A physical presence in his life once more. And as much as Jim wanted to forget the events of the past day, he could not get the old man's face out of his mind.

The late afternoon sun hovered above the tall trees and traced gray shadows across the flower gardens. The dissembled sections of white trellises, still stitched with peach satin ribbon, leaned against the tan brick building. Jim picked up a folding chair, opened it, and sat in the middle of the courtyard—eyes closed, the sun warm against his upturned face. He breathed deeply and tried to make some sense out of all that had happened.

My father. Bob Carlson—the same Bob Carlson I played 18 holes of golf with, that I was just talking to by the putting green. My father. No, it couldn't be. I haven't had a father since I was a little kid. Had any of this really happened? Or was he dreaming? Jim's mind was a swirling vortex of faces, feelings, events, emotions. No beginning, no end. A frenzied spin of twenty–five years of living that whirled in an orbit that designed itself.

But the truth came thundering back. Bob Carlson was real all right, and Jim knew with absolute certainty, that his life would never be the same again. He sighed. It was no use. Trying to make sense out of any of it at this moment. Exhausted, he closed his eyes once more, listened to the recurrent rush of waves rasp across the sand only a few hundred yards away. Savored the touch of the warm, moist sea breeze against his skin. Slowly, he began to relax, to breath deeply, to drift.

"Jim."

Jim jumped when he heard the voice. "Hi, Mr. Keeler."

"Sorry, Jim. Didn't mean to startle you."

Hans Keeler pulled his wheelchair closer.

"I just spoke with your dad, Jim. Heard about your experience out there today. On the Savage. That was some accomplishment. Getting it so close in three."

"But I missed the putt."

"Yeah, I realize that. But still...to get it that close. You've got a game, young man. One hell of a game."

"Thank you."

"Did John tell you about the time he missed a two–footer for par?"

"On the Savage?"

"That's right, on the Savage."

"No, he didn't."

"It was just two years ago. I think almost to the day. I was out there with him." Keeler smiled when he saw the look of surprise on Jim's face. "No, I wasn't playing. I just ride the course every so often. Just to experience the flow of a round of golf. I'll admit, it's sometimes frustrating not to be able to join in and play, but it's nice just to get out there and feel it all. You know the highs and lows, the beauty of the surroundings. Everything."

"When John missed his putt, did he hit three 9–irons to the green? The way he did on Friday?"

"Yes, he did. But he didn't use the gold ball or that old hick-ory–shafted 9–iron. He just recently got it in his head to use them on the Savage. Still, on that day, he hit three beautiful shots. Left himself two feet above the hole. Just like you did. The pin was also on the upper tier that day."

"What happened?"

"It's hard to say. It seems like he got too cute with the putt. Read too much break, took too much time standing over the ball. Anyway, he pushed it right of the hole, about four feet past. Missed the putt coming back, too. Wound up with a double."

"Was he very upset about it?"

"Seems like he was more upset about disappointing me than with his own situation. But I was so proud of the kind of man he had grown up to be. Could have cared less about the putt. And besides, I myself played the course all the time, for years, and never got that close to parring the Savage. If anything, I always wondered if my being out there wasn't the reason he missed that putt. At that time, it was less than a year since John showed up at Caramus. And he sure wasn't used to having me be around when he had to make a tough putt. I figured I had no business being there."

"Did John feel that way?"

"Actually not. John handled it really well. The way he figured it...it wasn't his time. He figured that he just wasn't ready to par the Savage."

"I can relate to that. It sounds kind of similar to my experience."

"That's not where the similarities end, Jim. I just got through talking to your dad. I guess he told you that he and I are good friends. Have been for some years now. And believe me, the situations are more similar than you might imagine them to be."

"In some ways. But, there are also big differences. You and John have chosen to be together. Meeting my dad here was an amazing fluke."

"You're right about that. I just can't get over the coincidence. That you two would meet here. When I met you on Friday, I had no idea that you were Bob's son."

"How could you have known?" Jim stood up, arms folded, and walked a few steps before stopping. "I've been listening to the surf, but I didn't realize you can see the ocean from here."

"Yeah, you can catch a piece of it from this spot."

"This is a beautiful place, Mr. Keeler. A great golf course, but far more than that."

"Thank you, Jim. We like it."

"Are John and Tina going to settle here?"

"If I have anything to say about it they will. But I can't count on it. John's a wanderer. Always has been."

Keeler wheeled toward the flower garden and spoke with his back to Jim. "When I look at these flowers, I can't help but think of another meeting between father and son. John's and mine. You know, we were reunited after not seeing each other for thirteen years."

Keeler turned and faced Jim again. "Must make you wonder how a father can cut off from his son."

"Yeah, it does. My father couldn't even explain it."

"Your father's not very good at that kind of thing."

Keeler wheeled until he was opposite Jim, a few feet away.

"Maybe I can help you understand. He's talked to me quite a bit about you. I also think I've made a lot of the same kind of mistakes your dad did."

Jim looked at Keeler, silently for a moment, before speaking. "You and John have a close relationship. It could never be that way with my dad and me. We're strangers. He didn't *want* to run into me. It was a total accident."

"John and I ran into each other by accident too. And it wasn't my doing."

"What happened?"

"Well, I left John and his mother when he was eight. Came to this country to try and make it on the PGA Tour. I was a self–centered young man in those days. I'll admit that I thought about John sometimes, a lot of the time, but I just never made the effort to contact him. I was afraid. If enough time passes, sometimes it's easier to just let things go."

"How did you and John wind up together at Caramus?"

"That was John's doing. His mother told him I spent a lot of time in this area, and he decided to come and settle here. Did he tell you about how he met Tina?"

Jim shook his head.

"Tina's father has managed Wild Links for me since I bought it in 1981. I never could have made it without him. Especially when the multiple sclerosis got worse. Tina and her sister, Debra, were just kids back then. Beautiful little girls. Beautiful women now. Well, after their mother died in 1980, it was tough. Two young girls being brought up by a single dad. But, the three of them came to live here on the island. It was good for them, and just what I needed, too. Those little girls really kept our spirits up."

"Where does John come in?"

"A few years back, Tina met John at the club where he worked and they started dating. We needed someone to help with the groundskeeping, so Tina brought John by to meet her dad and me. I guess you can figure out the rest."

"So your meeting John was a coincidence?"

"That's right. Maybe not as unlikely as you running into your dad. It was probably only a matter of time before John would have found me anyway. But I know that if he hadn't come looking for me, I would never have seen my son as a grown man. Getting to know each other after all the time we lost is the best thing that's ever happened to me. I now have a son, a wonderful daughter–in–law, and who knows, maybe I'll have grandchildren someday. I think God's been looking out for me. I've made so many mistakes, and still have so much to be grateful for. I'm a very fortunate man."

Jim was silent. He stood and walked to the other side of the courtyard. He wondered how *his* father really felt about crossing paths with his son. Grateful? Guilty? Happy? Numb? For as long as he could remember, Jim had wanted to know all about his father. How he thought, looked, laughed. All Jim ever knew for certain was what his mother had told him. That Bob Carlson had fallen in love with another woman, and had chosen her over their family. Jim hadn't questioned it. But the tuition…she'd never told him about that. Still, the rest of the facts marked a hurtful truth. All those years without a Christmas card, a call on his birthday. Nothing.

Early on, the disappointments and longing were festering wounds—resistant even to his mother's efforts to heal them. But gradually, the scar cover grew tough, unbroken, unfeeling. Bob Carlson had abandoned them. Period. The issue was dead. Settled. Or was it? Thinking of the incredible events of the last few days— seeing his father, watching John become the first to par the Savage, *his* putt on the Savage, and now, listening to Hans Keeler. Jim wasn't sure that anything was settled.

Jim glanced around the wedding site. He saw where his father had proposed the toast. Heard the familiar voice from his child- hood. Recalled the sight of him doing yardwork. Remembered the criticism. A different place. A different life. Once upon a time when a little boy *did* love his father.

"Jim, I'm going to leave you now, but there's something I'd like to give you first."

Keeler wheeled to Jim, reached into his left pocket, and pulled out the gold ball.

"Before John left on his honeymoon, he gave this back to me. Said that since he'd parred the Savage, he didn't need it anymore. I'd like you to have it."

"The gold ball? I can't take this. What would John say?"

"He doesn't need it, and neither do I."

Keeler dropped the ball into Jim's outstretched hand.

Jim stared at the golden ball in his palm. No, nothing was settled he realized. But as he looked at the gleaming amber sphere reflecting the fiery rays of the late afternoon sun, Jim saw the possibilities—for elusive pars and the forgiveness that heals old wounds.

Jim closed his hand around the gold ball. Looking up, meeting Hans Keeler's steady gaze, he recognized the eyes of his father.

"Thank you," Jim said quietly. "I'd like to have it."

Epilogue

*T*he young boy threw his new set of Bullet junior clubs into the *back of the red station wagon, on top of his father's oversized black Fila bag. They had just played nine at Sunrise Acres, a par 29 executive course, and the kid was frustrated with his inability to hit the new clubs well. He never wanted to give up his old set— his father's cutdown Hogan's—but his dad insisted that once he got used to them, he'd hit the ball much better with the new, more forgiving design of cavity–backs.*

The boy slammed the front passenger door closed, fastened his shoulder belt, and watched his father signal left and turn out of the golf course's parking lot onto Ocean Avenue. His father had grown silent after his outburst on the par 3, 127 yard, 8th hole. The boy had finally struck a decent 5–iron, hit a green, and lagged his putt up to two feet of the hole. He looked to his father, who made no offer of a gimme, and proceeded to mark his ball.

Last time out, when he still had his old clubs, he shot a personal best 35, only six over par. On the first eight holes, he had made three pars, along with three bogeys, and two doubles. The day was topped off on nine, when he made his first ever birdie. Today, on the other hand, was a golfing nightmare. Two triples, three doubles, and four bogeys for a God–awful, sixteen over total of 45. On eight, the kid figured he would, at very least, salvage the day with one par. But it was not meant to be. His little two–foot putt rolled half way to the hole and died. That's when the kid proceeded to lose it.

The boy watched his father fiddle with the radio, find a station he liked, and quietly hum to himself. He was a great golfer, his dad was. Shot a 31 today. Could hit the ball a ton. But, he wouldn't tolerate the kind of anger his son displayed on eight. Believed there was no place in golf for that kind of behavior. He repeatedly warned his son that, if he didn't get a better grip on his temper, he wouldn't take him out at all.

The boy was starting to feel calmer and didn't want his father to remain upset with him. "Dad," he said, while the car waited at a traffic light.

"Yes, Robbie." His father turned and looked at him.

"Sorry I lost it out there today."

His father reached forward and lowered the volume on the car's stereo. "I'm glad you're sorry, Rob. And I understand how frustrating golf can be. I just want you to learn how to enjoy the game."

"I enjoy the game. Most of the time."

The boy's father laughed. "I know you do. But you've got to realize that not every day can be a good day."

"I just wanted to make at least one par today. I usually have two or three."

"I understand. We all want to make pars. But, it's not always meant to be. You'll have your share of pars. You're going to be a fine player."

"Do you think I could ever be as good as you?"

"Sure you can."

"What about Grandpa Bob. He was a pro. Could I ever be as good as him? Could I be a pro?"

The boy's dad didn't answer as he waited for traffic to clear so he could turn left onto Moore Avenue. A street lined with mid–sized suburban homes. Three blocks ahead, the boy's mother and younger sister would be waiting out front of their gray with red trim Cape Cod. Even though it was a Wednesday, it was April vacation week, and they would all go out to dinner and a movie at the mall.

"If being a professional golfer is important to you, sure I think you might be able to do it. But you can't make it your whole life. Especially if things don't go your way. You can't take it too seriously. There's so many things you can do well and there's so much more to life than golf. Sure, it's a great game, but you've got to accept the good with the bad. Just like life."

The boy sat back. He was finished talking. He heard this speech before and didn't mind hearing it one more time. Not if it meant that his father was no longer mad at him. As the red wagon pulled into their driveway, the boy's little sister—platinum curls, chubby red cheeks, a flowered sun dress—came running out from the side of the house. When she spotted their car, she broke into a face–breaking smile, ran more quickly, and stumbled forward. She jumped right up—no tears, but her lower lip in its finest pout position. Following right behind her was the boy's mother, and the little girl immediately began to cry as she ran into her mother's arms.

The young boy opened his window and stuck his head out. "She's fine, mom. She didn't even cry until she saw you."

The boy's mom held the girl in her arms, rubbed her back, shook her head, smiled in the direction of her husband and son. Her just–washed blond curls were aglow with the sun's radiance, her blue eyes sparkled, her smile reassured. His mom was the most beautiful woman in the world. The boy shifted his glance to his father. His chin rested atop his big, strong hands on the steering wheel. He turned toward his son and winked, then looked back in the direction of his wife and daughter—his faint smile, a meager reflection of his contentment and pride.

The boy felt a rush of joy explode from his belly up into his reddening cheeks. He loved it when they went out as a family, he loved to do things with his dad, he loved vacation weeks. He had already forgotten about his disappointing golf round. His dad was right. There is more to life than golf.

And his life was oh, so good.